DOCTOR WHO™

Short Trips: Monsters

A Short-Story Anthology
Edited by Ian Farrington

BIG FINISH

Published by Big Finish Productions Ltd
PO Box 1127
Maidenhead
SL6 3LN

www.bigfinish.com

Managing Editor: Jason Haigh-Ellery
Consultant for BBC Worldwide: Jacqueline Rayner

ISBN 1–84435-110-6

Cover by RED INK 2004
Original sleeve design by Clayton Hickman

First published September 2004

With thanks to
Robert Dick, Nev Fountain, Kirstyn McDermott,
Gary Russell, Steve Tribe and Vicki Vrint

Typeset in Quadraat

Printed and bound in Great Britain by Biddles Ltd
www.biddles.co.uk

CONTENTS

Best Seller

Ian Mond & Danny Oz

'... hand in hand they headed off towards the stars.'

Alan switched off the B-Tab and stared with a shaky smile at the fifty or so people crowded into the alleyway around him. Their faces were entranced, blissful, content. He took a sip of lukewarm water from the bottle someone had handed him several hours before.

Despite his parched throat, his fear and the presence of the broad-shouldered man whose gun still pointed unwaveringly in the direction of his left temple, Alan felt strangely blissful. It had been a good book. No, a great book, a masterpiece; well worth the two weeks' wages he had paid to the black marketeer the previous evening. Worth even the black eye, the bruised ribs and the threat of death.

Alan rose from the upturned milk crate on which he'd been sitting, knees cracking.

'Oi!' the broad-shouldered man said. 'What do you think you're doing?'

'Well... I... I'm going home,' Alan replied. 'I mean, it's over. That's the end of the novel. I've...'

The eyes of the crowd were losing their blissful gaze, pulling him into focus. They looked hungry.

'I've finished?' Alan asked hopefully.

The man shook his head and gestured with his gun, indicating Alan should resume his seat.

Alan did so.

'There,' the man said. 'Now, you're going to read it to us again.'

Charley was eating something called a risotto when the riot started.

She and the Doctor were dining alfresco, enjoying the gorgeous autumn weather. Mario's was located in an inner suburb of Melbourne called Fitzroy. Charley hadn't been sure what to expect from the Antipodes. As a young girl, she'd imagined a wild, adventurous, swashbuckling land filled with horrifying creatures, cannibal tribes and knife-wielding convicts.

Fitzroy didn't entirely match up with those expectations.

Nibbling at her food, Charley watched a tall man with thick, ropy bands of hair and a lady with a horrid rat on her shoulder chat in front of the Brunswick Street Bookstore. Close by, a woman with jewellery in her nose, lips, chin and eyebrows handed out leaflets. Further down the street, two men wearing tea cosies on their heads were smoking and laughing.

The Doctor, of course, fitted right in. He looked so casual in his open-necked shirt and green velvet waistcoat. At the moment, he was engrossed in an animated conversation with a bald man in orange robes.

Charley speared a mushroom with her fork as a delivery van pulled up beside the bookshop. Two men dressed in drab uniforms emerged from the front cabin, armed with rifles. Although the weapons were a stark contrast to the relaxed atmosphere of the street, no one seemed to mind. Perhaps, Charley pondered, delivering books with guns was an eccentricity of the period. With brisk efficiency, the men unloaded several boxes and left.

Charley returned her attention to the endless variations of strange and exotic people that paraded before her. Everything was so laid back, so relaxed, you could sit here forever and never feel the time pass you by.

'Tristan!'

Charley jumped in her seat.

The Doctor was shouting at the orange-robed man who was racing across Brunswick Street, only narrowly missing an automobile. The screech of tires grabbed everyone's attention: they were now searching for the cause, their eyes focusing on one place in particular.

The Brunswick Street Bookstore.

Someone had just put up a large painted sign in the display window: '*The Darvias Saga* – now available here.'

'Doctor, what's –'

But the Doctor was already heading towards the bookshop, his face a picture of concern. Charley followed, her skin prickling, only for him to grab her by the shoulders.

'Go,' the Doctor said to her. 'Go now!'

And then it happened.

A crowd of people was suddenly surging towards the shop like a tidal wave, separating Charley from the Doctor. They came from everywhere, the footpath, the other shops, even from vehicles abandoned and left running in the middle of the street.

She tried to keep her balance, but the seething mass of humanity caused Charley to slip and fall. Immediately, someone fell on top of her. Struggling for breath, she attempted to crawl but a shoe came crushing down on her hand, forcing a strangled scream from her lips.

Charley knew she was seconds away from being trampled to death. Gritting her teeth, ignoring her throbbing hand, she dug her fingers into the ground and pulled herself away from the body on top of her. The pain was ghastly, but she fought past it, made it to her feet – and nearly fell right back down.

The only thing that saved her was grasping hold of the very table she'd been seated at. Charley watched in horror as most of the crowd were swept aside or slammed up against the display window.

Gripping the table, she tried to locate the Doctor. For a brief moment, she thought she caught sight of him, standing completely still in the middle of the carnage – the sad, calm eye at the centre of the storm.

And then he was gone.

The sound of breaking glass drew her attention back to the bookshop. A slender woman screamed, her arms and legs covered in blood. There was so much to take in, so much screaming, so much blood, so much shattered glass, so many people.

So many people!

'Get away from the bookshop,' she could imagine the Doctor saying. 'Get away from their focus.'

She looked for the thinnest part of the crowd and headed in that direction. Three or four times she nearly lost her balance, yet miraculously remained on her feet.

A flash of colour caught her eye.

She turned –

– nearly collapsed –

– and saw him –

– the man in the orange robes –

– climbing out of the second-storey window of the Brunswick Street Bookstore –

– clutching something to his chest.

Charley closed her eyes.

She knew what was going to happen next.

The Doctor hadn't been forthcoming with the details, but from what she could gather, Tristan had survived the fall only to be kicked to death by a young lady. 'So sad,' the Doctor had whispered. 'He was such a clever, imaginative fellow.'

Following the riot, the Doctor had wanted to stay and investigate, perhaps assist the police or help some of the injured. But Charley had insisted they leave. She wanted to be far away from the blood and the shattered glass. The sound of Tristan hitting the pavement still reverberated in her ears. Sometimes, closing your eyes didn't help.

So now they were sitting in a café, looking out onto a beach. The setting sun was casting an orange glow across the sand. She wanted to enjoy the moment, bask in the twilight and pretend they'd only just arrived, but the riot kept intruding on her thoughts. 'What could have made them so angry?'

'It wasn't anger,' the Doctor said, pulling something from his pocket. 'It was desire, the overwhelming need to have something so badly that it didn't matter who you hurt.' He placed the object from his pocket onto the table. It was a metal tablet with rounded corners and a hinged cover. 'That's what killed poor Tristan; he was holding it when he jumped. What do you make of it?'

Charley wasn't sure whether she wanted to touch the contraption, but her curiosity got the better of her. On the cover, there was a picture of a good-looking, dark-haired man, surrounded by spaceships and multi-coloured explosions. The words 'The Darvias Saga' were engraved into the metal. Opening the cover, Charley discovered a single sheet of shiny paper with a small, iridescent metal square located on the top left-hand side. Below the paper, there were five buttons, one of which she pressed. Letters formed on the paper, but in no language she could understand.

'It's a book,' Charley said, handing the tablet back to the Doctor. 'But I can't read Chinese.'

'It's not Chinese,' the Doctor said. 'This is a Biblio-Tablet and it uses memory paper to display written text. Once it's activated, the tablet programs itself to be read only by a single retinal pattern, making it unreadable to anyone else. Tristan must have activated it before... before he left the bookshop.' The Doctor pulled an assortment of odd tools from his pocket and started to poke at the device. 'I'm also detecting a slight alien influence in the design.'

'How do you know that?'

'I'm a connoisseur of technology.' The Doctor smiled and returned his attention to the tablet.

Charley was suddenly awash with a prickling sensation – similar to what she had experienced moments before the riot. She glanced around the café and noticed that three quarters of the room were watching the Doctor.

Oh... oh, please, not again.

'Doctor,' she whispered. 'Do you think you should be doing that here?'

But the Doctor was absorbed in his work, muttering about needing his eyepiece and resetting the retinal scanner.

Some of the crowd were whispering and pointing, and Charley sensed they were but moments away from another outburst of violence. She leaned across the table, reached out with her leg and kicked the Doctor hard in the shins.

'Charley!' the Doctor yelped, dropping his tool. Then he noticed his audience. 'Oh, hello.' He grinned and waved. 'Silly thing hasn't worked right since I bought it.' As if to prove his point, the Doctor began hitting the tablet against the corner of the table. 'And I paid a pretty penny for it as well.'

The ruse worked. Everyone in the café appeared to relax, turning back to their coffees, their food and their chatter. The Doctor immediately returned his attention to the tablet, leaving a nervous Charley to take deep, steadying breaths. Honestly, she couldn't take him anywhere.

A newspaper lay discarded on a nearby table and Charley, needing something to keep her mind occupied, quickly picked it up. No such luck. A good deal of the publication was devoted to *The Darvias Saga*, with headlines like 'How *The Darvias Saga* changed my life! True Confessions of a Serial Killer', 'Could Gary Oldman play the role of Darvias?' and 'Madonna embraces Darvias's teachings' shouting at her from the pages.

The paper was also brimming with reports and opinion pieces on the upsurge in riots and general violence. Each article was written with lurid detail, including pictures of bloodied people, broken limbs and body bags.

'Doctor, this is horrible. The publishers are actually limiting the number of books they print. They say they want the tablet to retain its "collectable quality", whatever that means. It all sounds utterly monstrous.'

'Cheer up, Charley!' The Doctor began packing away his tools. 'I've set the retinal scanner so that anyone can read it.'

'Well, if you don't mind, Doctor, I'd rather not.'

'No, I don't think you should either. I'm guessing there's subliminal encoding built into the retinal scanning matrix or maybe a carrier signal that activates certain areas of the human brain. Either way, it should have little or no effect on me.'

Charley's eyes widened. 'You don't intend to –'

'Of course I do.' The Doctor tucked the tablet back into the pocket of his coat. 'And while I'm embarking on a fantastical journey of heroes, villains and evil from the dawn of time, there's something I'd like you to do.'

Charley left the TARDIS the following morning equipped with local money and a fluorescent green mobile phone. She was feeling a little nervous, dressed in only flip-flops, shorts and a t-shirt. Most of the bits of flesh she'd spent years trying to hide were now on show for everyone to see. Sissy would have been horrified; her mother would have been proud of her.

The Doctor had asked her to find out all she could about the publishers, Chulka Biblio Tablets. But now that she'd arrived at their Melbourne offices, Charley wasn't sure how that would be possible. A massive crowd surrounded the office building and, while they showed no overt signs of violence, most of them were shouting, singing, and even praying, for a copy of *The Darvias Saga*. After yesterday's events, Charley had no intention of moving closer to the crowd. She'd had her fill of people left violent and addled by their need for the book.

Then she spotted a smaller group of bystanders, standing off to one side of the rabble. They were waving placards that read 'Stop the Saga!' and 'Movement for Real Literature' and, her personal favourite, 'You want a real Saga? – Read Proust!'

Relieved to find that not everyone was obsessed by the book, Charley marched straight over to the group. They really were a rather queer collection of people, not the sort you'd expect to see demonstrating on the street. In fact, they reminded her of stuffy old teachers from school. The man with the Proust sign was tall and chubby with thinning white hair. He wore a pair of brown trousers, a knitted pullover and brown boots that were badly scuffed.

Charley pointed at his placard. 'Personally I always thought Proust was overrated, until I heard about Darvias.'

The man paused, then offered a friendly, if slightly worried, smile. 'You, er... you don't like the book either?'

'Well, I haven't actually read it, but something this popular can't be good, can it? I mean, look at them all.' She gestured towards the crowd further down the street. 'Hardly the crème de la crème of the intelligentsia. Not people of learning.'

The man visibly relaxed, lowering his placard so he could shake her hand. 'I'm Professor Bruce Gillespie.'

'Charlotte Pollard,' Charley said. 'It's a pleasure and an honour to finally meet people who detest Darvias. I was beginning to think that I was the only reasonable human being left. If it's not an imposition, could I join your group?'

'Really? You'd like to join us?' Professor Gillespie looked about ready to fall over. He regained his composure and turned to his fellow colleagues. 'People, I think we should retreat to headquarters.'

The group seemed excited by the suggestion. They crowded around Charley, all wanting to introduce themselves, wanting to know how she had discovered them, wanting to know whether she was good at painting placards.

'Oh, leave the girl alone,' Professor Gillespie moaned. 'We really must stop frightening off potential members!'

* * *

Headquarters was actually Professor Gillespie's house. Inside, each room was filled with bookshelves, brimming with hundreds of books and thousands of small, silver discs in glass sleeves. Everything smelt of cat.

The Professor – who had asked Charley to call him Bruce – led the group into the living room, where immediately everyone seemed to take up pre-assigned spots, whether on the couch, a patch of carpet or a small stool brought in from the kitchen.

Bruce made sure Charley had a seat on the large, comfortable sofa and thrust a cup of tea into her hands.

'You say you've worked with resistance groups before?' Bruce was constantly wringing his hands together as if expecting something horrible to happen. And yet the group was quite happy to defer to him. 'You seem a little young for that sort of thing.'

'Well, oppression doesn't care how old you are, Bruce. My guardian and I have travelled all over the world fighting for the downtrodden.'

Several members of the group nodded approvingly.

'And you hadn't heard of the book until you landed in Melbourne?'

'No. The Doctor and I had just returned from helping native tribes in Africa and the first we knew about Darvias was the newspapers at the airport.'

'Africa? But that's where the publishers are based! You didn't hear anything about the book while over there?'

Charley took a sip of her tea. Making up stories was quite easy; the Doctor really was a bad influence. 'Well, we heard rumours of a magic tale that had people in its thrall, but those sorts of stories are common in Africa. It wasn't until we returned to civilisation that I realised how serious it was.'

'And this guardian –'

'The Doctor.'

'This Doctor, he'd help us, too?'

'Oh, yes, the Doctor is all for literature.'

'Good, good. Only you see, we've gathered lots of information but we don't actually know what to do with it.'

Charley sat back and smiled. 'Well, you can start by telling me all you've found out.'

The Doctor had decided that reading indoors was no fun at all. So, with the help of the TARDIS, he'd found himself a stunning little spot in the Botanical Gardens.

He lay on a grassy embankment overlooking the city of Melbourne, occasionally breaking away from the novel to enjoy the beauty of the gardens around him. But before long he was drawn back to the text. At the end of the previous chapter, Darvias's long time friend, Fyfen, had been caught reporting sensitive information to a mysterious stranger. The Doctor was about to start the next chapter when a shadow fell over him.

Looking up, he saw a boy of about seven.

'Hello,' said the boy.

'Hello,' said the Doctor with a huge smile. They regarded each other silently for a few moments.

'Whatcha readin'?'

'A book about a man who travels the universe righting wrongs with his band of dear friends.'

'Any good?'

'It's wonderful!' The Doctor laughed. 'Would you like me to read you some?'

The boy nodded and sat down. Realising it would hardly be fair on the young boy to continue from the middle of the story, the Doctor turned back to the beginning of the novel.

'Okay – what's your name?'

'Mitch.'

'Okay, Mitch. *The Darvias Saga*, Chapter One. Ready?'

The boy nodded.

The Doctor cleared his throat and started to read.

Charley sat and listened.

All the group members took turns to speak. They spoke about a book that had mesmerised the populace, a book that was eating away at the cultural soul, a book that had forced bookstores around the world to employ armed guards.

'I loved visiting the Brunswick Street Bookstore,' said a small woman with long, silver hair tied in a plait. 'I begged the owner, *begged him*, not to order in that horrible novel. But it's the margins you see; the publishers sell the B-Tabs for an extraordinarily low price. It's like dangling a juicy worm in front of a trout.' The old woman shook her head, tears running down her face. 'Michael said he didn't want guards because he believed it would make the shop look unfriendly. And now his shop is gone.' One of the other members placed a comforting arm around the old woman's shoulder, and she quietly sobbed.

'We're not against popular culture,' Bruce explained. 'Well, not entirely. But this book is an addiction. An insidious force, impossible to escape. They want you to need it, to hanker for it, and then... and then they purposely limit the print run, making it impossible to share.' He was close to shouting. 'And when anyone tries to transcribe the book, they disappear.'

'Disappear?' Charley shuddered.

Bruce nodded and rattled off a list of names. It was a long list.

Charley's heart went out to these poor souls, the rare few who'd been able to fight the book's lure. 'My friend and I will do all we can to help.'

'Thank you so much, we –'

Bruce never finished his sentence. A stalk-like man loped into the room holding a silver disk. He was huffing and puffing and looked liked he might collapse from exhaustion.

'Henry,' whined Bruce. 'I was in the middle of a sentence. What is it?!'

'Put... put this in... in the machine.'

'It had better be important.'

Seconds later they were watching an interview with the author of *The Darvias Saga*, Nathaniel Clamp. This was Charley's first look at the man responsible for so much insanity. His features were unmemorable, except for a wide smile that never seemed to falter.

The group jeered and laughed their way through most of the interview until something caught Bruce's attention. Flapping his hands about, Bruce shushed everyone, then asked Henry to replay the last part of the interview.

'The prequel is being released next Sunday in New York,' Clamp said. 'Smaller print run, they tell me, but each book will be able to be read by up to five people, so everyone can share!'

Bruce stopped wringing his hands. His face hardened and Charley saw something in his eyes that made her shudder.

'The bastard must die,' he said.

'Doctor! Where have you been?! I thought this portable telephone contraption was broken. Look, they're going to kill him and we have to stop them or at least stop the publishers or –'

'Charley, slow down. Who is going to be killed?'

'The author. These people I met want to kill him before the publishers bring out the new Darvias book. But we can't let them! I've tried to explain that violence is never the answer, but they won't listen. Oh, Doctor, how can one book do all this?'

'Well, it has no hypnotic effect, no hidden messages; it's just a really cleverly written story that's easy to read with likeable characters. You care about these people, Charley, they *matter* to you.'

'I'm not sure I understand.'

'Don't you see, Charley; it's the marketing and the execution. Supply can't help but fall behind demand, and they've advertised the Saga to the hilt. All of this points back to the publishers... and with the release of a new book... Charley, what's the release date?'

'Next Sunday.'

'Only eight days... it goes against every marketing principle, Charley. No time for anticipation, no time for speculation.'

'Since the announcement, riots have started everywhere. It's as if people can't stand living without possession of this horrid book.'

'The riots will only get worse; I need to stop this now. If I fiddle with the TARDIS sensors and lock in on the signal the tablet sends out –'

'What signal?'

'Didn't I say? Each tablet broadcasts information on a frequency that no one from this planet could detect. The TARDIS, however, has better ears. Anyway, I dare say all the books transmit back to head office. Tell your friends to wait until you hear from me before they move on the author. Charley, I'll speak to you in a few hours, by then all this will be over.'

'But Doc –'

The Doctor hung up the mobile phone and tucked it back into the pocket of his coat. Perched on the roof of the TARDIS, he turned to the sea of expectant, excited faces.

'Terribly sorry,' he said through a loudspeaker. 'But I can only read another couple of chapters, and then I really must be off.'

'We still haven't heard from your friend, Charley. We must go ahead with our plan. The madness must stop!'

The prequel was to be released in less than four days. As the Doctor had predicted, the riots had grown in their violence and intensity. Charley knew they were running out of options, and Bruce had already planned a trip to New York.

'Please, just give the Doctor more time,' Charley said. 'He'll come through, he always does.'

Bruce put his hand on her shoulder. 'Charley.' His voice was gentle. 'He's vanished, just like so many others. I have no doubt that he was a great man to inspire so much faith in you, but you have to face facts. He's gone.'

Charley lowered her head, fearing that Bruce was right. The Doctor could be a trifle featherbrained at times, but he would never procrastinate when so much was at stake.

Charley I'll speak to you in a few hours... by then all this will be over.

The Doctor was in awful trouble or he was dead.

Either way, she was on her own.

* * *

At first, Bruce had resisted the idea of Charley travelling with him to New York. It was clear he saw himself as her new guardian and couldn't bear the thought of putting her in danger. But, as Charley had pointed out, it wasn't as if the group was clamouring to help. 'You can't do this by yourself,' she'd argued. 'If you fail, then someone else needs to step into the breach.'

With sad eyes, Bruce had finally agreed.

But if Charley was going to come along, they would need to organise a fake passport. And then there was the unseemly issue of purchasing weapons from someone 'hush hush' in New York.

Assistance came from a most unlikely source.

No one knew that Henry – shy, gawky and an admirer of James Joyce – was also a member of a right-wing group called Uprising. But what would have disturbed (and possibly frightened) everyone only weeks before proved to be precisely the help Bruce needed. Henry knew all about fake passports and guns and planning assassinations. He just didn't like to talk about it much.

Bruce, Charley and Henry arrived in New York two days before the release. Clamp's publishing machine had decided to launch the prequel at the author's favourite Barnes & Noble in New York City.

Hours after they'd landed, they were met by a scary, fat man named Clint. He drove them to a farm in upstate New York where, for the remainder of the day, they practised using Clint's collection of ceramic guns. Bruce had been nervous with the weapon, nearly shooting off his own foot. Charley had been frightened as well. But she focused on the terrible things she'd seen over the last few days – the riots, the death, the grieving families – and slowly it became easier to pull the trigger.

And every shot she fired pushed thoughts of the Doctor further from her mind.

Mr Tluss and the board liked to watch.

A bank of monitors filled one wall of the boardroom, the screens flashing gorgeous images of violence. In less than five hours, *Darvias: Beginnings* would be released and the people were putting on the most wonderful variety of riots in anticipation. Tluss had discovered long ago that no two riots were alike; each had its own unique mixture of blood, death and destruction.

While the board groaned in ecstasy, Tluss's notebook began bleeping.

'There's something happening in the warehouse,' he said.

Thin fingers danced across the laptop keyboard. Mass riots and general insanity were replaced by different angles of a massive warehouse.

'Boooooring,' a board member complained.

'The internal sensors are detecting... ah...' Mr Tluss and the board watched as a blue capsule materialised in the centre of the warehouse. From the capsule emerged a man, with curly, shoulder-length brown hair, wearing a frock coat and trousers. He was holding a dull grey box and sporting a wide smile.

Mr Tluss shuddered with excitement. He knew potential when he saw it.

'I didn't know these people had transmat technology!' one of the board remarked.

'They don't.' Tluss grinned. 'This must be an alien incursion.'

'Alien! Could it be a spy from a rival network?'

'Perhaps,' said Tluss. 'I've initiated a cross-check.'

The man looked ready to do something with the box and, for a moment, Mr Tluss wondered whether the intruder was actually holding a bomb. But then the man paused, as if only just realising the warehouse was mostly empty.

The intruder began speaking to himself, so Tluss activated the sound.

'... no, no, no,' the man said. 'Where could they possibly be?'

'Could he be looking for the tablets?' a board member asked.

'Fascinating,' Tluss said. 'I wonder how he knew where to find the warehouse. We went to so much trouble to hide it underground, and he just transmats in.'

After running through most of the warehouse, the intruder discovered a series of crates that had yet to be shipped to bookstores. He pocketed the grey box, slid open the crate and removed a Biblio Tablet.

'We must stop him!' shouted a board member.

'All in good time,' Mr Tluss said.

Tablet in hand, the man raced back into his box.

'He's going to escape!'

'We will track him with the tablet,' Tluss said.

The box moaned and groaned out of existence, only to reappear a few seconds later. Once again, the intruder emerged, still holding *Darvias: Beginnings*. His face was a picture of determination, his eyes blazing.

Mr Tluss chuckled. 'I think it's time we invited our guest up to the boardroom.'

The Doctor burst into the boardroom, only to be brought up short by what confronted him.

'Cookies and tea!' he shouted, racing over to the table.

Mr Tluss smiled. 'Please make yourself at home.'

In the short time since the Doctor had arrived, Mr Tluss had discovered how to tame this particular beast. The Doctor sat down opposite Tluss, poured himself a hot cup of Roobios tea, spooned in three sugars, added a dash of milk and gathered together a plate of cookies and cakes. 'How delightful,' he said, smacking his lips together.

Tluss sat and watched as the Doctor sipped his tea and nibbled at his cookies. He found the man's mood changes exciting, and his mind raced with possibilities.

'You must really love watching television.' The Doctor gestured towards the dark bank of monitors.

'A little obsession of mine, but at the moment I'd rather we chatted, Doctor.' Tluss said.

'How wonderful: you know my name.' The Doctor put down his cup of tea. 'Did you hack into top-secret files, or did you just put my description into Google?'

Mr Tluss laughed. 'A little bit of this, a little bit of that. You're really quite an interesting fellow. So, how did you find us?'

'Well, Mr...?'

'Tluss.'

'Well, Mr Tluss, obviously you never thought anyone on this planet could use the books' broadcast frequency as a homing beacon.'

'My dear Doctor, are you implying that I'm an alien?'

'Well, of course! I mean, you've done a very good job at copying the human form, but it's not quite right. The nose is too long and thin, the cheekbones a little too low, the smile about a centimetre too wide. Sorry to seem so critical.'

'I'm always in favour of constructive criticism,' Mr Tluss said.

The Doctor scoffed down a vanilla slice. 'So,' he said between mouthfuls. 'Why have you decided to go into publishing on Earth? I mean, there are plenty of worlds on the lookout for new works of literature. Why this one?'

Mr Tluss activated a secret switch below the redwood table and heard the secret panel slide open behind him. He watched the Doctor's face carefully as his compatriots slithered, crawled and squelched their way into the room.

'In answer to your question, Doctor, may I introduce the Board of Directors!'

The Doctor's reaction was immediate. He grinned, leapt from his chair and immediately shook appendages with what resembled a haggis having a bad hair day, then greeted each of the board members in turn, asking again why they were doing this.

'Our kind love to watch the antics of the lower races, Doctor,' Mr Tluss explained. 'When we find a world that looks promising, we find a hook. Something simple that everyone will feel a connection to and desire most strongly. On Zassaph in Dimension 16 it was a ceremonial headdress, on Kelpa it was a wooden toy –'

'And on Earth it's a book,' the Doctor cut in.

'Yes. Oh, it wasn't easy, Doctor; we spent years researching the psyche of the average human, their dreams, hopes and fears. Humans like stories. So we constructed them an epic science fantasy for the modern age. Didn't we, Mr Marg?'

Mr Marg – who, except for the mandibles, looked rather like an inside-out rabbit – edged forward and spoke in a gurgling voice. 'I did most of the actual writing, with some help from my friends here.' The butcher's shop assortment of creatures did their own equivalent of a modest nod.

The Doctor clapped. 'Then congratulations are in order, my dear chap. It really is a most engaging tale.'

'I'm so glad you liked it. I didn't overdo it with the evil female twin, did I? Only I –'

'Anyway,' Mr Tluss interrupted. 'Now you know all about us, Doctor.'

'Not at all. Given your rather varied nature, I'd say these aren't your true forms.'

'We come from the upper dimensions and moving through them is quite difficult. We arrive in a non-corporeal form and then start assembling matter from discarded cells. It can take months to come up with a functioning body, let alone one that looks like it belongs to one of the native species. I was the first to come close.'

'And Nathaniel Clamp used your research to build a body for himself.'

'Exactly.'

'But what's the point of it all? You can't transfer the money between dimensions and you're restricting your sales to a ludicrous degree...'

'Oh, it's not about sales, it's about havoc. Our public adores mayhem and destruction; it rates so well. Every book is a transmitter that allows us to send images back to our own dimension. We show only the choicest moments, the most violent and amusing incidents. We do this on world after world and our ratings are always brilliant. We couldn't believe our luck when we discovered this planet had yet to be tapped by any of the other networks. It should have been done centuries ago. Not many sentient species are so easily provoked into fighting amongst themselves.'

The Doctor slammed an irate fist down on the table, nearly knocking over his cup of tea. 'You're treating humans no better than roosters in a cockfight,' he growled. 'Turning people against one another for the amusement of a bunch of intergalactic couch potatoes. And with the sudden, unexpected release of the prequel, think of the atrocities that will occur.'

Mr Tluss laughed. 'Yes, I know. The ratings will be marvellous!'

'Please...' the Doctor whispered. 'Please don't do this. Please don't force my hand.'

'Force your hand!' Tluss clapped. 'You really are a comedian, Doctor.'

He activated the bank of monitors, the screens displaying a massive crowd waiting outside a bookshop. A large clock hanging over the doors to the store was counting down the amount of time before the prequel would be released.

'Gentlemen, if you need to use the amenities, please do so now. In less than an hour, the show begins!'

Charley fidgeted, watching the clock count down to madness.

They'd arrived at the Lower East Side very early that morning. As expected, the publishers had set up security posts in a one-mile radius around the Barnes & Noble. There was also a sizeable police presence that was on the alert for any obvious troublemakers. Immediately, the three split up and, for the first time in over a week, Charley found herself alone and totally calm.

I'm going to stop the insanity, Doctor.

Her first hint of nervousness came as she was confronted at a security post by the thuggish-looking guards and their black wands. Clint had been confident the ceramic weapon (small and compact) would evade detection, but there was always the risk.

In the end she had no troubles at all. There were so many people, so much shouting and screaming, so many random acts of violence; the guards didn't bother with her.

Charley had found a grand vantage point outside a neighbouring florist. Despite the amazing number of people surrounding the bookseller, she still had a good line of sight. Charley was really pleased, until the reality hit her. She was happy about having a clear shot at an innocent man.

No, not innocent! If he was innocent, how could she...?

Deep down, Charley knew there were holes in Bruce's plan. What if Clamp never showed his face? What if her shots were suddenly blocked by bystanders? And most of all, what if she couldn't pull the trigger? It was the biggest 'what if' of them all, and Charley realised she *still* didn't have an answer. How strange. She had been so sure when she'd woken up that morning that she could.

Where are you, Doctor? You left me to save the world on my lonesome. You don't know what I've seen, the awful things I've witnessed, all because of this stupid book. I don't want to kill anyone... but... maybe... maybe it will stop this madness.

'You don't really believe that, Charley.' She could almost believe the Doctor was standing right next to her.

'Please go away,' she whispered.

A sudden ripple of anticipation and excitement ran through the crowd as a long, expensive-looking car approached. It was inky black and gleamed in the afternoon sun.

Somewhere nearby a mobile phone rang. For a brief moment Charley thought it was hers, hoping briefly that the Doctor was contacting her to say he was about to save the day. But it was someone else's phone. Saving the day would be her task alone.

This was it. This was her moment. This was where all the 'what if's became a reality.

The door to the car opened.

Nathaniel Clamp emerged, waving to the audience.

Charley raised her gun. Destiny was granting her wish. She had a perfectly clear shot.

Her gun fired twice.

Everyone in the boardroom was on the edge of their seat. All eyes, be they in heads, on stalks or randomly placed somewhere else, focused on the screens.

When the shots rang out, Tluss and the board stood and applauded.

The cameras focused on a familiar face.

'Oh, Charley,' the Doctor whispered.

It happened so quickly that it took seconds for Charley to realise what she'd done.

Clamp had been in her sights –

– she'd had a clear shot –

– and, in a sudden bloom of anger and hatred and fear, Charley had pulled the trigger.

Twice.

So why was Bruce clutching his shoulder, blood seeping through his fingers? And why was Henry glaring at her, his gun now pointed in *her* direction?

I shot them! I shot my friends.

She'd used violence to stop violence – the irony of the moment forced a manic giggle from her lips.

Around her, chaos had erupted. People were either trying to get away from the gunfire or looking to get closer to Clamp, as if meaning to throw themselves in front of the bullets. Henry was still aiming his weapon at Charley, his eyes cold and calculating. His intent was obvious, but the mob kept blocking his shot. And then the inevitable happened: he and his gun were noticed. Someone tackled Henry to the ground and, before Charley could whisper sorry, he was engulfed by a mob of screaming, frenzied people.

Charley took a step backward, not afraid of the mob, not afraid for her life. She only wanted to find Bruce, wanted to apologise, to explain why she'd shot him, why she'd betrayed them. But he was lost in the crowd and she knew, deep down, she would never, ever see dear Bruce again.

Charley backed up against the wall of the flower shop. She dropped the ceramic gun, closed her eyes and thought sweet thoughts of her parents and the Doctor. Another mobile phone rang; again it wasn't hers.

And then another rang.

Seconds passed.

Charley cringed in anticipation of the ripping and the scratching and the punching.

But then someone seemed to whisper in her ear.

'On the internet... on the internet...'

No, not one person; a chorus of people. And they were no longer whispering. They were speaking aloud...

'On the internet... on the internet...'

...and now they were shouting: 'DARVIAS IS ON THE INTERNET!'

Tluss and the board watched in surprise as the crowd began to disperse. Through the speakers, they could clearly hear the people chant, 'DARVIAS IS ON THE INTERNET!'

All eyes turned to the Doctor. 'What did you do?' Mr Tluss asked.

The Doctor smiled innocently. 'A magician never reveals his secrets.'

'If you don't tell us, we will kill you!' screamed Mr Marg, his mandibles chittering in anger. Poor Mr Marg, he'd been really looking forward to the reviews.

'No, we won't,' said Tluss. 'We will be letting you go either way, Doctor. We're not savages.' Tluss spared a glance at Mr Marg. 'Well, most of us aren't. I am merely curious.'

The Doctor poured himself another cup of tea before launching into a breathless explanation of how he'd outwitted them.

It seemed that his transmat capsule was capable of limited movement through time. The Doctor had arrived later than intended and the laws of time prevented him from going back to an earlier period.

'My initial plan was to arrive here a week ago and wipe the data encoded in the tablets with this box.' He produced the dull grey device he'd been holding in the warehouse. 'But I hadn't counted on the TARDIS having one of her funny turns. When I realised I'd arrived on the day of release, I had to conjure up an alternative plan. So, I stole one of your tablets, nipped back into the TARDIS and entered a temporal orbit. Not a move I'm proud of, but it did give me time to read and then transcribe the new book.'

'Ahhhh... and that was when your capsule disappeared. What seemed like a moment for us, was in fact hours for you.'

'Yes.'

'You cheated!' Mr Tluss found himself laughing with delight.

'I did say I wasn't proud.'

'It's not fair,' grunted Mr Marg. 'If we'd known you were time-active we would have set up a quantum dispersal field. Your capsule would have been turned inside out.'

The Doctor winced. 'Yes, well, if it makes you feel any better, gentlemen, you put me in a position where I had to bend the laws of time. Anyway, there's more...'

'Oh, please go on.' Mr Tluss said. 'This is most entertaining.'

'Once I'd finished the transcription process, I materialised back into the warehouse. Then, before leaving the TARDIS, I uploaded the contents of your book onto your own website.'

'You hacked our site? How brilliant.' Mr Tluss laughed, checking his notebook. Sure enough, the three sample chapters on the website were followed by the rest of the book. 'Ha! You used our own marketing to defeat us. It's not often we experience the thrill of being outwitted.'

The members of the board gave the Doctor a polite, if slightly squishy-sounding, round of applause.

'If I'd been able to talk you gentlemen into releasing the B-Tabs properly, I would have warned you the book was on the site. You could have deleted it before it was seen by too many people. In the end, you defeated yourselves.'

'Indeed we did. Well, Doctor, it was lovely chatting. We will have someone take you back to your capsule.' Mr Tluss stood and shook the Doctor's hand.

'Really?' The Doctor appeared a little nervous, as if expecting someone to shoot him.

'Yes, Doctor.'

The Doctor seemed to consider this for a moment, looking deep into Mr Tluss's eyes. Then, with a broad smile, he leapt to his feet and made a round of the room, shaking appendages again with all the members of the board and finishing with Mr Tluss.

'Before I go, the people of this region you employ to run this complex; I hope you intend to look after them, I wouldn't want them to suffer the moment you leave.' There was an edge of warning in the Doctor's voice.

'Not at all,' Mr Tluss said. 'We're quite happy to help those who've assisted us. Now that there's nothing left for us here, we plan to give the natives of this region ownership of our reader-limitation process. Many companies and governments will pay them a fortune to use that technology. As I said earlier Doctor, we are not savages.'

'Yes...' the Doctor's smile vanished. 'Though considering how many lives you've ruined, some might disagree. I will be keeping an eye on you.'

And with that final threat the Doctor was gone.

There was silence in the room for a few moments.

'Such ingenuity,' Mr Tluss sighed.

'Had to cheat to beat us,' said Mr Marg.

'Yes, but I liked that. Touch of the rebel about him. Traditional heroes are so passé.'

'Pity. From the research, I was hoping he'd blow this place up,' Mr Marg chattered. 'Would have made for better ratings.'

'Nonsense!' Mr Tluss grinned. 'People love a feel-good ending from time to time.'

Charley was sitting in a café in New York, pondering the future, when her phone rang.

'Charley?'

'Doctor! Where on earth are you?'

'I'm standing right behind you.'

Charley turned, dropped her phone and ran to hug her friend. Without letting go, Charley told him about the attempted assassination of Clamp and how, at the time, killing him had seemed the only option.

'Where were you?' she asked, her face streaked with tears.

'The TARDIS had one of her turns. You know I would never leave you, Charley. It must have been horrible.'

'I saw so many ghastly things... and I just wanted it to end.'

The Doctor gave Charley another hug. 'Like everyone else on this planet, you were infected by the Darvias bug. Even I saw the attraction.'

'I wish I could see Bruce again, I wish I could tell him how sorry I am. But I had to do it Doctor...'

'There, there, Charley. He may not appreciate it, but you've saved him. Killing Clamp would only have made things worse. Even if the crowd hadn't torn him apart, the action would have haunted Bruce for the rest of his days. Besides, guns wouldn't stop the organisation itself, even if they could have killed the author. It was never about money, you see, it was all about the...'

'...ratings!' Mr Tluss turned the sound down as the 3D figures of the Doctor and Charley continued to talk. He looked at the Board of Directors, who all nodded approvingly.

'We shall soon have a ratings boom on our hands! Our research has shown that, whatever organisation the agents designated "Doctor" work for, they are inevitably sent to trouble spots. Alien incursions, totalitarian regimes, mad scientists – the variety is quite amazing. *And* all the agents appear to have inquisitive assistants, thus negating the need for a narrator to explain what is happening to the audience.'

'Always a chore finding a good narrator,' sighed Mr Marg.

Mr Tluss nodded. 'We are setting up listening posts throughout this dimension, all looking for the specific materialisation signature of the Doctor's transmat capsule. The N-Dimension nano-cameras are in place and set to a rolling frequency to avoid detection. They will continue to breed and secrete themselves on him, his capsule, his friends, the other agents when he meets them. We will get unlimited access to all that they encounter.'

'There will be death, explosions and nastiness – all at a fraction of the set-up costs we normally incur,' Mr Marg gurgled.

Mr Tluss smiled, displaying far too many teeth.

'The viewers back home are going to love watching... *the Doctor*.'

From Eternity

Jim Mortimore

> My heart was fashioned to be susceptible of love and sympathy; and when wrenched by misery to vice and hatred it did not endure the violence of the change without torture such as you cannot even imagine.
>
> Mary Shelley
> *Frankenstein or, The Modern Prometheus*

> Why do we only remember the past?
>
> Stephen Hawking
> *A Brief History of the Universe*

Four hundred billion generations passed before I realised they were intelligent. By the time I understood that they had been trying to communicate with me it was too late. By then they were a sub-cognitive organic slime, trickling sluggishly through an ocean of amino acids, blasted by lightning from the burning atmosphere of their molten planet.

I watched their sun shrink, curl up and implode.

It was the first time I'd seen anything like it.

I wondered if it was important.

All right, Doctor, I can see you have a lot of questions, so let me start at the beginning.

I was born in darkness. At least, by the time I was mature enough to form questions concerning my origin and destiny, I had never known light. I had no word or icon for light, the absence of darkness. And yet I would come to know it, all too briefly, in stuttering moments at the very end of my life.

What am I?

Matter, like you. Atoms and molecules, divided by empty space, intimately linked by an underlying quantum foam of fluxing possibilities.

Rephrase the answer?

All right, all right, let me think... well, I'm afraid I can't. But I can add this: when I was younger, it was easy to determine the properties of quantum particles. Their choices were apparently much more limited then than now.

But that's obvious, isn't it? I mean the universe was a much bigger place then.

Parents?

Define the word, please, Doctor.

Oh, I see.

The simple answer (always the best, don't you think?) is that if I do have parents, I don't remember them. I could have any number of origins. As far as I understand the term, I could have been the result of cellular fission, though I don't think I was a familial clone because as far as I can remember there was no one before me. I was the first. The first to exist, the first to gain self-awareness, the first to pose questions, to seek understanding. I would suggest your term 'immaculate conception' best describes me but for the obvious fact that the term clearly implies a progenitor. To be honest, I simply can't remember. I'm quite old now. Even when I was young I couldn't remember every thought I ever had. Could you?

How old?

Well, quite old, Doctor. Immeasurable, I should think.

I can only surmise this, of course, but it seems to me that to be what I am, I must have been born in a coalescent storm of fundamental particles. Matter itself, coming into being, created me. I was smashed together in the most violent of births imaginable, and all matter in the universe with me. Given that I was born during a time of flux between a universe without physical matter and a universe composed of physical matter, then time as you understand it is meaningless, or rather, has a meaning that changes depending upon which state we inhabit.

No, I'm sorry, I can't simplify that statement. Except to say that the oldest physical matter that currently exists in the universe is something I remember coming into existence.

Well, yes, of course I remember *that*. It was the first time in a life whose earliest memories I was already having a problem finding room for that I'd encountered anything like the physical matter you are made of.

I made a special note.

Wouldn't you?

Ah! Thought you'd caught me out there, didn't you? Yes, I'm composed of physical matter, everything in this universe is. But the matter I am composed of waxes and wanes, whilst I continue, unbroken.

You don't? Oh, I'm sorry, Doctor, I'll try to rephrase.

Think of it like this: the chemicals and electrical charges that make up your memories are in constant flux. Matter and energy decays and reforms, changing its state in countless ways all the time. The physical substance of your mind fluxes more violently than any war, yet do you notice an interruption in the continued existence of self? Of course not.

Neither do I.

It's simply a matter of scale.

Yes, all right. While we're on the subject, why don't we talk of war?

Time passed. In another part of the universe a new sun sprang abruptly to life. This time, I observed the process a little more carefully.

Where before the star had erupted spontaneously from a tiny but rapidly expanding globe of iron to form a sharply incandescent blue-white orb, here the process was quite different.

This second atomic furnace began life as a contracting shell of gas and energetic particles. Over time, gravity bound this material together into a lump of hydrogen, which ignited under its own weight. When the radiation flash subsided, the sun was a huge, sullen mass, still shrinking, though now surrounded by smaller, cooler lumps of rock and heavy metals, recently disgorged by the ever-brightening photosphere. Red light brightened slowly to yellow as stray particles of energy combined with free atoms to form molecules bound in the rigid structures unique to physical matter. The area of space surrounding the red star's birth was far less cluttered than had been the space surrounding that of the blue star.

I waited, wondering if anything else I observed would resonate with what had gone before. My patience was rewarded when, after a while, a countless number of symmetrical metallic objects appeared out of the depths of the universe, moving rapidly sunwards. The lumps coalesced around the inner planets of the solar system, weaving paths between them as intricate and beautiful as those of any atomic nuclei.

Here at last were the patterns I had been searching for.

The paths intelligence walked between lonely stars.

I started listening then. Sure enough they began to talk. But unlike those who went before they never noticed my existence. I wondered briefly what they might be thinking, but all too soon they stopped. Before long, they had also stopped moving around between planets. Their intricate patterns collapsed into chaotic motion driven only by the gravity of natural bodies. Soon all of them that remained were concentrated on one planet, and even their numbers were dwindling fast. As their ability to communicate faded so too did their understanding of the universe around them, of language, of tools. As had the first ones before them, so too this new species withered and died, their last moments illuminated by a frenzy of self-destruction. And then the inevitable liquid dissolution followed by the implosion of their sun.

As quickly as that they were gone from the universe.

In all my time I had never seen anything like this: two distinct species of intelligence so far apart in the universe that the crawling light from their suns could never have met; destroyed by the same inevitable process.

I knew fear then, for the first time. I didn't have a name for it, of course. The name would come later, intricately bound with another word.

War.

All right, don't think of it as war. Think of it as inevitable change. That's all war is really. The violent exchange of one state of being for another. It's a universal process. I see it everywhere, now. It wasn't always like this, though. For the longest time imaginable, longer than the lifetime of suns, there was peace in the universe. Cool, unchanging peace. Then war came.

I beg your pardon?

Yes, of course, I'm sorry, Doctor, you're quite right. Perhaps a better word would be *infection*. Yes, that feels right. An infection, spreading from star to star, people to people, Mind to Mind.

I was the first Mind. I watched it happen. Watched Mind bloom, fade and die, victim of some nameless, unidentifiable infection.

I learned about pain then. Loneliness and regret.

And death. I learned of that, too, for the first time.

They were my responsibility, you see.

I had to warn them all.

About the infection.

About the war.

You know, Doctor, talking to you now, watching your harshly angular face, your thumb-tucked arrogance, I feel like I've made a mistake. That's what you make me feel. That I am inadequate, somehow, and should feel guilty for those inadequacies. If only you knew the lifetimes I have walked, the lives of galaxies I have forgotten. If I could but allow you a glimpse of –

I beg your pardon?

I'm sorry, of course, you're right. The time for self-pity is long past. Now we must speak not of justification but of explanation and redemption. We must ensure that what has gone before never occurs again. The time is long overdue for a new pattern to form.

Let's begin again.

I am nameless.

I am evil.

I beg to learn contrition and earn forgiveness for my sins.

* * *

Yes, Doctor, I quite agree. Now would be a very good time to revisit those sins.

Time passed, and light spread throughout the universe. Stars, no longer too far apart for their photonic emissions to meet, infected the universal darkness, blooming, gathering into clumps, fuelled by gravity, their mass enticing the smooth, cool beauty of the universe to form knots and whirlpools. Lumpen galaxies formed, at first distantly, then closer together. Some collided. Energy abounded. The universe became frenzied, a dervish of existence, of change.

And eventually, inevitably, I encountered Mind again.

This time, communication between us was immediate. I was hopeful of a better outcome but my hope was not to last. Although we were able to define a common frame of reference containing a lexicon of symbols and convergent language icons, it proved impossible to sustain a meaningful concept-thread during any exchange. This Mind, while clearly intelligent, possessed a frighteningly short memory. Continuity, for them, was impossible. It was as though each generation of Mind was born with less knowledge than their forebears.

For the longest time I was convinced, given the circumstances, that this new Mind was being deliberately obstructive.

I learned frustration then, and anger.

It was then, in desperation, I became violent.

Now I understand how wrong I was; then it was very different.

At that time I had an overwhelming need to help them. Having met Mind other than myself, I now had a framework within which to understand the meaning of isolation. I was lonely and, because of my new understanding of time, I realised I had been lonely for a period whose duration would have induced insanity in any other than myself. Worse, I was afraid that, if this unnamed infection and destruction of Mind persisted, I would remain alone throughout all eternity in the universe. Having experienced that, it was something I now wanted to avoid at any cost.

It was then I became desperate. Clearly my duty was to nurture these emergent Minds, protect them from the infection to which they inevitably fell prey, in the hope that one day I would be able to forge lasting relationships with them.

Love?

Define the word please.

Oh, I see. Yes. Well, if you put it like that, Doctor, I suppose you're right. I wanted love and I couldn't get it.

That's why I began to hurt them.

Tell you what I did?

I'm not sure I...

I mean, the memories are...

Yes, all right, I know I will have to revisit those times if I hope to earn redemption.

It's just very painful for me. Knowing the things I know now, relating that knowledge to my actions of so long ago.

How would you like the memories presented?

Very well. A simple description to begin with, I agree. Though I must admit to being extremely frightened by this process.

No, Doctor.

Thank you for the offer, but I will decline.

Mainly because I do not rest. But, more specifically, I sense from my interaction with your species of Mind that any delay in the assessment process now might make a successful resolution moot.

Will I become violent again?

I can only say that I do not have that intention now.

Of course the Lords of Time will have to decide for themselves whether I speak the truth.

Restraints?

Doctor, I don't understand. We have already agreed that it is impossible for one of your kind to place me under any sort of confinement, compulsion or restraint.

Promise?

Can you define the word?

I don't understand. Can you redefine the word using different propositions?

All right. I think I see.

Well, if you are sure that an unenforceable statement of intent will suffice, then I will happily give my word.

I solemnly promise not to hurt you or anyone else gathered here to assess my intention in seeking absolution for my sins, for any reason whatsoever.

Will that do?

You're welcome. How shall we proceed?

I see. Very well. Here is a simple description of my relationship to the species of Mind known as the Iarcho.

I will try to remain calm.

I encountered the Iarcho in the same way as all the other doomed species of Mind I had previously met. The difference was, this time I knew what to expect. I knew I had to get my warning over as quickly as possible, before they could succumb to the infection ravaging the universe. In my experience, the infection rate was one hundred per cent and the recovery rate was zero. Every species that became infected was destroyed, and every species I had ever encountered contracted the disease. Ancient as I was, and powerful, I felt powerless against this unnameable nemesis. I had to do something. My previous attempts at communication had failed, to my cost and that of other Minds. I was failing in my responsibility. Now I had to try something different.

My first encounter with the Iarcho took place in the gulf between galaxies. I met one of their outflung symmetries, an ancient metallic object loaded with suspended organic material travelling at what they would consider enormous velocities between stars. I contacted the extension of the symmetry responsible for decision-making and guidance of the object and described the extinction threat that its species faced. The intelligence responded with curiosity but no fear. I sought to further amplify the danger. The intelligence indicated that it felt no personal threat. Knowing that my time was short and that successive generations of the Iarcho Mind would not be able to maintain a coherent and consistent communication, I determined the only effective course of action was to provide an immediate threat to the existence of the intelligence with which I was communicating. My intent was to provide an opportunity for it to comprehend an actual, immediate danger and therefore learn enough to protect itself when the larger threat arose in the future. Given adequate time for preparation, the Iarcho might survive.

I destroyed the organic cargo.

The symmetry did not respond in the way I had hoped. It showed no fear. It did not attempt to communicate with any of the other components of the Iarcho Mind.

I was not surprised by this reaction. It had been my experience that Mind often behaved irrationally, in defiance of the logical order of things. But I had planned carefully for this eventuality and I knew what to do next.

My second encounter with the Iarcho Mind came inside a shell they had built around a small blue-white star. By their standards, the shell was gargantuan, an incredible achievement. The shell orbited the blue-white star equatorially, the polar regions supported against solar gravity by moon-diameter pipes containing water pumped at orbital velocities at right angles to the shell's rotation. Night and day cycles were provided by gigantic sails orbiting within the shell. It was an engineering feat to stagger the imagination, yet the Iarcho I met used resin data crystals containing the history of their people as fuel for fires and lived in caves while their magnificent cities were home only to scavengers and rampant jungles.

I wondered if the Iarcho Mind had already contracted the inevitable infection.

I managed to communicate after a fashion, by assuming the guise of a figure I took to be one of their deities, but the exchanges held little meaning. I showed them ancient cities and the ruin to which they had come; I allowed them to glimpse the greatness that had brought them across the universe to their new home.

They saw all and comprehended nothing.

I told them of the sickness of stars that would swallow them if they did not heed my warning. They cowered and writhed, and killed their young in my name. But they did not understand.

Finally, I rained blue fire upon their tribal communities from holes I made in the skin of their world. They reacted as I had come to expect, their life bleeding away into the jungle as the air they breathed bled into a larger universe they no longer believed in.

I couldn't bear their pain and fear, so I left the Iarcho to their inevitable dissolution, instead following their ancient tracks further back towards their point of origin.

The Iarcho were a star-travelling species of Mind. I could afford to let this component die, a sacrifice made willingly if it would save the central intelligence.

My third encounter with the Iarcho Mind came in a galaxy-sized geodesic construct orbiting a black hole almost as large as that from which I had watched the first matter in the universe emerge in a storm of free electrons. Here lived the Mind that had long abandoned elements of itself among the outflung regions of the galaxy, fuelled by the ingenious conversion of stray electrons falling free of the event horizon.

Here, where death and life were more intricately linked than at any time in Iarcho history, would the hoped-for meeting of Mind finally take place.

Here also, my hopes were finally abandoned.

For although the Iarcho were an extraordinarily advanced species of Mind, they had by now come to suffer greatly from the inter-generational information loss that had proved such an insurmountable obstacle to my previous attempts to communicate with other Mind in the universe. In fact, their lives were shorter now than they had ever been, a sure sign of advanced infection and incipient death.

I had no recourse but to abandon communication in the hope that a simple attack would provide the impulse necessary for any sufficiently aware components of the Iarcho Mind to prepare themselves for the major infection I knew would follow.

I changed the strong-force interactive bond between the molecules of the matter from which their geodesic edifice was constructed.

I watched in hopeful anticipation as the construct fell into the black hole. There were individual Iarcho here without number, and I saw that each perceived the moment of death with terror and madness. Yet still no warning came from their deaths to other elements of the Iarcho Mind.

As the last Iarcho fell to its death, torn silently apart by gravity's tide, I wondered if I might not have made a mistake. I watched stray electrons escape from the event horizon, and I considered my actions carefully.

No. I had acted with good faith and the best of intentions. I had observed, as only a being of my longevity and power could, the evolution and actions of every intelligent species of Mind I had encountered. Their birth, coalescence, the ignition of their intelligence, their long fall to the inescapable infection – all had all been charted and remained, intricately patterned, within my memory. My actions against the Iarcho Mind had been carefully considered and flawlessly executed. I had made no mistake.

The fault clearly lay with the Iarcho themselves.

Something about their intellectual make-up made them incapable of anticipating or even comprehending their own destruction.

Fortunately, the Iarcho still existed in the universe. Following older, even fainter traces and symmetries, I eventually reached their world of origin, and here my final encounter began. But time was against me now, for I knew that soon the infection would become terminal. The Iarcho would regress to an animalistic state, blast each other apart with internal warfare as their intellect failed, falling eventually to liquid dissolution while first their world and then their star dissipated into the void. Then another Mind, unique in all the universe, would have vanished never to return, taking with it one more of my ever-dwindling opportunities to find love.

Sadly, this phase of my attempt to save the Iarcho was briefest of all. For none now but one could understand me and that one had already given herself to prescient madness. I watched as her peers dressed her in thorns and sacrificed her in the name of her mother, and knew then that I had failed.

I could but mourn the passing of another Mind.

Unable to bear the last inevitable death throes, I altered the atomic mass of hydrogen within the Iarcho star.

Their end, at least, was thankfully brief.

Merciful?

Of course I believed I was being merciful. Why else administer the *coup de grâce?*

I did not know then what I know now: what you, Doctor, and the Lords of Time have brought so brutally to my attention.

I did not realise time for me moved in reverse of time for every other living thing in the universe. I did not know I was born at the end of all things, not the First Mind but the Last. That what I perceived to be a terrible infection was simply the natural order of evolution for all life other than myself.

If we are lucky, understanding comes before the end. In this I consider myself unjustly rewarded for my sins. For the desperate truth is that my understanding came at the price of many such species of Mind as the Iarcho.

I do not plead innocence, for I know I am guilty of evil beyond measure by any judgement you are capable of making. In truth I hope for nothing more than to have demonstrated my tragic intentions, and offer nothing in retribution beyond the knowledge that I will exist throughout all of time, arriving at last at that place you consider the beginning of all things, and find my lonely end there, in the singularity that for me is the inevitable destiny of the ever-contracting universe.

In all this time I will never know love.

Redemption?

Of course I wish for it. But I know now I can never earn it. Even I cannot turn back time.

And so, Doctor, I leave you, in full knowledge of my all too human tragedy, with such apologies as one so misguided as I can give.

As ever I wish you well and hope for more.

Goodbye.

Time passed, the brief, stuttering moment of light at the end of the universe. I waited through the collapse, feeling my own structure contracting with the universe. The end would be soon, I knew it. The Iarcho had gone, their ancestor species had gone, the Doctor and his kind had gone. Now only I was left. Time and matter shrank. Heat increased, a steepening ramp I was happy to climb, in search of a final end at what for Mind to come, would be the beginning of all things.

The walls of the universe pressed down upon me, confining me as no Mind ever could. I was defined by the space in which I lived and now that space was ending.

Senses overloading, finally, I sensed the end was near. I felt no pain. Just light, packed so densely now it was a physical pressure against me.

The pressure became overwhelming, unbearable.

Was this what it felt like to die? To have life ended? To know the frustration that everything you hoped and strove for was all for nothing, that it would vanish in a moment of time so small as to be unmeasurable?

I had watched the end of all Mind, all life in the universe. Now it was my turn, alone at the end of all things, crushed from existence in what, for them, would be a singularity of meaningless potential.

Their birth, my death.

I waited.

The last moment in the universe ended – but I did not.

Instead, a sudden truth ripped through me.

I was not alone! I was not even dying. I screamed, I sang, every part of me altered now, bursting with new life and energy. Truth came then, and with it an understanding I could never grasp while bound by a single universe.

The truth: that there are many universes, each one expanding endlessly within its own higher dimensional membrane. That the 'branes move within a still larger space, in directions I could never previously conceive. Colliding, potential existing within the 'branes releases energy. Singularities give birth to universes, each cradled in its own eternity of time.

At the end of such a universe, I am born. I believe I am alone forever. But I do not yet comprehend what forever is. Other universes mean other Minds. Other Minds like me. An infinity of Others, living and touching, if briefly and infrequently, for eternity.

The 'branes approach, touch, part, leaving new singularities kindled where only potential had previously existed. In a space of time without measure, the moment of destruction inverts.

I am alive.

Alive!

And finally, endlessly, I know love.

Last Rites

Marc Platt

The tannoy bing-bonged.

'All remaining passengers are advised that Flight 600386W, the 1830 hours to Sehebra Space Junction, is now boarding at Gate 91. This is the final personnel flight from Epajaenda Resource Sphere. There are no more flights after this. Remaining time to planetary closure six hours and 45 minutes.'

A squall of brown rain hurtled against the giant windows of the spaceport lounge. Lights on the tall control tower and landing concourse outside rippled and turned a baleful yellow. The Doctor appeared in the doorway from the observation balcony, shook out his smoking umbrella and threaded his way between rows of empty seats until he reached Ace.

'Bank holidays, eh?' she said with a grin.

The Doctor frowned and sat down. He shuffled the bulging plastic bag he was carrying under the seat.

'It's traditional,' she went on. 'Book the whole family on a week in Marbella and spend most of it at the airport.'

'Ah,' he said and studied a hole in his umbrella where the acid rain had eaten through the fabric.

The lounge was empty, apart from a village of six domed tents at the far end, between the *Bureau de Change* and the dried-up fountain. The tents were grey and battered, adorned with faded blue and white squiggles that might have been religious iconography or alien graffiti. Steam wisped from vents at the top as if the inhabitants were simmering lightly.

The lounge's retail outlets were shuttered and abandoned. Anything not welded down had been looted. Torn streamers and the occasional battered glitter hat were strewn across the functional fittings – detritus from any number of leaving parties. Something like a blue tumbleweed tumbled past, heading for the line of check-in desks. An airy mass of fibrous veins apparently liberated from the clumsy nuisance of the flesh. When a sharp-suited security guard appeared in its path, it stopped, rocked gently back and forth for a moment and turned sharp right, tumbling instead towards the bathrooms.

The security guard stood watching the encampment of tents, mumbling into his earphone. A flap on one dome opened and a wide, grey-green head protruded. Its large frog eyes blinked and its throat swelled and sank. The creature raised its hands, made a circle with its spindly fingers and spat through the hole at the guard. The guard gave no reaction. The creature gave a belch of defiance and retreated again.

'That was Crospa,' said Ace. 'He's their spokesman. Well, more like *croak*sman really.'

'Still resisting deportation,' observed the Doctor. 'Either they have no homes to go to or an exceedingly good reason for staying.'

Another brown squall clattered acid hail against the windows. The Doctor stared with narrowed eyes at a spike-haired black rat sifting through the detritus of a litter bin. He edged one foot back against the bag under the seat as if checking it was still there. Ace was aware of a smell. It was somehow familiar, acrid but sweet, like rotting fruit, but she couldn't remember what it reminded her of. She leaned out of her chair, reaching for the bag. 'What did you find?' But he smacked her hand away sharply.

'Always questions.'

'That's a *nothing* then.'

'Nothing of anything,' he declared with an abruptness that could only mean *plenty* and *mind your own business.*

She sat down again in disgust. 'We've been here twenty-nine hours and I can't work everything out myself! They keep announcing the final flight, but there's no one here to get on it.'

'Probably all gone already.'

'Apart from the Travellers. And they don't seem to care. And another thing...' She was getting into the mood for this. 'I wouldn't ask so many questions if you occasionally told me what you were up to.'

He sighed, delved into a pocket and produced his gun-shaped scanner. Figures danced on the display screen. Here comes the *blind me with science* bit, she thought.

'Local tachyon flare levels are 86 per cent above normal. Emissions are increasing at a rate of 2.69 TERPSecs over 31.'

'Oh, right. And in simple terms?'

'That *is* simple.'

'If your name's Einstein.'

The Doctor shrugged. 'I went outside.'

'Outside the terminal?'

'Not a pleasant experience, given that the air is a corrosive soup of pollution. I did a tour of the spaceport perimeter. I needed to take some more readings.'

'Of the tachyon flares?'

He nodded grimly. 'That was the intention. But there was a hole in the perimeter fence. As if something had chewed its way in. Something large.'

Ace's eyes darted towards the streaming windows. There were fewer lights outside now. The darkness seemed to grow. 'Something that lives out there? In that?' The floor suddenly trembled. She gripped the sides of her seat. 'Earthquake!'

His hand planted on her shoulder. 'Just the planet shuddering.' He ignored her glance of alarm. 'There's a fissure in local space. A fault-line. The TARDIS picked it up.'

'What? Like the one under San Francisco?'

'Big enough for the whole planet to fall through... if it opens.'

Ace looked around the weather-beaten passenger lounge. 'That'd be worth seeing. Will there be an explosion?'

'Probably the reverse.'

'An implosion? Boring.'

'You are a slave to the instant gratification of the loud bang,' he snapped. 'The discerning find far more pathos and resonance in the whimper.'

She did a mock cringe. 'You're not going to take me to another opera, are you?' When he didn't rise to the bait, she added, 'Don't suppose anyone will miss this planet anyway. The state it's in.'

His eyes narrowed. 'Who have you been talking to?'

'No one.'

'Apart from Crospa, the spokesman for the Travellers over there. And the security guard whose name-tag describes him as Safensound.'

'That's his security company. His name's Essjee 78.' Damn, she thought. Fell into that one.

'Aha! And what did you find out?'

'He's all right. Bit of a plank, but his eyes are this amazing electric green...'

The Doctor fluttered his fingers in irritation. 'Not the guard, the situation!'

'What is this? Continuous assessment?'

'It's helpful to me.'

From the distant tents, came a sound of croaking. A frog chorus like night-time around a pond. The Travellers were starting their protest song again.

Ace took a deep breath and told the Doctor about the planet Epajaenda Resource Sphere. A video-brochure she had picked up called the planet 'a treasure house of indispensable resources, serving the galactic industrial machine for over three hundred local years with supplies of unique mineral wealth'. But now that the place had been thoroughly gutted, the companies were moving on to the next treasure house.

'And?' said the Doctor.

'Everybody out,' she added. 'The place has been cleared and the planet closes down. Once everyone's off, it'll be a tip for industrial by-products and radioactive waste.'

'The atmosphere is already turning into mulligatawny. I've rarely seen anywhere so toxic.'

'Essjee reckons that's all the place is good for. They've got to put the stuff somewhere.'

'Suppose they didn't produce it in the first place. In a few hours, the Gug-Truckers and their dumper ships will arrive and start spewing down the galaxy's industrial and unmentionable residue. If the planet's still here.'

The frog chorus was getting louder. The Doctor stood and walked slowly towards the encampment.

'Time to get moving, sir,' said a man's voice. A tall, dark security man with alarmingly green eyes, was looming over them.

'Hi, Essjee,' said Ace.

The Doctor raised his hat. 'We have our own transport, thank you.'

'There are no other ships, sir. Flight 600386W is the last. No one is allowed to stay. Please show me your identity permits.'

'Sorry. They're in our ship.'

'There are no other ships, sir. Flight 600386W is the last. No one is allowed to stay. I require your identity permits.'

Ace and the Doctor exchanged glances. 'Have I been chatting up a robot?' she said.

'An android,' the Doctor observed. 'Quite a sophisticated model. You could have done worse.'

Ace swore under her breath.

'Is this your baggage, sir?'

'What?' snapped Ace, and then realised that Essjee 78 was eyeing the plastic carrier under the seat.

'All unattended luggage will be confiscated by security forces and may be destroyed.'

'It's not unattended,' announced the Doctor, hurrying back. 'It's a personal souvenir of our trip.' He snatched at the evil-smelling bag, but Essjee already had a hand on it.

'Please may I see the contents, sir.' His voice was unerringly, unnervingly polite. Ace realised, with alarm, that his eyes had flickered from acid green to flame red. She suddenly remembered where she'd caught that rotting smell before. She'd worked in enough fast food outlets both on Earth and elsewhere to recognise it. It was the behind-the-fridge smell that appeared a week after the Rentokil man had been round, when there was a rush to clear away the evidence before the Environmental Health Inspector arrived.

'It's private!' The Doctor wrenched the bag back, but the guard's grip was firm. They both tugged for a moment before the cheap plastic stretched and tore, spilling the contents to the floor with a dull thud.

'Strewth!' announced Ace.

Seven dead rats in a circle, laid out like slices of pie, their tails knotted together, giving swollen vent to their sickly corruption. Little horrors with yellow chisel teeth. Ace covered her nose and mouth.

'Alert. Assistance required in lounge three.' Essjee was registering no emotion at all. Curious frog-heads were appearing from the flaps in the tent village.

The Doctor poked at the arrangement with the tip of his umbrella. 'A *Rattenkoenig*. A Rat King. Not an uncommon anomaly on a dying world.'

'Where did you find this, sir?'

'Down by the perimeter fence near Terminal Two.'

Essjee turned smoothly towards them. 'Areas outside the terminals are restricted for civilian workers.'

'Very sensible. You don't want just anyone wandering about. It's not safe out there.'

Ace was aware of more Travellers emerging from their tents, nudging each other and croaking with interest. Several had hopped up onto the seats for a better view.

Two more sharp-suited Safensound guards were striding towards the Doctor and Ace. One was carrying a bunch of shiny white isolation suits. The other held a large canister with a nozzled hose. 'Please put these on, sir, and come with us,' said the first. 'Your identities need to be validated.'

'Official mumbo jumbo,' intoned the Doctor. The second guard unleashed a spray of acrid disinfectant at them. Ace choked and fell against a seat.

'That's enough!' The Doctor darted in front of Ace and opened his umbrella to stave off the spray. After a second, he looked out and levelled an accusing finger at their persecutors. 'Is this any way to treat the public? There's been a serious breach of security in this spaceport for which I hold you responsible. Why was the electric perimeter fence turned off?'

The three guards stared implacably. Ace, her own eyes still stinging, could see that the range of Safensound production models was limited. Her Essjee had the same nose as the Essjee with the spray. Both back-up Essjees had the same mouth. The mode of all three's eyes flickered down in unison from red to orange. 'The Resource Sphere is closing for business. All systems are shutting down. You have violated the integrity of the *cordon sanitaire* that surrounds the spaceport.'

The Doctor nodded at the dead rats. 'You don't let anyone outside, but you've let something else in.'

With accustomed skill, one of the guards produced a piece of plastic sheeting, which he threw over the dead rats, and scooped up the evidence.

'Very neat,' observed the Doctor. 'But that specimen was dead. And just a forerunner for what I'm sure you know came through the fence.'

'If you have been on the surface without protection, sir, you will have been contaminated by the atmosphere.'

The Doctor pushed aside the proffered white suits. 'Not today, thank you. I tried not to breathe and I had my umbrella. My companion has been in the safety of the terminal all the time.'

'Why did you break through the fence?'

'I did not. Check your security cameras. Or have you turned those off, too? We are neither terrorists nor environmental protestors.'

There was a moment of scrutiny. Ace could hear the croaking commentary of the Travellers behind them as the guards' eyes scanned the Doctor. He smirked in the superior way that humans reserve for mere machines and aliens reserve for humans. And something squeaked nearby. In the corner of her eye, Ace noticed something scurrying... several black things moving so fast they were lost behind the seats. Then she realised the guards had turned towards her.

She coughed uneasily under their gaze and the Doctor hurriedly waved a hand. 'Could I have a word? Please excuse my companion, she is an authority on combat and strategy and, as such, any explosive devices she may be carrying on her person can easily be explained away as items of research.'

The first Essjee spoke calmly, but his eyes went back to red. 'Quantities of crude explosive devices hidden on the female subject. Both will be taken into custody and deported for interrogation on Sehebra Central.'

Hands seized Ace and the Doctor, pushing them out of the lounge. Then they heard the scream. The lowest, slowest scream Ace had ever heard. More a squishy death rattle of a last gasp as, out of the corridor to the bathrooms, came what was left of the blue tumbleweed. No longer capable of even half a tumble, it was crawling, its fibrous body all strung out and broken, smearing the floor with blue blood. Around it, harrying and biting, surged a small stream of black rats, their squeaks of delight drowning the tumbleweed's final screams as they tore it to pieces.

The guards acted quickly. Letting go of Ace and the Doctor, they drew pencil guns from their jackets and set about picking off each individual rat in the turmoil. Unimpaired by human foibles, they were precision marksmen. But more rats kept appearing from the corridor, from out of litter bins, squeezing through impossible gratings in air vents.

Compelled by fear to watch, Ace felt a gentle touch on her shaking arm. She turned, expecting to find the Doctor, but she was face to face with the permanently broad green smile of one of the Travellers. 'Shelter,' it croaked, and Ace saw the Doctor was beckoning to her. She nodded and they ran and hopped towards the village of tents.

Behind them, the guards were apparently too absorbed in coping with the seething inundation of black vermin to either notice or care that their prisoners were making an escape.

The tannoy bing-bonged.

'This is the penultimate call for remaining passengers on Flight 600386W, the 1830 hours to Sehebra Space Junction, now boarding at Gate 91. If Group Nine passengers from the DC Mining Corporation are in the spaceport, please report immediately to Gate 91. This is the final personnel flight from Epajaenda Resource Sphere. Take-off will be in 25 minutes. There are no more flights after this. Remaining time to planetary closure five hours and 55 minutes.'

From the tent, the sound of the gunshots and the squeals of dying rats had long ceased. Apart from the announcements, an ominous silence had descended on the spaceport lounge.

'This can't be safe,' muttered Ace. 'They must know we're in here. Why don't they follow?' But she resisted the urge to look outside.

'Oh, yes.' The Doctor sipped at the bowl of warm green tea he had been given by their hosts. It was like a sauna inside the domed tent and smelt like a greenhouse. In the centre of the area, a large bowl of liquid was steaming gently over a single tiny flame. Swathes of coloured beads dripped from the roof. Through the vapour, seated on the floor opposite them, was Crospa, the Travellers' leader, resembling some ancient green sage. His thin webby toes splayed out under long legs built like levers. His knees rose above his head. He wore rough-cut tribal clothes woven with more beads and had a resigned smile, the way most frogs do.

'Well, go on,' the Doctor urged Ace. 'You've known Mr Crospa longer than I have. You make conversation.'

'I only said "All right" to him. And we swapped names.'

'It was a start. You've opened relations.'

But she was otherwise preoccupied, watching a small brown fin circling in her bowl. 'There's something alive in my tea.'

'Just smile and remember your manners.'

'I don't think I want any manners.' She watched the fin complete a neat figure of eight.

'If the ooflu distresses, return it to the pool,' suggested Crospa. His voice was liquid, like the dark gurgling of a drain.

'Ooflu?' She stared at the bowl. 'No. Really, it's fine. I just got spooked by the rats out there. I'm not really thirsty... or hungry.'

'Hungry?' Crospa's throat ballooned alarmingly, bigger and bigger, until the chieftain erupted with an enormous croak of laughter. Flaps all around the tent opened and other frog heads appeared, all split wide with pink, tongue-waggling amusement. 'The ooflu gives spice to the drink, but not to the inside.'

'I think the fish is a sort of seasoning,' said the Doctor. 'But you don't eat him.'

Crospa rocked back and forth, which seemed to be his way of nodding. 'If the ooflu goes down, he soon comes back up!'

Ace tried to force a laugh, but it came out as a large uncontrollable burp. She cringed with apologetic embarrassment. The Doctor ignored her and dabbled a finger at the ooflu in his own bowl. To her amazement, Ace saw that the Traveller's chieftain was slapping his feet on the floor with delight. 'We thank you for the compliment,' he said and waited for the laughter to subside and the heads of his followers to withdraw. His huge black, red-ringed eyes met hers through the vapour. 'Why do you stay here?'

'I was just going to ask you that,' said Ace. 'You know this planet's finished.'

There was a general croaked reaction from outside the tent. 'No, no,' insisted Crospa. 'Not finished. After the cold dark time comes the light to wash the dark clean. New birth and new growth. New beginning.'

The Doctor leaned towards Ace like a royal advisor. 'I think he's talking about seasoning again. Well, seasons to be exact.'

'I'd figured that,' Ace muttered. She turned back to Crospa. 'Are you planning to settle here? Coz, if you are, you're in for a bit of a shock. Not a good idea. They've already scraped out the planet and once everyone's off, they'll turn it into a giant rubbish tip. All the muck and radioactive rubbish from other worlds will get dumped here. It's what they call sweeping under the carpet.' She caught the narrowing of Crospa's eyes. 'Sorry. Maybe you know that. I suppose you might like that sort of thing.'

The Traveller chief slapped a foot on the floor, but now he was angry. 'Is this true? We had an agreement.'

'Agreement?' interrupted the Doctor. 'What agreement's that?'

Crospa inflated his throat and made a popping noise. Instantly another

Traveller bobbed into view, carrying what resembled a short, decorated stem of bamboo. Crospa bowed to the object in deepest veneration. He reached a finger inside the tube and extracted a scrolled document. 'Our agreement between the peoples of Epajaenda and the Derris-Cuthbertson Mining Company.'

'May I?' asked the Doctor. At a nod from Crospa, the Keeper of the Deed ambled round the tent and unrolled the document, holding it up for the Doctor to peruse. The Doctor bowed reverently to the sacred paper and studied it, his eyes darting back and forth in mounting disbelief. 'Crospa, am I right in thinking this was once your planet?'

The old Traveller nodded. 'It remains so, Doctor. Epajaenda... our mud and stone, air and water. There are no words about rubbish or radiation.'

'But this deed was signed over three hundred years ago.' He squinted at the signature at the bottom. 'Who's this? Abraham Dennis Custardson?

'Derris-Cuthbertson,' insisted the Traveller. 'He signed, we spat on a shaken hand.'

'But they may have spat on the contract too. Spitting's different where they come from. According to this, you've sold away the rights to all of your world's mineral wealth. Now there's nothing left except a worthless shell. How could you agree to that?'

There was rumble in the ground and the air. The tent rattled and its beads shivered and clattered together. Crospa set both webbed feet on the floor as if trying to steady the uneasy planet. His voice was calm and rich with the weight of his heritage. 'The world was old and we were old too. We had been in the pool all spring and summer. When our ancestral spawners saw that dark winter was approaching, they knew that it was time to sleep. But there is too much to forget when we close our eyes and are lost in dreams. Then, out of the stars came Derris-Cuthbertson with gifts of ships to travel and visit other worlds and other summers.'

'How very generous,' muttered the Doctor. 'You make him sound like some kind of saviour.'

Crospa lowered his head in benediction. 'He was a mining prospector with a good heart.'

'He'd have been one of the Sixty-Two-ers in the old Earth land rush. They'd stake a claim on any old lump of rock they flew past.'

'And you believed this bloke?' interrupted Ace.

Crospa puffed out his throat and went grey with astonishment. 'Derris-Cuthbertson promised and we agreed. Hospitality is everything. Have some more ooflu water.'

'Erm, thanks. But I haven't finished this one yet.'

'We have travelled far,' croaked Crospa. 'We are Travellers of many moons. We never stay long anywhere. Other worlds do not welcome us. Many are too dry, their summers too hot or too quick. Their people angry and arid. We give them greeting. They give us dust.'

The Doctor studied the deed again. 'And now you've returned to claim back your world. Do you still have your ships?'

Crospa shook his heavy head. 'They were ancient and unsteady. We sold them to a vintage spaceship dealer to get fares home for some of us. The rest await our signal.'

'One born every minute,' muttered Ace.

'The circle is complete,' continued Crospa. 'Derris-Cuthbertson gave his word that Epajaenda would be returned to us.'

'You may have noticed that the tenants haven't exactly left your world in the state that you'd like to find it. It's polluted and infested with vermin. When a world is dying, that's when the rats claim their dominion.'

Ace shuddered. 'It looked like they were hunting in packs.' She fancied she could hear distant squeaking again.

'That's just the start. When they get the upper hand, rats have their own little social evolutionary tricks to play.'

'The Rat King.'

'The *Rattenkoenig*. Rats aren't exclusive to Earth. They've got a claw-hold on most inhabited planets. Always scavenging on the rotten pickings of so-called civilisation. The stuff we sweep under the carpet.' He paused to take another gulp of his drink as if it might take the nasty taste away. 'The Rat King is a trick they try out every so often when the conditions seem favourable. It's another step up the evolutionary scale. Several rats with knotted tails to make a collective beast that increases its power and intelligence. If it doesn't work, they still have plenty to scavenge off.'

'And if it does work?' said Ace.

The Doctor smiled at her and Crospa. 'Maybe it would be better if you went with the last flight to Sehebra and registered a claim for damages with the authorities there. I'm surprised the port authorities here haven't already tried to force you. If you hurry you might still get on board.'

'Derris-Cuthbertson made a promise. We honoured our part of the contract. He will honour his.' Crospa raised his hands, made a circle with his fingers and spat through the hole.

The Doctor raised an eyebrow. Then he stood up and bowed low. 'You're nothing if not optimistic, Crospa. But I fear that, after three hundred years, your friend Derris-Cuthbertson may no longer be alive, let alone honouring contracts. If you will excuse us...'

Ace nudged him. 'The fault.'

'Not now,' he hissed in irritation.

'Fault?' asked their host. 'Whose fault is this?'

'Ah, we all have faults,' mused the Doctor with a degree of nonchalance that verged on the absurd. 'Unfortunately in this case, the blame lies at the door of the universe itself.'

'Doctor!' Ace protested.

'Quiet! I'm being diplomatic.' He waved a hand airily. 'Probably nothing to worry about, but the spatial location of Epajaenda appears to be sitting on a fault-line in the temporal continuum. I was attempting to pinpoint the anomaly, but so far it eludes me. It should be an easy thing to find, but you'd almost think it was deliberately dodging my readings.' He produced his scanner-gun again and completed a sweep of the tent, watching the figures fluctuate and resolve on the little screen.

Far from looking alarmed, Crospa simply beamed. 'We are aware that the ice is thin here, Doctor. But we cannot leave.'

The Doctor chewed his lip and frowned at his readings. 'This may be your last chance to get away.' But Crospa's only response was a throaty gurgle. The Doctor pocketed his scanner and bowed low. Nudging Ace to follow suit, he added, 'Thank you for the rescue and the tea. If the universe was a fair place, your hospitality in such unfortunate circumstances would be the stuff of legend. I'll see what I can do.'

'Thank you, Doctor and Ace. But your efforts are unnecessary.' The Traveller chief closed his first and second eyelids and appeared to sleep. His guests were turning to leave when he re-opened one eye and added, 'We intend to enjoy the last few hours. We will be happy if you can join us.'

There was a sudden sound of gushing water followed by an outbreak of delighted croaking. Crospa threw back the tent's main flap to reveal the spaceport lounge's abandoned fountain. Water was spilling from the top of a tall cone, down mirrored surfaces into a wide marble basin. Several of the Travellers had already clambered over the parapet and were splashing and hopping about in the pool amid the floating litter.

One of them turned towards Crospa. 'We found it! The way to start the water. Look! Epajaendan water at last!' And he splashed them vigorously. The Doctor, with a look of extreme concern, shook the water from his hat, fetched out his scanner again and directed it at the fountain. Before he could take any readings, his arm was grabbed and Ace was pointing away across the lounge.

A group of at least twenty Essjees was standing staring at them. Evenly spaced, sharp-suited, implacable, looking for trouble. Red-eye mode. One of them pointed, singling out the Doctor and Ace. Behind them, the lounge floor was strewn with the bodies of dead rats.

The tannoy bing-bonged again.

'This is the final call for passengers on Flight 600386W, the 1830 hours to Sehebra Space Junction, now boarding at Gate 91. If anyone knows the whereabouts of Group Nine passengers from the DC Mining Corporation, please report immediately to Gate 91. This is the final personnel flight from Epajaenda Resource Sphere. Take-off will be in eight minutes. There are no more flights after this. Remaining time to planetary closure five hours and 38 minutes.'

The Essjees were moving in. Ace had lost track of which had been her original guard. Behind her, she could hear the Travellers splashing in the fountain and croaking their protest songs.

'Shouldn't you be getting on board the last flight?' called the Doctor as the guards loomed.

'Yeah,' yelled Ace. 'Don't you have homes to go to?'

'Probably not,' the Doctor suggested. 'Androids are sad like that.'

A cold hand landed vice-like on his arm. An Essjee towered over him. 'Sir? Are you a passenger with Group Nine DC Mining Corp?'

'No, I am not!' snapped the Doctor.

'Say yes,' mumbled Ace.

'What?'

'Are you sure, sir?' the guard intoned.

'Why?' The Doctor regained his composure. 'People not checked in, holding up your flight? Didn't make it to the spaceport? Couldn't have run into a little rodent problem, could they? That'll go down well with the environmentalists.'

The guard ignored the remark and turned to Ace. 'Madam? Are you a passenger with Group Nine...?'

'Who are you calling *Madam*?' bawled Ace. 'Yes, we are with Group Nine.'

'Ace? What are you doing?' The Doctor was plainly mystified.

She met the guard's red-eyed stare head on. 'Our shuttle came down in the storm. We lost all our IDs. And my friend here is stressed and confused. Look at the state of his clothes. This is gross negligence on the part of DC and we demand immediate recompense!'

As the Essjee turned to its colleagues, Ace nudged the Doctor. '*How To Complain*. Chapter Three. It's in the TARDIS library.'

'One of Tegan's, I expect,' he said, dusting down his jacket and still looking puzzled.

'Oh, come on, Professor. DC Mining Corp – get it? Derris-Cuthbertson!'

'Oh, that. Yes, of course. Just testing your powers of observation.'

'Good, eh?' she grinned. 'And check his lapel badge too.'

The Doctor squinted at the guard's badge inscription. It read

'Safensound is a subsidiary of DC Investment Corp.' The Doctor started to smile. 'Nothing like a finger in every pie, eh?'

At that moment, the Essjee turned back. 'You are not recognised as members of Group Nine. You are already under arrest for possession of illegal weapons and contaminated materials. Deportation to be instigated with immediate effect.'

'Just one moment,' declared the Doctor. He turned and pointed to the fountain. 'What about our friends here? Surely you are not going to leave them to perish on this extremely inhospitable planet?'

The Travellers stopped their splashing and stared.

Twenty pairs of Essjee eyes went directly from red to green mode. 'Diplomatic immunity, sir,' said the leader.

'You don't say?' exclaimed the Doctor. 'Is that a direct order from the good old DC Board of Directors themselves? It must be close on three hundred years since Abe Derris-Cuthbertson first made his fortune panning in the Yukon with one pack-mule and a sledge. That was before he went on to far grander things in them newfangled spaceships.' The guard's eyes flicked up to orange mode, but the Doctor was in full flow by now. 'Still, the Board of Directors at DC must be chock-full of Abe's sons and grandsons by now, all fat and wealthy on grandpappy's pickings. So you tell them from me that these good people here had a deal with old Abe over the rights to this planet. And I aim to see that deal through.' He dabbed a finger at the guard's chest which was on the same level as his own head. 'You listening to me, sonny?'

Ace had been trying not to laugh. Surely no one could fall for that. But she reckoned that it might confuse a few stupid androids.

The Essjee pushed the Doctor's finger away. 'Please come with me, sir.' As he lifted his prisoner bodily into the air, there was a chorus of disapproval from the Travellers. Ace found herself similarly airborne, slung over a guard's shoulder. So maybe these androids were *too* stupid to get confused. But as the Essjees turned en masse to go, their path was suddenly full of leaping frog people, bounding in right over the guards' heads and brandishing bamboo staves to block the way. Several guards raised their guns.

At the front of the Travellers, Crospa stood his ground. 'These people are our guests. Release them now. You are guards, not warriors. Why do you attack rather than protect?'

'Stand aside, sir... please.' The Essjees took one unified step forward.

Crospa weighed his stave in his spindly hands. 'That is not hospitable.'

From his tilted viewpoint, clutched under the guard's arm, the Doctor called, 'You don't seem too bothered about moving the Travellers on. Or is it better for your Board of Directors if the embarrassing locals don't survive to tell the tale at all?'

'We bought shares in the company, too,' insisted Crospa. 'Release our friends now!' The Travellers, bobbing on their long legs, raised their staves in determined anger.

'No!' called the Doctor. 'Don't fight on our behalf!'

The floor thundered again. A jagged claw of blue lightning hissed through the high ceiling and struck the mirrored fountain. The edifice imploded and vanished completely, sucked out of reality in the briefest cloud of steam. There was a roar of energy. A wind, fresh and clean, tinged with ozone, blew at them, instantly reminding Ace of wet holidays in Weston-super-Mare.

In the air, above where the fountain had stood, an impossible throat of churning water had opened. A silver vortex like the surging tunnel inside an ocean roller, spitting foam and dribbling water from elsewhere into their reality.

'Get back, all of you!' yelled the Doctor. The guards were suddenly in confusion. Their eyes flickered, changing colour at random, like insane traffic lights. The Doctor struggled free and stumbled forward against the tide of fleeing travellers.

In a moment, Ace was beside him, her hair tangling in the sudden gale. 'Is this the fault?' she called.

He nodded. 'I should have stayed indoors. It was in here all the time. We're looking through into another dimension.' He glanced back at the Traveller chieftain, who was ambling up to join them. 'Crospa, you no longer have a world to stay on. Better get your people on that flight now before this window opens completely and swallows us all.'

'We stay, Doctor.'

'No one stays in this! Just go!'

Something boomed loudly at the lounge's tall observation windows. And again. A dark shape, at least twelve feet high, only visible by the exterior lights it blocked out, was throwing itself at the glass.

'Ah,' said the Doctor, full of foreboding. 'I thought the conditions might be favourable.'

'For the rats?' asked Ace. 'Is that one big rat?'

'No,' he growled. 'That would be evolutionarily impractical and look silly. This is rather worse.'

The Travellers and guards sidelined their differences and stared as the black shape rolled at the window again. This time, the impact cracked the glass into an opaque mosaic of numberless tiny jigsaw pieces. The huge shadow withdrew a little and then rushed again with a shriek like a thousand murderous flutes. The mosaic burst asunder. Glass showered down as an immense greasy sphere barrelled into the light, glinting with myriad tiny black eyes. Several thousand rat heads packed tightly together on the surface of an undulating globe of living filth, squealing their hatred and hunger.

'The King of Rat Kings,' whispered Ace.

The Doctor grimly surveyed the entity. 'A *Rattenkaiser.* An Emperor Rat. Top of the verminous ladder.'

The Essjees were already opening fire on the monster, but their guns were too precise, only able to pick off one rat at a time in the moving mass of rodents.

The Rat Kaiser advanced, rolling forward, oblivious to the shots. Behind it, more rats scampered through the shattered window and across the floor. With them came the stench of the rotting, flyblown carcass of the planet Epajaenda itself.

The Travellers were withdrawing towards their encampment, content to let the android guards carry out their defence, but lone rats were already scurrying between the tents. Beyond that, the cold wind blew in flecks of spray from the gaping throat of the vortex.

Ace was going through her pockets, fishing out the cans of explosive that the Doctor knew about, and the back-up emergency batch that she never admitted to carrying. 'Four for you,' she said, handing him the fresher cans. 'And four for me.'

The Doctor sniffed one. 'What's the expiry date on these?'

She shrugged. 'Time is relative, yeah? A couple might be down to a four-second delay.'

There was a crescendo of squeals above the shots. The Rat Kaiser had flung out a string of rats like a tendril. It wound around one of the guards, reeling him in until he was absorbed into the mass of the collective creature.

Ace tore off a ring-pull and flung one of her bombs. It struck the Rat Kaiser squarely on the side and was swallowed into the monster's depths. Several hundred rat heads turned and squealed their hatred at her. Then the side of the sphere blew out in a spray of blood and dead vermin. But the brute didn't stop. Immediately, a small inrush of rats scampered across the floor and took their places, filling in the writhing wound.

'Round the other way,' yelled the Doctor to the Travellers. 'Then make a run for the last flight!' But they were crouching together, mumbling a last half-hearted protest song.

'Go on!' yelled Ace, but her words were drowned by the scream of jet engines. Though the windows, a set of lights was angling up into the darkened sky. The last flight had gone.

Then the lights veered sharply to the side as different lights appeared from above. They approached until they blazed through the windows. A sleek, silver craft, honed like an arrowhead, was descending onto the landing area outside. Below it, caught in the fierce glow of its lights, the ground was seething with black rats, scurrying and scrambling over each other in desperate attempts to escape the burning down-thrust of the spaceship.

Moments later, a ramp descended and down he came, a tall figure cowled in darkness, before whom even the fearless rats fell back.

In the lounge, the Essjees stopped their barrage against the Rat Kaiser. The croaking song of the Travellers died as the dark, hooded figure entered through the window. The monster, seeing all ways at once, had no need to turn. It hissed its loathing, and began to roll at him. The figure waved a hand and a glittering energy field instantly circled the brute. It rocked back and forth in a rage, striking sparks as it tried to escape.

Ace wiped the blood-clotted hair out of her face. 'Who's this? One of those "daisy ex machine wash" geezers? Come to save the day?'

'A deus ex machina?' murmured the Doctor.

'That's the one.'

'I seriously doubt that. More like a death's head undertaker, come to say the last rites before the planet gets buried permanently.'

Ace nodded towards the Travellers. 'They don't seem to think so.' The group were ambling towards the figure like schoolchildren summoned before the headmistress. There was a smell like mothballs in the air.

Crospa raised his arms in greeting. 'Derris-Cuthbertson? Is it you? Are you really returning?'

'Is it him?' Ace whispered. 'Was all that Yukon stuff true?'

'Never even heard of him before,' sniffed the Doctor.

The figure, numinous and exuding power with every step, raised a hand in response. The hand was withered and skeletal. The voice, frail and weary. 'This is the time that I promised. I cannot forget. I made a pact to gain such power. That is my burden. I signed away my life for such wealth as your world has given me. And in return, I must do good deeds for ever.'

The Travellers began to sing again, praising their saviour.

'Sanctimonious Faustian twaddle,' called out the Doctor. 'You've been doing penance very nicely on the proceeds ever since.'

'Three hundred years of wandering.'

The Doctor glanced through the window at the ship. 'Very luxurious wandering from the look of it. It always pays to read the small print before you sign anything.'

The figure threw back his hood to reveal his skully head and eyes sunken almost without trace. 'The Board of Directors is agreed. It honours our original contract.'

There were cries of joy from the Travellers, but the Doctor started a slow handclap. He walked up to the imprisoned Rat Kaiser and squinted through the energy field at the ravening monster. 'I should hope so, considering all the damage you've caused.' He pointed towards the watery vortex. 'I take it this is part of your plan, too.'

Derris-Cuthbertson bowed his head. 'I forgive you your doubts. This temporal duct was created by our award-winning engineers in the workshops of DC Mining Corp. It will channel the filtered ocean of the planet Dirrijali in Om Ceti directly into this world, cleansing and replenishing Epajaenda for the original tenants.'

'Inhabitants!' snapped the Doctor. 'Original inhabitants and rightful owners!'

The ancient creature nodded, but the Doctor was incandescent with fury. 'And the inhabitants of Dirrijali?'

'Their world will be restored when their contract is up.'

'And you've plundered their mineral resources. One world after another. You've climbed on a treadmill and now you can't get off!'

'It is my burden and my curse,' agreed Derris-Cuthbertson. He advanced on the Travellers, who were still staring in a state of near trance at their redeemer. 'Please make your way to the viewing galleries at the top of the control tower, where you will have a good view. The security officers will escort you.'

There was much bowing as Crospa and the Travellers made their farewells and hopped after the guards to the lifts. Then Derris-Cuthbertson turned back to the Doctor. In his hand, he held a small transmitter. 'You should leave too. I must withdraw from this area before I order the sluice from Dirrijali to be opened.'

'Come on, Ace,' the Doctor said. 'The TARDIS is in the VIP lounge.'

But Ace blocked the old man's path. 'What about the dumping?'

His thin lips tried to smile. 'An oversight by the marketing department. It has been revoked.'

'Just in time,' she snapped.

The Doctor shook his head. 'Oh, dear. All that extra revenue you could have raked in from selling the licences. What will you tell the shareholders?'

The thin smile grew thinner. 'Are you from the press?'

'I could be,' smirked the Doctor. 'It depends. I can be anyone you dislike.' He walked towards the stairs leading to the VIP suite with Ace following. The old man, a figure of commercially marketable death for the economic universe, stood alone in the terminal lounge.

The Doctor and Ace were halfway up the stairs when they heard the squeaking. Below, a torrent of rats was streaming in through the broken window. More and more, all homing on a single point, crawling under each other, jamming themselves in tight, raising the shape of a new Rat Kaiser from the top down, so that it seemed to grow from the sea of vermin.

The old man, standing below, suddenly lifted his head towards his persecutors on the stairs and cracked a rictus grin across his stony face.

'Into the TARDIS now!' yelled the Doctor, throwing the key at Ace. She ran for shelter, but he lingered, just for a moment, on the stair.

The successor to the first Rat Kaiser was already half as big again. It grew still higher, seething its button-eyed, yellow-toothed rage. Emperor of its world.

'Goodbye, Doctor,' called Derris-Cuthbertson, dwarfed by the monster. He pointed the transmitter towards the churning sluice gate and, as the Rat Kaiser swallowed him whole, he pressed the button.

The Touch of the Nurazh

Stephen Hatcher

Jack Canning knew that it had just been bad luck. He had been in the wrong place at the wrong time. There was no way he could have known that the junior government official whom he had been cultivating would walk into the offices of the small electronics company at just the moment that he was passing himself off as a maintenance engineer. He had been able to make a quick exit from the building, but the game was up and it was no longer safe for him to remain in Bulgaria.

The journey from Sofia had passed relatively without incident. Canning knew, however, that to attempt to cross into Greece by road would be impossible. So, abandoning his car, he continued on foot, moving through the forest along the many paths created during the war by partisans, and used more recently by poachers and smugglers (the supply of Greek ouzo was surprisingly plentiful in the local villages).

It was just after nightfall and Canning was within five kilometres of the border when he became aware of his pursuers. The howl of a hound and the sound of voices alerted him to the danger. There was nothing to do but keep going. He pressed on further into the forest, taking to the bed of a shallow river, hoping to throw the dogs off his scent.

The stream became deeper and slower as it came down the hill towards the stretch of cleared land that marked the frontier with Greece. Canning knew that this would be the most dangerous part of his escape. The deforested strip was pockmarked with craters where unfortunate wildlife, not to mention earlier would-be escapees, had discovered the whereabouts of landmines. A chain of wooden observation towers gave their heavily armed occupants the clearest of views over the last stretch of Bulgarian soil.

The sounds of the dogs and their handlers were now close by. Canning knew that he had a stark choice, either to run for it or to wait for certain capture. Keeping to the edge of the forest until the last possible moment, Canning tensed then sprang. Head down, he ran literally for his life, cutting from side to side in the hope of avoiding the mines and the inevitable bullets. He was spotted almost at once. A shout rang out, followed by the first shot. Canning was lucky; it hit the ground no more than a foot to his right. Another shot came even closer. He looked up to see the border fence and the Greek checkpoint almost within touching distance.

At that moment, the third shot found its mark. Canning felt the force of the blow, which bowled him over seconds before he was overtaken by the searing pain in his right leg. He lay on his back, barely conscious, awaiting his captors. The men came out of the mist that was enveloping his vision, and as Canning lapsed into the relief of unconsciousness, their leader spoke.

'*Kalispera*, Mr Canning. Welcome to Greece.'

He sniffed the air and cast a penetrating gaze around the plain. In the distance he spied what appeared to be the ruins of a long-destroyed and abandoned city. This wasn't right. There should have been a civilisation here, people. This was a dead world, of no use to him. He couldn't understand it. Perhaps he had come to the wrong planet, or to the right planet at the wrong time. He had to check. He turned to go back to his capsule, but stopped. He had felt something. There had been a touch upon his mind. He was not alone.

'Hello, who is there?' He sent the words out telepathically. Before he could react, the creature was upon him – not physically, but in his mind. The traveller was under a mental assault, the like of which he had not encountered before. But he was strong and his assailant was weak and the outcome of the struggle was predictable, the traveller fought off his attacker.

As he turned once more to leave this world, he felt the creature's touch on his mind again, but this time it was different. Now even weaker, it pleaded pathetically. 'Help me! Do not leave me here!' The traveller gave an unpleasant smile. He stopped and addressed the creature.

'Who are you?'

The scene was one of utter carnage. At 31 for 5, the cream of England's batting had been swept aside – defiant Boycott, stubborn Edrich, elegant Luckhurst, plucky d'Oliveira and the blond giant, Tony Greig, were all back in the pavilion having found no answer to the ferocious pace of Lillee and the guileful swing of Massie.

Jack Canning sighed and briefly considered giving up on the cricket on the television. However, he stayed, reflecting on the good fortune that allowed him still to be able to watch the game – even if the Australians were winning. He settled himself even further down into the deep high-backed armchair and prepared to watch the horror of the English batting at Lords with a renewed satisfaction. As he adjusted his position, he felt a twitch of pain in his right shin. He grimaced, but almost immediately forgot his discomfort as M.J.K. Smith came close to losing his head to a vicious Dennis Lillee bouncer. His fellow cricket-lovers groaned, but Jack just smiled to himself and looked around the room.

There was Ted, whom Jack had come to know quite well in the six months that he had been here, and Alec Thomas, whom he had worked with in the aftermath of the Keller business. Jack didn't know the other two, except by sight.

But he did know that, like everyone else here, they were intelligence personnel – MI5, MI6, UNIT or whatever other organisation that even Jack didn't know about. Injured in the course of their duties, they were being cared for in the ultra-secure environment of Kenstone Hall.

Jack turned his attention to the next ball, another short-pitched delivery from Lillee, which Smith got right behind and played safely to the ground. Before the demon bowler could collect the ball to prepare for his next attempt on Smith's wicket and/or life, Jack was disturbed by a call from the doorway. It was Tony Maple, one of the nurses.

'Mr Canning, you've got a visitor. Your niece is here to see you.'

Jo Grant had enjoyed the train ride up from Paddington to Leamington Spa. Until her first visit to see her uncle Jack, about a month earlier, Warwickshire had been a part of England that she hardly knew at all. It had come as a delightful surprise to discover that the rolling hills of Shakespeare's county were one of the most green and pleasant places imaginable.

The taxi took her through the little spa town, with its somewhat faded Regency prosperity, and out into the countryside. After about twenty minutes' drive through increasingly narrow country lanes, she was deposited at the locked gates of Kenstone Hall.

She rang the bell and, after a wait of no more than half a minute, a small car drove up the gravel drive and came to a halt inside the gates. Two burly and forbidding men jumped out to investigate the visitor, the outlines of their handguns scarcely concealed beneath their jackets, incongruous in the warm sunshine. Jo flashed one of her most winning smiles and bade them a cheery hello, holding out the letter from Brigadier Lethbridge-Stewart. Seemingly won over as much by her smile as by her letter, the two security men smiled back at Jo, opened the gate, ushered her into the waiting car and drove her up to the hall.

Jack was delighted to see Jo again. His sister's daughter was his only niece – and consequently a favourite of his since her childhood. He was also very aware of the rules that forbade visitors to the hall. It was only Jo's position within UNIT that had allowed her to pull the strings necessary to bend those rules.

When he found her, she was waiting in the hallway, chatting to the security guards. Jack walked smartly across, his gait betraying only a very slight limp, and embraced his niece. 'Jo, my dear! What an absolute delight to see you!'

Jo returned the embrace and then took a step back to look at her uncle. 'Uncle Jack, you really are looking well, and you're out of that wheelchair already!'

Jo and her uncle spent the next couple of hours reminiscing about happy times and discussing each other's plans for the future as they wandered around the grounds in the late-June sunshine.

Jo's mind went back to her previous visit. On that occasion, Jack had been feeling very low. Not only was he clearly in a lot of pain from his shattered leg, but he had not yet come to terms with the bad prognosis for his injury. The doctors had made it quite clear to him that he would in all likelihood never walk again without the aid of a stick. Even that limited amount of mobility had seemed a long way off. Jack had been confined to the hated wheelchair, his leg unable to do so much as support his weight.

Jo had been shocked and upset to see her uncle in such a bad way and had pushed him in his chair, around the grounds, then sat chatting in the lounge with Jack and his friend Ted Parrish, both trying their best to cheer him up.

She would have come back to see him again much sooner if that had been possible, but things at work had got a little out of hand, what with the business with the Sea Devils and an unexpected mission to the planet Solos in the thirtieth century. And so it had been a month since she had visited; yet, looking at Jack, it was hard to believe that a much longer span of time had not passed. Jo checked mentally with herself that it had indeed been only a month. After travelling a thousand years into the future and back again, she could have become confused. But no, it had been five weeks at the most. The extent of Jack's recovery was quite amazing.

'So, will you be going back to work soon?' Jo asked, as they crossed the lawn towards the ornate fountain.

'Not quite yet. I've just about had it as far as being an agent in the field,' Jack smiled ruefully, 'but they are going to give me something to do in Whitehall. I suppose, at my age, that was going to happen sooner or later anyway, and I don't think I'm going to miss all of the rough stuff. But anyway, they want me to stay here for a while yet, just to be sure that everything's OK – probably until the end of next month.'

'Well,' said Jo, 'at the rate at which you're getting better, they'll want you in Munich for the Olympics.' Her uncle chuckled and they turned back towards the house. As they walked, Jo happened to glance around at some of the other residents enjoying the sun and fresh air. At the edge of the lawn, two men were playing tennis on a fenced-off court. With a start, Jo realised that she knew one of the men. 'Uncle Jack,' she began. 'Isn't that Tom Berkeley over there?'

'Yes, that's Tom.'

'But he was in a worse state than you were.' Jo remembered Tom, an old UNIT acquaintance, from a month previously, sitting in the communal lounge of the hall, paralysed from the waist down, yet here he was running around the tennis court.

'Yes, well,' said Jack. 'It looks as if he's on the mend, too.'

Jo didn't reply, but began examining the residents more closely. The more she thought about it, the more they seemed to be in remarkably good health – and the more Jo began to think that something was not quite right. These suspicions solidified into certainty when Ted Parrish walked around the corner of the building towards them, smiling broadly.

'Hello, Jo,' he said. 'How nice to see you again.' Jo froze as Ted held out his right hand for her to shake – the hand that Jo clearly remembered had been blown off. She recovered quickly from her shock and managed to shake Ted's hand, checking as she did both that the hand was real and that she hadn't simply been confused as to which hand was missing. Ted was clearly in possession of a full complement.

Once Jack's friend had walked on, Jo confronted her uncle. 'OK then, Uncle, just what's going on here?'

'I don't think anything's going on, Jo. What do you mean?'

'All these people, looking so healthy. And what about Ted's hand?'

Jack's expression suggested that he was almost remembering something, and then he looked puzzled, shook his head slightly and smiled indulgently at his niece. 'Well, they are all here to get better, you know. What about Ted's hand, anyway?'

Jo told her uncle what she had remembered of Ted's injury from her last visit. As the words passed her lips, she began to feel increasingly foolish – she must have imagined it, mustn't she? When Jack assured her that Ted had always had two good hands, Jo would almost have been inclined to accept it, if she hadn't noticed the strange blank look that came into her uncle's eyes as he attempted to reassure her and disappeared almost as soon as it had appeared.

Feeling uneasy, Jo accompanied Jack back to the hall and was taking her leave when Miss Caxton approached them. Jo had met the matron on her previous visit and had found the small, slightly built, very feminine woman in her mid forties to be efficient, caring and very charming.

Jack embraced his niece goodbye. Jo promised to return soon, and Miss Caxton walked her to the car, which would take her back to the gate, where a taxi would, by arrangement, be waiting. Jo asked the older woman about her uncle's condition.

'He's doing very well indeed,' came the reply. 'We'll soon have him out of here and back at work.'

'Yes,' remarked Jo. 'It's been something of a miracle cure all in all. I've noticed that a lot of your patients seem to be making remarkable recoveries.'

'We put most of it down to rest and clean air. And to our good care, of course.' The matron laughed. 'Well, goodbye, Miss Grant. Do come and see us again soon.' Miss Caxton ushered Jo into the car and shut the door.

Jo sat back in her seat, deep in thought as the car reached the gate and she transferred into the waiting taxi.

From an upstairs window, he had watched Jo Grant leave. He shook his head sadly and spoke under his breath to himself.

'Off you go, Miss Grant. I'm sure that you haven't seen anything that you shouldn't have, but I'm afraid that is a risk that I am not prepared to take. What a pity you came here.' He left the window and walked over to the desk.

By the time they had been driving for fifteen minutes, Jo was once more beginning to wonder whether she had, after all, imagined the whole thing.

The taxi slowed down as it approached the flashing warning lights, clanging alarms and descending barriers of an unmanned railway crossing. Jo looked up from a paper that she had begun to read to watch the train pass. As she did so, the car, which had almost come to a complete halt, suddenly shot forward, flinging Jo back into her seat and crashing through the barrier.

The car stopped on the line. With the sound of the crossing alarm still filling her ears, Jo called out to the driver, now slumped over the steering wheel. No reply. Jo reached through to the front seat of the car and pulled the driver upright. There was no mistaking the fact that he was quite dead – a trickle of blood ran from each of his ears.

In the distance, Jo could hear the train coming. She had to get out and quickly. She pulled on the door handle – locked! The other side was also locked. Jo clambered into the front of the car and manoeuvred herself into the passenger seat – the front doors, too, defied her every effort to open them.

Realising that she had only seconds before the car was crushed – and her with it – Jo began to pull at the body of the driver. Despite her relative lack of bulk, she found that she was able, more through desperation than anything, to move him from the driving seat and sit behind the wheel. From the corner of her right eye, she could see the oncoming train.

She turned the key, the car restarted and moved forward, just failing to clear the line as the train passed. She felt the force of the impact as the locomotive clipped the rear of the car, spinning it around and clear.

Jo, unhurt but shaken, climbed back over the seat and out of the newly smashed rear window. She scrambled to her feet and, in fear that it might explode, hurried to put as much distance between herself and the wrecked taxi as she could.

The local police couldn't have been more helpful. Once Jo had been given a clean bill of health by a doctor and a cup of tea by a friendly desk sergeant, they took a statement then put her on her train. Nevertheless, it was past midnight by the time Jo reached home, so it was not until the following morning that she had a chance to discuss the day's events with the Doctor and the Brigadier.

In Lethbridge-Stewart's office at UNIT HQ, they listened intently as Jo told her story. The two men had already heard about the incident on the level crossing, and Jo was quite touched that, before she could even begin her account, they both made sure that she was fully recovered from the shock and was quite uninjured.

The Doctor stood up from where he had been perched on the edge of the Brigadier's desk. 'Well, Jo,' he began, 'whatever is going on at Kenstone Hall, the people behind it have made a rather big mistake.' He looked at her, scratching the side of his nose. 'To be quite honest, my dear, if it hadn't been for the attempt on your life, I think I might have put it all down to your imagination...'

'Well, thank you very much,' Jo interjected crossly.

'Yes, well, anyway... The fact that they were prepared to go so far, suggests that they were worried that you might have seen something. Don't you agree, Brigadier?'

'For once, Doctor, I agree absolutely. Kenstone Hall is a high-security establishment. Among its residents are some of the highest-ranking intelligence operatives that this country possesses. These are men with access to the highest levels of the military and civil defence establishment. Furthermore, many of them are some of our best deep-cover agents.'

'What you mean, Brigadier, is that these chaps are highly trained spies and killers!' retorted the Doctor.

'Well, I wouldn't use that word.'

'What word would you use then? Assassins perhaps?'

'Let's just say, that if a foreign power were to get to these men, then a very dangerous situation could develop.'

'A foreign power? Well, maybe!' The Doctor began pacing around the room. 'Certainly not one from this planet, unless you really think that the Russians or the Chinese have suddenly developed miracle cures and powers of mass hypnotism.'

'Well, who then, Doctor?' asked Jo. 'You don't think the Master...'

'Well, I must admit that was my first thought, but I don't think miracle cures are his style really, do you?'

The Brigadier picked up the dossier from his desk. 'I think perhaps you'd better pay a visit to Kenstone Hall, Doctor, see what you can find out.'

'Yes, I think you're right. Who's in charge up there?'

'The director is Professor Geoffrey Thynne, very respected chap, worked for the MoD for years – specialises in post-traumatic stress and that sort of thing.'

At that moment a knock on the door was followed by the entry of the burly figure of Sergeant Benton. He flashed Jo a quick smile and handed a note to the Brigadier.

'Thank you, Benton.'

The sergeant left as his superior read the note. 'Now that is interesting. Your taxi driver was no such thing, Miss Grant. His name was Captain Kevin Charlton, and he was a resident of Kenstone Hall!'

The Doctor picked up his cape and headed for the door. 'Well, that settles it. Come along, Jo, we'd better be going.'

Jo followed him, scarcely having time to give the Brigadier a goodbye smile as she left the room.

After stopping for lunch at a pleasant country pub just outside Banbury, the Doctor and Jo reached Kenstone Hall in the early afternoon. The yellow Edwardian car, referred to by everyone at UNIT as Bessie, pulled up outside the gates. The Doctor alighted and rang the bell. After a moment, the two security guards arrived in their small car. Jo noticed that, in contrast to the day before, the two men's demeanour was distinctly unfriendly. The Time Lord addressed them as they left the car and approached the gate.

'Hello there, I'm the Doctor. I believe you've already met Miss Grant. We would like to talk with Professor Thynne please.'

Without answering, one of the guards returned to his car and spoke into a telephone receiver. Neither Jo nor the Doctor could catch the conversation but the guard, having received a reply, nodded to his colleague, who opened the gates and called out, 'Follow us please.'

The two cars proceeded in convoy up the drive. As they drove through the peaceful grounds, many of the residents could be seen, some strolling and apparently chatting, others playing tennis or bowls or sitting reading in the sunshine. The Doctor reflected silently on how normal everything looked – in fact, just a little bit too normal.

The Doctor and Jo were shown into a small, functional office, where they were joined almost immediately by Miss Caxton. The matron greeted Jo with a somewhat artificial warmth. 'Hello again, Miss Grant. I didn't expect to see you again... so soon. And you are?'

'I'm the Doctor.' He flashed his UNIT pass. 'Miss Grant and I happened to be in the area, so we thought we would call in. We were hoping to talk to Professor Thynne. Would you be so good as to let him know that we are here?'

Miss Caxton, as if unused to being addressed in so peremptory a manner, seemed momentarily lost for words, but quickly recovered. 'I'm afraid Professor Thynne is unavailable at the moment – he is seeing patients. Is there anything I can help with?'

'No, I shouldn't think so. In that case, perhaps we can pay a call on Miss Grant's uncle, Mr Canning, before we leave.'

'Again, Doctor, I'm afraid that is quite impossible. Mr Canning is currently undergoing treatment. Besides, we have a very strict policy of no visitors at Kenstone Hall – and certainly no casual visitors! Miss Grant was accorded a very exceptional privilege, at the express request of Brigadier Lethbridge-Stewart. I am disappointed that she has chosen to abuse that privilege.'

'No, of course, I quite understand.' The Doctor smiled and shook the matron's hand energetically. 'Well, we've wasted too much of your time already, Miss Caxton. Please pass on my regards to Professor Thynne.'

'And say hello to Uncle Jack from me,' added Jo.

Jo and the Doctor were ushered out of the building and back to Bessie before being escorted out of the gates, which were locked behind them.

'That didn't get us very far, did it, Doctor?' Jo asked. 'But we can't just give up. I'm absolutely sure that there's something going on in that hall.'

'My dear Jo,' the Doctor reassured her, 'I have absolutely no intention of giving up. Of course something is going on, and unless I am very much mistaken, it's a very dangerous something indeed – and one that doesn't originate on this planet. Did you notice that woman's eyes, Jo? They were completely dead. She seemed to be looking right through us, and she didn't blink once.'

By this time, they were driving along a wooded lane beside the high brick boundary wall, around the corner from the main gates. The Doctor pulled off the road and parked Bessie between the trees, concealing the car beneath some loose branches and undergrowth. He and Jo then walked over to the ivy-covered wall and began to examine it, the Doctor standing back, his hands on his hips.

'What are we going to do then, Doctor?' asked Jo. 'This wall's a bit high, but I dare say I could get over it if you gave me a bunk-up.'

'A bunk-up? Steady on, Jo, there's no need for that. Come and have a look at this.' The Doctor pulled back a section of the ivy to reveal an old wooden door. 'I thought so, an old gardener's gate from the days when the hall was a private house. You couldn't have the servants coming and going up the main drive, you know. Let's see where it leads, shall we?'

Jo smiled admiringly at her friend and nodded enthusiastically. The Doctor tried the latch, but the gate was securely bolted.

'Oh! Ah, well, we'll just have to try and open it in a less orthodox fashion then.' The Doctor took a step back, then with a loud 'hi-ya!' he gave the door a clinical yet brutal blow, not unlike a karate chop. The old wood splintered and what remained of it swung open.

'Now, come on, let's see what's going on in there.'

Inside the walls, the Time Lord and his companion crept unseen through woodland, until they came to the edge of the open lawns, which surrounded the hall.

'There's nothing for it, Jo, we're just going to have to brazen it out. Come on!' The Doctor strode out across the grass as if he had every right to be there, Jo following him. They were fortunate in that none of the residents or staff were too close by, and they managed to reach the rear of the hall, without being challenged. Now out of sight, the Doctor began examining windows, trying to gain entry. At the third attempt, he found one slightly ajar and was able to open it fully. Silently beckoning Jo to follow, the Doctor climbed through the window and into a small storeroom, used for keeping disused wheelchairs, crutches and the like. The pair looked at each other and sighed with relief.

It is doubtful whether the Doctor and Jo would have felt any relief at all had they noticed as they crossed the lawn that they were being observed by the same figure who had watched Jo's departure the day before.

'Ah, my dear Doctor, how delightful,' he chuckled to himself.

* * *

The door into the house was not locked. The Doctor opened it slightly, and then closed it again at the sound of approaching voices. Miss Caxton and Tony Maple walked by, the matron giving the nurse instructions. 'The first ones must be ready to leave today – see to it without fail.'

'Yes, Miss Caxton.'

'And where is Thynne?'

'I think he is in his office, Miss Caxton.'

'Good, I need to talk to him. Now go, you have things to do.'

The pair separated, Maple going towards the residents' lounge, while Miss Caxton set off towards the main staircase, in search of the director.

The Doctor tried the door again. The coast was clear. He turned to Jo. 'Now let's find your Uncle Jack.'

'His room's on the first floor.'

The pair made their way up the stairs and along an empty corridor past a number of closed bedroom doors, before Jo indicated one in particular. 'I'm almost sure that it's this one.'

The Doctor tried the handle. It was unlocked. They crept in. Although it was the middle of the afternoon, they found Jack lying in bed.

'Uncle Jack,' whispered Jo urgently. The Doctor hurried to examine Canning, an expression of deep concern on his face. Jack was clearly alive, not asleep, but then again not really awake. He seemed to be in some sort of dream state, his unseeing eyes staring towards the ceiling.

'But I don't understand it, Doctor,' said Jo. 'He seemed so well yesterday. Oh, Uncle Jack, what have they done to you?'

At the sound of his niece's voice, Canning stirred. His eyes flickered in recognition and he croaked out her name and then a word that she missed.

'Uncle Jack, what was that? What did you say?'

He looked at her with desperate eyes and gasped the word out again, 'Nurazh!' Jo reached for the water on the bedside table, to pour a glass for her uncle. The Doctor looked very thoughtful and repeated Jack's word to himself under his breath. 'Nurazh'.

At that moment, Canning jumped violently to his feet, knocking the glass from Jo's hand. As he lunged and grabbed the Doctor by the throat, the girl noticed that all trace of her uncle had left his eyes. He stared unseeingly ahead. The Doctor struggled in vain to release Canning's hold on his windpipe. Jo attempted to pull her uncle off her friend, but it was all to no avail. As it seemed inevitable that the Doctor would lose consciousness, the door burst open. Canning relaxed his stranglehold and six more residents entered the room, each staring ahead with sightless eyes. They grabbed the intruders and held them firm.

* * *

In what appeared to be a doctor's consulting room, the Doctor looked over to his companion, like him strapped tightly to a hospital trolley. 'Are you all right, Jo?'

'Yes, Doctor, I'm fine – although I can't move. Are you OK?'

'Yes, I'm fine, and at least we know now what's going on.'

'Do we?'

'Well, yes, didn't you hear your uncle? Before he attacked me, he said one word. "Nurazh". I've come across them before. Nurazh are extremely nasty mind parasites from the Horsehead Nebula.'

'So you think some of these Nurazh are here on Earth?'

'Oh, no, Jo, not some of them – just one. One Nurazh can control many thousands of minds at once – especially those of weaker species. They are solitary creatures – beings of pure thought energy, which drift from world to world, colonising living beings. They take them over, live off their mental energy for a while, and then consume them. In a very little time, a single Nurazh can devour an entire planet. It's all so obvious now, I should have realised. Before a Nurazh can inhabit its host, it carefully nurtures and heals any imperfections it finds in it – which explains all of these so-called miracle cures. If they weren't such rapacious creatures, the Nurazh would be the most efficacious physicians in the universe.'

'But how did it come to be on Earth, and why here at Kenstone Hall?'

'That is a very good question. The only way that a Nurazh could be here on Earth is if someone brought it here and is using it for his own ends.'

'You mean...'

At that moment, the door opened and Miss Caxton and Jack Canning walked in, led by a man dressed in black.

'The Master,' said the Doctor, without an ounce of surprise in his voice.

'Good afternoon, Doctor, Miss Grant. How very pleasant to see you both again.' His voice possessed a rich intensity, which compelled attention. 'We must have a little chat. I hope you are not too tied up to spare me a moment.'

'Professor Thynne, I presume?'

'For the moment, Doctor, yes,' said the Master.

'And the real professor?'

'Let us just say that all his problems are now very much little ones.' The Master gave his captives a meaningful and self-satisfied look. Jo was left in no doubt that Professor Thynne had become another victim of the Master's favourite weapon, the tissue compression eliminator.

'I find it very hard to believe that even you would bring a Nurazh here,' said the Doctor. 'The consequences could be quite simply catastrophic.' He was now clearly very angry. 'What do you hope to achieve by this?'

'Be careful, Doctor, you are talking about my ally,' warned the Master. 'I happened upon this particular Nurazh, lost, alone and starving on an isolated planet. It had consumed all of the available food...'

'You mean all the life!' interjected Jo in disgust.

'As you say, Miss Grant... all of the life, but there had not been enough of that life to provide it with sufficient energy to leave the planet and look for more food, until I was able to offer a little assistance.'

'So you brought it to Earth, where it could eat its fill!' the Doctor spat out the words.

'In return for which, it will provide me with an army of people willing to do my bidding. Oh, I pride myself that I have certain talents in the field of mind control, as I am sure you will testify, Miss Grant...'

Jo looked away, remembering her first encounter with the Master and how it had led to her attempting to murder the Doctor.

'However,' continued the Master, 'the Nurazh has mental powers greater than even I could imagine. Within the next few hours, my patients, every one of them a person with power and influence, will begin to leave here and return to their work – except now they will be working for me. I will have access to every cog in the machinery of state. I will be in a position to do just what I want – run this country, maybe start a war or two. What do you think, Doctor? Perhaps I might even disband your precious UNIT.'

The Doctor's anger seemed to have been replaced more by concern. 'But you can't work with a Nurazh. Their sole concern is food. A Nurazh doesn't have friends or allies. As soon as it has got what it wants from you, it is just as likely to make your mind its next meal. You simply cannot trust the creature.'

'I have no worries about that, Doctor. The Nurazh tried to take my mind when I first found it, but my intellect was too rich a diet for it, it couldn't manage it and ended up begging for my help.'

'But it was in a weakened state then! For heaven's sake, man...!'

'Enough, Doctor, it is time for Miss Grant and yourself to join my cohorts. Nurazh, come feed on them!'

At his words, Miss Caxton stepped forward and began staring intently at Jo. 'The girl first, I think,' she whispered. Although Jo couldn't see the Nurazh, she felt its touch on her mind, at first gentle like a swish of silk, then increasingly strident and demanding: a heavy crashing, battering down the doors of her consciousness, demanding entry.

'Jo, look at me!' the Doctor shouted 'Jo!' The girl turned and looked into the Time Lord's eyes. 'Jo, think of your friends and family – your parents, Uncle Jack, think of the Brigadier, Sergeant Benton, Mike Yates, everyone you love and who loves you! Jo!' The pressure on her mind was becoming unbearable. 'Think of me, Jo, think of our friendship! Jo, remember who you are! Remember!' Still holding the Doctor's gaze, Jo gave a little nod, as she felt her resistance crumbling.

Jo had lost consciousness, then a second or two later her eyes sprang open: they were dead, unseeing eyes; the eyes of a slave of the Nurazh.

As Jack Canning began releasing his niece from her bonds, the creature turned its attention to the Doctor, his face contorting with the pain of the assault and his body writhing within the trolley's restraints. The Master looked on in delight. After a few moments, the movement ceased, the Doctor lapsed into unconsciousness.

The Master was concerned. 'That was too easy.' He turned to Caxton. 'Have you taken him?'

'Not yet. He is very strong and is fighting back. It will take time, but he will be mine. I am already deep in his mind. Let us go and prepare our plans.' Caxton made to leave the room. The Master hesitated.

'But don't you need to stay here to feed on the Doctor?'

'The location of the body through which I am speaking is of no concern. We can go to your office, the Doctor will still be mine.' Caxton left the room, followed by Canning and Jo Grant. The Master looked back in triumph towards the inert body of his rival, before following them.

In the office of Professor Geoffrey Thynne, the Master made himself comfortable behind the desk, the bottom left drawer of which contained its true owner's dead and miniaturised body. 'My dear Nurazh,' – he addressed Miss Caxton in a tone of smug superiority, '– with your invaluable assistance I will rule this little island within a week. And, of course, this is merely the beginning. This entire planet will soon be mine to do with as I wish. But did I say mine?' The Master seemed to realise that he had allowed his ambition to show a little too plainly. 'Of course, I mean ours.'

Caxton looked at her partner silently for a second, then spoke. 'My dear Master – ' she imbued his name with irony ' – do you seriously believe that I have any ambitions to rule this pathetic little world?'

The Master rose from the seat. 'No, of course not. I shall rule – with you by my side.'

'This planet is of no use to me, other than as a source of nourishment. I will feed on all of the primitive minds that infest it and when I have consumed all life, I shall leave and move on until I find the next food source.'

As Caxton pronounced their planet's death sentence, Jack Canning, Tony Maple and Jo Grant stood passively by, showing no reaction.

'But what use is a dead planet to me?' The Master was alarmed. He could see his alliance with the Nurazh unravelling. 'I saved you. You were dying. You promised me your help.'

'Yes, you saved me. You brought me here, you let me feed, and now I no longer need your help.' Caxton's dead eyes continued to stare ahead. 'Our alliance is no longer relevant.'

Alarmed, the Master realised that he was now in danger. He felt the touch of the Nurazh on his mind. He clutched his temples and called out. 'No, you tried that before. Mine is not some inferior mind, you will fail again if you try to take me!'

Caxton began to laugh as the Nurazh continued the assault. The Master reeled around the room, aware that he was losing the fight. He staggered into a corner and crashed into a grey metal filing cabinet. The Master turned to the cabinet and inserted a key into the lock. The cabinet seemed to grow bigger, then split open, spilling a soft light into the room. The Master stepped into his TARDIS, and turned to Caxton. 'I will remember this betrayal. I will remember,' he called out, before slamming the door of his time and space machine.

The sound of the one word – 'remember' – in the voice of the Master, began echoing through Jo Grant's mind, repeating over and over. She shook her head slightly. Still the Master's voice insisted, 'Remember, remember.' Then the voice changed, taking on the familiar well-loved tones of her friend the Doctor: 'Remember, Jo, remember.'

She staggered forward slightly, then straightened. She was back in control. The realisation dawned that the Doctor had saved her. Somehow, before she had fallen under the influence of the Nurazh, he had placed a telepathic trigger in her mind that had allowed her to break free.

Looking weakened, Caxton, leaning with one hand on the desk, did not notice Jo slip out of the room. Jo made her way swiftly back to where the Doctor still lay strapped to the gurney; she found him conscious – and still himself.

'But I don't understand, Doctor,' she said. 'How did you manage to defeat the Nurazh?'

'I didn't, Jo.' He grimaced as Jo released him from the straps. 'The truth is that the creature still has its claws in me. I can feel it even as I talk to you, trying to get control. I'm still fighting it Jo. The Nurazh seems to be working mainly from inside the mind of the matron, Miss Caxton. If we can help her to break free, that'll weaken it considerably.'

The Doctor and Jo ran along the corridor back to the director's office. The matron had just about recovered her strength as the pair burst in.

'Miss Caxton,' the Doctor called out to her. 'Fight it. Fight the Nurazh.' He stepped up to the woman and seized her head, turning her face to look directly into her eyes. The Doctor whispered urgently, 'Miss Caxton, fight the Nurazh!' The woman's eyes seemed to flicker in confusion. The Doctor was getting through to her. Then, with an inhuman roar, the Nurazh reasserted control. Caxton's arms came up and hurled the Doctor off. She called to Canning and Maple, who had until now remained unmoving and disinterested.

'Seize them both!'

With a shared look, the Doctor and his companion pushed past the two men and out of the door. In the corridor, more residents, all under the alien influence, blocked their escape.

'Come on, Jo – upstairs!' shouted the Doctor. Narrowly evading the clutches of their pursuers, the pair vaulted up the staircase. They found no exit along the first-floor landing, which was also blocked by their enemy's agents. Continuing up the stairs onto the second floor and beyond, they came at last to a wooden door, under which Jo could feel a strong draft. She tried the handle, it opened, and they came out onto a flat terrace on the roof of the hall. The sounds of their pursuers could be heard no more than half a dozen steps behind them. Jo slammed the door shut and looked for something that she could use to jam it closed – there was nothing.

'Jo, quickly,' the Doctor called to her, pointing to the other side of the wide expanse of terrace. 'There's a fire escape. Come on!' At that moment, the door opened and the pursuing puppets of the Nurazh poured onto the roof. Before the Doctor and Jo could reach the fire escape – their only way off the roof – the dead-eyed creatures had them cornered. The Doctor and Jo stood with their backs to the roof's edge. Jo glanced briefly over her shoulder at the vertiginous drop and quickly dismissed any idea that she might have entertained of jumping – that would be suicide.

As if heeding a silent command, the crowd parted and Caxton walked through. 'Leave him to me. Hold the girl,' the Nurazh host snarled. As Jo was grabbed by Maple, she saw Caxton hurl herself with an unearthly scream onto the Doctor. The pair seemed evenly matched. Caxton's hands reached for the Time Lord's throat, but he pushed her off and the two fell into a violent grapple. As Jo remembered it later, the final moments of the struggle seemed both to be over in an instant and to last an eternity. One of the two, either Caxton or the Doctor – Jo couldn't be sure which – seemed to lose their footing on the edge of the roof. To Jo's horror, she saw her friend, together with the possessed woman, disappear over the edge. Caxton's horrified scream was cut short as she hit the gravel below.

In contrast, the Doctor made no sound as he fell to certain death.

Jo's scream was almost as loud as Caxton's had been. She shook herself free of her captor, who in common with his fellows seemed confused by the evident death of his leader's host body. Most of the residents stood motionless, a few shook their heads slightly. Jo took the opportunity and ran for the door, but there was no longer any thought of escape in her mind. She had to reach the Doctor. He had to be all right, he couldn't have died.

As she bounded down the stairs, Jo was scarcely aware of her surroundings. In her head all she could see were images of her friend and of the adventures that they had shared. Autons and Axons, Dæmons and Daleks not to mention trips in the Doctor's extraordinary TARDIS to Peladon and Solos; and then there was the Master, he who was ultimately responsible for all of this, but who had disappeared again to leave the Doctor to deal with the consequences of his evil. Through all of this, of course, there had been the Doctor, with his way of reassuring her that he had seen it all before; with his sense of adventure and fun; with his often almost unbearably patronising manner. Jo loved him dearly – her best friend. He had to be alive! She needed him to be.

As Jo came out of the front door of the hall onto the gravel drive, the men on the roof came to and began to follow her. With a glance, Jo took in the contorted body of the matron. There was no doubt that she was dead. Jo reached the Doctor, crouched down beside him and whispered his name tenderly.

At the sound of her voice he turned his head and opened his eyes. A half-smile played across his features as, with difficulty, he spoke her name. His eyes closed once more and his head fell back. Jo knew that he was dead.

But something was happening. As Jo looked at the body of her friend it seemed suffused with a strange light. In disbelief, she saw the familiar features begin to change. The hair turned darker and became curlier, the nose – no less prominent – assumed a different shape, the teeth seemed to grow to fill the new mouth and the Doctor's body, while remaining tall, seemed to fill out, assuming even grander proportions. Within a matter of seconds, the body lying before her was no longer the familiar one of her friend. The new Doctor began to stir, but before his eyes could open, another change seemed to seize him. As Jo looked on in wonderment, the Doctor's form began to revert to how it had been before. The Doctor, Jo's Doctor, was reborn. He opened his eyes and sat up.

'Hello, Jo!'

She threw her arms around him and began sobbing in relief. The Doctor patted her reassuringly. 'It's all right, Jo, everything's all right now.'

With a start, Jo collected her wits. 'But, Doctor, what about the Nurazh?'

'Look, Jo, everything's all right.'

Jo turned to where the Doctor was looking. The men who had pursued her down the stairs were in some disarray. Several of them were sitting on the ground holding their heads. Others staggered around in confusion. They began talking to each other in bewilderment. From those nearest to them, Jo could see that they were all themselves once more.

'They are all free now, Jo. The Nurazh is dead.'

Jo heard a voice call her name and turned to see Jack Canning hurrying towards her. She embraced her uncle warmly.

'But what I don't understand, Doctor, is just what happened to this Nurazh creature.' Brigadier Lethbridge-Stewart put his copy of Jo's report back down on his desk. 'From what Miss Grant saw, it was quite clearly still alive after the death of the unfortunate Miss Caxton, but your... er, recovery seems to have killed it.'

The Doctor considered for a moment. 'It's really quite simple, Brigadier. Don't forget that all of that time the Nurazh was still struggling to take my mind. Now, I was just about managing to keep it at bay, but when I was... ah, killed...' – the Doctor paused as if reflecting on that word, ' – I began to regenerate. Now my future selves, like my former selves are all still very much me – the same person, so to speak. However, in another sense they are also all different. For a split second, at the moment of regeneration, there were, in effect, two minds in the same body – and that was too much for the Nurazh, it caused it to overload.'

'But you said that the Nurazh could control thousands of minds at the same time,' interjected Jo.

'True, but I was talking about human minds. Don't forget, Jo, I am a Time Lord, my mind is infinitely more developed than any human one. Two of us... of me, that is to say, were far more than the Nurazh could take.'

The Brigadier's eyes rolled towards the ceiling as he gave a slight sigh, but he said nothing.

Jo continued. 'So this person that you turned into, he was you as well, then?'

'That's right, my future self – but his time hasn't come yet.'

'But he was nothing like you, Doctor. He had these enormous teeth, and wild curly hair, and...'

'Jo, Jo, please stop,' the Doctor cut her short. 'It really isn't very wise for me to know too much about my own future, you know.' He smiled kindly at her. 'All teeth and curls, eh? That doesn't sound very promising.

Anyway, there's nothing I can do about it, Jo. Sooner or later, I will become that curly, toothy chap, whether I like it or not.'

'Well, let's hope it's not too soon anyway, Doctor,' Jo said.

'I intend to be around in this body for a while longer yet.' He smiled. 'I think I'd better try and look after myself a little better. I could do with a little rest. Perhaps in a nice convalescent home in the countryside somewhere. What do you think, Brigadier?'

The Brigadier sighed indulgently and Jo, laughing quietly, shook her head. 'Oh no you don't, Doctor,' she said. 'Oh no you don't.'

Flashpoint

Matt Grady

Archaeologists have discovered the wreckage site of an ancient Roman slave-trader ship off the northern coast of Sicily. Surveying has uncovered pottery shards, coins, iron shackles and one very special find.

'It's a well-preserved marble bust of Emperor Nero,' reports Dr Orlando Dirossi, who is heading the recovery. Nero ruled the Roman Empire from 54 to 68 AD, and there is speculation that he masterminded the Great Fire of 64 AD, which covered nearly two-thirds of Rome.

The bust, thought to date from around the time of Nero's death, has puzzled archaelogists since its discovery due to an odd phenomenon.

'It leaks,' says Dr Dirossi. 'At first we thought sea water had collected inside. But after a week, it's still leaking condensation out of a crack in its base. Very peculiar – an inner heat source of some kind.' The Nero bust is currently on display at the Palermo Museum in Rome.

Giornale di Sicilia
15 March 1999

Tanned locals and sunburned tourists shuffled past red-figured vases, bronze statues and a sculptured sarcophagus, into a large showroom. A crowd of visitors inched forward and stood on tiptoe, muttering to each other as they struggled to catch a glimpse of the display. A young guard stood in the corner, observing members of the crowd.

A little boy slipped loose from his mother's grasp and edged past the towering adults to the clearing ahead. Reaching the roped-off section at the front of the room, the boy saw a marble head on top of a clear column. Drops of water passed through a screen and fell into a shallow pool at the column's base. The head took no notice of the boy and continued staring blankly at the curious, fixated crowd.

The boy ducked under the rope and approached the head. With a grin, he looked up the nostrils of the aquiline nose, then tapped on the column. Chuckles and whispers rose from the front row. The boy reached up to the head and ran a finger over the marble surface. It felt cool in some spots and, oddly, warm in others. He placed his hand on the chin and suddenly jumped back. Wiping his hand on his shirt, the boy's face reddened and he began to cry.

The guard awoke from a reverie and pushed his way through the crowd. The boy's mother ducked under the ropes, grabbed the crying child and dragged him out of the room.

The commotion subsided as the crowd's attention returned to Nero's unflinching gaze.

'Have you explored much of the city, *signora?*'

'Besides what I've seen out the car window? The Colosseum, the Pantheon, the Forum, the Spanish Steps... but just in passing.'

'Be sure to visit the countryside, if you can,' the driver said. The car pulled up to the pavement. 'Here we are, *signora*.'

Dr Elizabeth Shaw turned her attention away from the window. 'The countryside?'

He chuckled. 'No, the university.'

'Pity.' She exited the car and called over her shoulder, 'See you this evening.'

The driver waved as he sped away. Liz ascended the concrete steps of the University of Rome's Science building, silhouetted in the bright morning light. Passing through the entrance, she flashed her security pass to the male guard at the front desk.

'*Buon giorno*.'

The guard nodded. '*Buon giorno, dottoressa* Shaw.'

Liz proceeded down a whitewashed hallway, lined on either side with offices and laboratories. She returned nods from passing professors, on their way to classrooms. Turning a corner, she stopped at the first door on her left and fished out a set of keys from her handbag. The door opened onto an office with a metal desk surrounded by filing cabinets. Liz threw her jacket over the desk chair, stirring the pages of a university newsletter. Gathering back her hair, and trying not to think about the streaks of grey, she tied it up into a bun.

Except for greetings in Italian and better coffee, her morning routine here differed little from that at Cambridge. But at least there, the long hours she spent at the research lab were productive. Here in Rome, she was making little progress. She frowned, realising the chances of turning this assignment into a paid vacation were slim.

Her lab coat hung on the adjacent wall, beside the door to the lab. Liz tensed, noticing the dim light through the door's translucent window. She crossed the room and checked the door handle: unlocked. Had the caretaker – Claudio, that was his name, wasn't it? – forgotten to lock up? From her brief conversation with the man, she'd gathered he'd been with the university for some time. He wouldn't be so careless, she thought.

She hesitated a moment before turning the handle and opening the door a crack. She peered through the dim lamplight and spotted a man sitting at the lab table, his back facing her. Liz considered alerting security. Surely the stranger had heard her come into the office? Or maybe he was too absorbed in his work. If so, he was a rather bold spy, or a rather foolish one.

'There's no need to call security,' the stranger said. The voice was friendly, disarming.

'Who are you and what are you doing here?' Liz said in her best authoritative voice. 'This lab is off-limits to the public.'

'And for good reason.'

'Then I'd appreciate it if you left at once.'

The stranger retrieved a leather wallet from his coat pocket and held it up to her, his attention still focused on the table.

Cautiously, Liz entered the lab, grabbed the wallet and stepped back. She flipped it open to reveal a familiar identity card: 'United Nations Intelligence Taskforce: scientific adviser.' The photo showed a youthful, fair-haired man grinning for the camera. She read the name: 'Dr Jonas Smythe.'

'Yes, how do you do. The security guard was kind enough to let me in.'

'You should have waited at the front desk with him.' Liz relaxed a little and placed the wallet on the table. 'Why are you here? I was under the impression UNIT had selected me as science advisor for this assignment.'

The man swivelled around on the stool to face her, a pair of half-moon glasses perched on his nose. He flashed her a grin. 'I'm your assistant. Colonel Chaudhry thought you'd be happier if you weren't stuck with all the work.'

'How kind of her,' Liz said, straight-faced. 'Unfortunately, I've reached an impasse and haven't made any progress all week. Unless you have a wealth of radical ideas, I'm afraid you were sent here for nothing.' She studied Smythe for a moment. Over a cricket sweater and striped trousers, he wore a beige lab coat with a sprig of celery pinned to one lapel. 'Where were you seconded from, Dr Smythe?'

He snatched his glasses away from his face. 'Nowhere in particular. I travel around.'

She moved to the side of the table, on which was a marble bust on a perforated metal plate, resting on a shallow pan. Chiselled locks of hair surrounded a round, corpulent face: puffy cheeks, double chin, wide nose and small mouth. Water droplets formed at a crack in its base and fell into the pan.

'Did anyone brief you on our friend here?' Liz retrieved a file from a drawer in the table.

'A bust of Nero Claudius Caesar Augustus Germanicus, found at the site of a shipwreck, well-preserved save for a small crack. It houses an unexplained source of heat, which is causing condensation to form inside. Hence its leaky nature.'

'So, yes, then?' said Liz.

Smythe stood up and paced the room. 'What tests have been performed on the bust so far?'

Liz opened the file. 'Let's see... CAT scan, ultrasound, thermal imaging, Geiger counter – all inconclusive. Readings wavered, images came out blurred.'

Smythe glanced over Liz's shoulder at the contents of the folder.

'How about a fibre optic camera, as used in surgery?'

'It's been tried. The camera shorted out – twice.'

'Did it really? How interesting.' He bent over the table and peered into the marble eyes, then traced the eyelids with his finger.

'Smythe, you may – '

His face winced and he withdrew his finger.

' – want to use gloves if you're going to touch it.' She nodded to a pair of workman's gloves on the table.

'Curious. I suddenly felt disoriented, as if I stood up too fast. Did you experience a similar sensation, Liz?'

She cleared her throat. 'Pardon me, Dr Smythe, but I wasn't aware we were on a first-name basis.'

Smythe rubbed the back of his neck. 'Sorry. Dr Shaw, I should say.'

'In my initial briefing from UNIT, I was advised to use gloves when handling the sculpture. One of its strange traits: prolonged, direct contact results in dizziness and fatigue.' She flipped to a report in the folder. 'Apparently, one of the Palermo Museum staff fainted while transporting the bust. When co-workers woke him and removed the bust from his grip, they noted burn marks on his palms.'

Smythe slipped his hands into his trouser pockets. 'No wonder the scientific community is showing such an interest.'

'And archaeologists are fighting them in the courts to prevent the bust from being cut open,' Liz added.

Smythe glared at Nero. 'Cutting him open would do far more harm than good.' He turned to Liz. 'Were any photos taken of that museum worker's hands?'

She flipped through the folder and handed him a colour photograph. The image showed a close-up of the man's right palm. The skin was red and swollen. Smythe reviewed the attached medical report.

'According to this physician, the burns originated beneath the skin. The first-degree burns on the skin hid far worse tissue damage underneath.'

Liz took a look at the photo. 'More like an extreme allergic reaction or infection.'

'It's as if the warmth in his hands rose to searing levels.' He handed her the image.

'Like an isolated fever? I've never heard of such a case.'

Smythe sat down and wiped his brow. 'The air conditioning seems to be malfunctioning. I adjusted it when I entered the lab, but it's still warm in here.'

Liz walked over to the thermostat and turned the dial a full revolution. 'It's like this every morning. You have to turn it to full to have any effect. I checked with the professors in the offices around the corner, and they rarely need to have it on as high as I do.'

'Have you noted anything else peculiar?'

'Yes.' She returned to the table and slid back the metal plate on which the marble bust rested. Running her fingers through the water in the pan, she grabbed something and placed it in Smythe's hand.

'A dead fly?' He examined the shrivelled insect in the lamplight. 'Ah, a cooked dead fly.'

'I usually find a couple of them a week – the occasional spider, too.'

'Or a museum worker had he been found an hour later.'

Liz sighed. 'Yet they insist on putting such a dangerous object on display. The investors of the archaeological survey are keen to recoup every penny and then some.'

'It's put on display here at the university?'

'Yes, in the afternoon from twelve to five, at the gallery. Analyses and research are conducted in the mornings and evenings. The rest of the day, I try to be a tourist.'

Smythe grinned thoughtfully. 'Seems ages since my last visit to Italy... Electroencephalograph.'

'What?'

He sprang from his seat and turned his bright eyes on Liz, causing her to take a step back. 'Does the university have an electroencephalograph – EEG equipment?'

'A brain-wave monitor?' Just what did he have in mind? 'I'm sure I could secure one from the Medical Studies building. Though not till this evening, or perhaps tomorrow.'

'This can't wait. Let's see if we can pull some strings.' He hurried out of the room, stirring loose pages in his wake.

What an odd man, Liz thought. Where on Earth did UNIT find him? He seemed bright enough though, asking many pertinent questions. His keenness and spirit reminded her of her younger self, eager to change the world after completing her first Ph.D. She locked up the lab, put on her lab coat and followed after him.

Claudio Terrizzi finished his sandwich and checked his watch: 11.46 a.m. He wiped his mouth with his handkerchief and tucked it back into his coveralls pocket. Checking his cleaning cart, he grabbed a few supplies off the metal shelves lining the narrow caretaker's room. Satisfied, he hit the light switch and pushed the cart into the hallway.

He hummed a tune as he passed office after office. Apparently, the professors preferred the clicking of keyboards or the buzzing of lab equipment to his whistled symphonies. Their loss.

Making his way through the building, he stopped the cart before *dottoressa* Shaw's office. His wizened hands retrieved a ring of keys from his pocket and he flipped to the right one. *La dottoressa* seemed kind enough, pretty too, Claudio thought. He'd only spoken to the British scientist briefly, and her mind was somewhere else. Probably on her research.

The caretaker entered the office and unlocked the lab. Chill air washed over him as he opened the door. 'Every single day!' he muttered. You'd think someone from England would enjoy the warmth here, Claudio thought. But each day at noon, he discovered the air conditioning in *la dottoressa*'s lab set to full. Homesickness, indeed.

From beneath the desk lamp, Nero stared at him blankly. Claudio smiled. He put on his gloves and approached the marble bust. What a magnificent sculpture! While the public paid 8000 lira to see it in the gallery, he had the fortune of studying it daily as a perk of the job. Checking in the pan, he shook his head as he removed the dead insects. Couldn't she swat flies and throw them in the bin like everyone else? He'd have to have a polite word with her...

He gripped the sides of the pan and lifted the bust onto his cart. Locking up, Claudio headed to the elevator and descended to the first floor. He made for the back entrance and placed a plastic container over Nero before exiting. The concrete walkways of the courtyard glowed white in the midday sun. Students gave Claudio passing nods or greetings on their way to classes. As usual, everyone dismissed the overturned container.

If it were up to him, Claudio thought, he'd put the marble bust on display in the middle of the courtyard for all the students and faculty to see. On a column in the middle of a flower garden, yes, that would be ideal. And he wouldn't even have to water the flowers: Nero had that covered. The caretaker grinned.

But here at the university, the bust was nothing but a tool used by the investors to milk the public. Crowds of people raved and gushed over the sculpture as if it were one of those weeping portraits of Christ or statuettes of the Virgin Mary that appeared in the tabloids. And it was the attraction of such a crowd that caused museum curators around Rome to turn up their noses. But, for a percentage of the profits, the university was more than willing to showcase the dripping Nero in their tiny gallery.

Claudio pushed the cart to a building across campus, and eventually stopped at the back door of the gallery.

'Ready to face the crowds?' he said, removing the plastic container. He knocked on the door. A moment later, a small, balding man wearing spectacles peeped his head out the door. Claudio picked up the pan and held it before the curator. The man took it, but Claudio's grip remained firm.

'*Grazie*, Claudio,' the curator said with a nervous smile.

The caretaker hesitated a moment before letting go. The door slammed shut in his face. With a sigh, he turned his cart around and headed back, his footsteps echoing down the hallway.

Back in the caretaker's room, Claudio retrieved a sketchbook from his rucksack and sat in a wooden chair. He opened it at a page bookmarked by a Polaroid and removed a pencil from his breast pocket.

Liz left the Medical Studies building and took a sip of coffee from a paper cup. She held the door open as Smythe followed, cradling the EEG equipment.

'Are you sure you don't want help carrying that?'

Smythe adjusted his grip. 'Yes, I'm sure, thanks.'

'Coffee?'

'No thanks, I prefer tea. Mind if we take a detour to the gallery?'

'To see the Nero bust on display?'

'Yes, I'm curious to see what sort of crowd it draws. Besides, we have a few hours to spare.'

Liz took another sip of coffee. 'Follow me, then.'

She put on sunglasses and led her companion around the campus, weaving between groups of students. The sun glinted off car windscreens in the traffic surrounding the university. Liz kept a medium pace, grinning at Smythe's efforts to keep the decades-old equipment balanced in his arms.

They soon came across a line of people filing through the open doors of the Fine Arts building. Small children shuffled their feet and tugged their mothers' arms impatiently.

Liz and Smythe entered the building, where the line of people halted at the front desk. Liz spoke to a guard, who let them pass through a side door. Smythe set down the EEG equipment behind the desk. They entered a large, brightly lit room, its walls adorned with framed paintings, and sculptures on stands in the middle.

'Artwork by students and local artists. With only this room and the showroom, the curator regularly brings in new pieces,' Liz said.

'Short attention span, I suppose?' Smythe said, examining the collection.

People shuffled past them, paying little attention to their surroundings, and disappeared under an archway at the front of the room. Liz and Smythe followed. Inside, the curator greeted her, spotlights glaring off his head. A small crowd encircled a tall glass cylinder with the marble bust of Nero perched on top. Drops of water passed through the perforated top and fell into a bucket at the base. Its rhythmic drip reverberated through the showroom thanks to a microphone.

More people entered, pushing Liz and Smythe in an effort to get a closer look. Smythe put his hands in his pockets.

'What's your theory, Dr Shaw?' Smythe whispered.

Liz stirred from her thoughts. 'Pardon?'

'Your theory about what's inside the bust, causing people to pass out and suffer burns?'

'I believe it's an unknown radioactive element, with radiation that affects organic matter after prolonged direct contact,' Liz whispered.

Smythe nodded. 'That would explain the negative read-out of the Geiger counter.'

'Then why the EEG equipment? Are you suggesting there's something living inside the marble?'

A few people pricked up their ears. The curator shushed Liz.

'You want to be thorough with your testing, don't you?' Smythe whispered.

'I suppose so,' she whispered back. She'd exhausted all the obvious testing methods, so why not try a few outlandish ones. Otherwise, it would be another long day of reviewing research notes.

A man bumped into Smythe and forced his way to the front of the crowd. His hair was dishevelled, his white t-shirt wrinkled and spotted. His hands kneaded a sweater tied at his waist. He scanned the room and, as his eyes met hers, Liz glanced at her feet. She felt Smythe tense beside her.

'Did you hear that?' he whispered.

'Hear what?'

'That voice... Asking for warmth...'

They were both distracted by the t-shirt man as he began to circle the display, chuckling to himself. Liz spotted a guard stepping towards the crowd from the back entrance. The t-shirt man untied his sweater and rubbed it over his head like a towel while muttering a stream of words under his breath. Suddenly, he leaped forward and bundled up the sculpture in his sweater. The guard pushed through the crowd and tried to tackle him but, wielding his bundle like a ball and chain, the thief knocked the wind out of the guard with a sickening thud. Screams rose from the crowd as the guard crumpled to the floor.

Smythe tried to cut him off at the back entrance, but the thief charged into him. Liz checked on the fallen guard as he struggled to breathe. The guard from the front desk dashed into the room, spotted Smythe wrestling with the thief, and pushed through the crowd. The thief shouldered Smythe into the wall and ran off down a hallway. Shaking the stars from his head, Smythe ran after him.

The curator pointed out the missing showpiece to the bemused front-desk guard, who then fumbled for his radio and barked orders over the commotion of the crowd. Liz followed the guard out the back entrance, down the hallway and through the exit. Other security guards appeared around the corners of surrounding buildings and rushed to join them.

'Damn heels,' Liz muttered, wincing. She slipped off her shoes and ran after the guards. She spotted Smythe thirty yards ahead on the main campus walkway.

The thief turned right and the guards followed suit, disappearing between buildings. Liz soon found herself in the large courtyard, with the Science building at the opposite corner. The thief darted across the walkway, the Doctor on his tail. A cart suddenly rolled into their path, pushed by Claudio, who'd been attracted by all the noise, no doubt. Liz found herself watching a rugby match, as the thief collided with the cart, toppling it over; and Smythe, unable to stop, tripped over both and tumbled into the grass.

Liz ran to Smythe's side as the guards surrounded the thief. The area was strewn with toilet paper and bottles of cleaning fluid. The thief jumped up holding the sweater bundle over his head. The guards stopped in their tracks.

Smythe sat up with a groan.

Claudio joined them. 'He'll smash the sculpture!' He pulled at his thinning hair. 'The crazy fool!'

The thief's eyes shifted erratically in their sockets as he recovered his breath. He muttered several quick sentences, catching Smythe's attention.

Liz helped Smythe to his feet. 'What did he say?'

'He claims Nero speaks to him. That he asks for fire.'

Which Nero? Liz thought. The emperor – or the bust?!

'Take it from him before he smashes it!' Claudio told the guards.

The thief unwrapped the bust and tossed aside the sweater. His hands gripped the marble surface tightly.

'He'll pass out,' Liz told Smythe, who gazed at the marble bust intently.

Fire... inner fire!

The thought suddenly popped into Liz's head. Or was that a voice? It was almost a whisper. She looked at Smythe, who noted her confused expression.

'So you heard it too, then.'

Before she could comment, the thief's trembling hands caught Liz's attention. His eyes flickered and his head nodded forward. 'Catch him! He's fainting!'

The guards rushed forward as the man collapsed. The bust slipped from his grasp and hit the concrete face first, its nose shattering.

Claudio gasped.

The guards laid the unconscious thief down on his side. Chips of marble surrounded the bust. Wearing gloves, Claudio carefully turned it over.

'*Càspita!*'

Nero's new pockmarked complexion, with a flat, coarse patch in place of the nose, greeted him. Condensation trickled from the broken base. Claudio swept the chips of marble into a dustpan.

'Such a waste...' he muttered.

Smythe checked the thief's pulse then his hands, which appeared swollen. 'Probably just minor tissue damage,' he told Liz. 'He'll need a psychiatrist though.'

An emergency crew soon arrived with a stretcher, the curator in tow. He carried the EEG equipment. At the sight of the damaged sculpture, his eyes widened in shock.

'This is horrible!'

Claudio glared at him. 'See what happens when you display art as if it were a circus sideshow!'

'He was a madman! We tried to stop –'

'What's done is done,' Liz cut in. 'The exhibit is closed till we've assessed the damage.'

'How long will you need? A day or two?' The curator smiled nervously.

'Closed indefinitely.'

'The investors won't like this.'

Claudio's eyes bore into the curator's as he took the EEG equipment and placed it on his righted cleaning cart. He set the bust carefully beside it.

'The damage isn't too extensive,' the curator pleaded. 'At least let me keep it on display for the rest of the day. Those people have paid money after all.'

'Good day, *signore*,' Smythe replied. The curator opened his mouth to object but, with a nod from Smythe, he returned to the gallery with his tail between his legs.

Claudio unloaded the EEG equipment, marble bust and broken pieces onto the lab desk.

'*Grazie*, Claudio. We can handle things from here.'

'Will you be able to repair the bust? I took a picture of it a few days ago. That might help you.'

Liz smiled at him. 'No thank you, I have several pictures. And don't worry, it's in good hands. Now if you'll excuse us...'

'Of course.' Claudio smiled back and paid Nero one last glance before pushing the cart back into the hallway.

Smythe began setting up the EEG equipment.

'So you're convinced there's something sentient inside there?' She put on the workman's gloves and slipped a towel underneath the marble bust.

'I wouldn't rule out the possibility.'

He knows something, Liz thought. Some detail UNIT briefed him on but not me. Or maybe a fact known only to him... She considered how easy it would be to fake a UNIT pass. 'Jonas Smythe' did sound rather suspect.

'Would you mind attaching the electrodes, Dr Shaw?' He retrieved a multi-bit screwdriver from his coat pocket and unscrewed the cover of the equipment. Lifting it off, he prodded at the exposed circuitry.

Liz attached seven electrodes around the bust's head and stuffed one inside its base. 'Let's say there is something living inside here,' she said, recalling the whispered voice. 'The readings will be of little use when it's covered by a layer of marble.'

'That's why I'm adjusting the equipment sensitivity.'

Watching him work, Liz pictured another scientist from her days at UNIT. A much older man, of course. Always tinkering with gadgets, attempting to reverse the polarity of the neutron flow.

Smythe replaced the cover and flashed her a grin. 'There. Now a brain the size of a fly will cause the readings to go off the chart.' He plugged in the power cord and flipped a switch. The equipment beeped, then whirred to life. Paper passed through the printer with a hum. The eight pens remained still, tracing a straight line.

Liz turned her attention from the read-out to Smythe.

'It's warming up,' he said, fiddling with the amplifier and filter settings.

'Maybe I should adjust the electrodes?' Liz pulled one off the forehead.

One of the pens twitched.

She quickly replaced the electrode. 'Sorry, my fault.'

'Perhaps... May I borrow one of your gloves?'

Liz removed her right glove and handed it to him. He slipped it on and approached the bust. Keeping his eyes on the EEG read-outs, he waved his gloved hand before Nero's eyes. Then he placed his palm on the forehead.

Several pens twitched.

'Interesting.' Smythe pulled off the glove and pressed his bare fingers against the forehead.

All eight pens twitched wildly.

He snatched his hand away, and the pens continued dancing on the graph paper for a moment before resuming a straight line.

'You were right!' Liz exclaimed. 'And it obviously thrives on body heat.'

'Heat in general, which would explain the warm room each morning. But it can manipulate body heat far faster.'

Liz stood back from the table. 'This certainly justifies UNIT's interest. I suppose we should contact Colonel Chaudhry right away? She's probably itching to create a cover-up.'

'We'll contact her later. First, we need to know what exactly we're dealing with.'

'How the hell did a creature get in there?' Her mind raced over her knowledge of geology. 'Either it can manipulate the structure of rock and hide in it like a hermit crab. Or it was caught in a lava stream that cooled into igneous rock, then metamorphosed into marble.'

'I doubt it would have remained encased in marble for two thousand years on the Mediterranean seabed if it were capable of escaping. So it was probably caught in lava.'

'But from lava to marble, millions of years would have passed. Unless there are other such creatures beneath the Earth's crust, it's certainly not from this planet,' Liz said.

Smythe nodded. 'Precisely. It probably penetrated through the Earth's crust as a meteorite.'

'And a large volcano or seismic event cast it up to the surface, where it was caught in lava?' Liz suggested.

'That would be my guess. The lava probably drifted into an ancient sea, cooling before the creature could manipulate the heat.'

'This creature remains dormant in cold environments then,' she concluded. 'That's how it survived through space.'

'Then we should move it to a sub-zero environment, to be on the safe side. What's nearby... Antarctica, Europa, Pluto –'

Liz snickered. 'I suppose you have a rocket at your disposal?'

Smythe blushed. 'No, of course not.'

'There are several freezers in the building. We could store it in one until we find a better solution,' Liz suggested.

'Yes, cold storage.' Smythe's eyes lit up. 'Liquid nitrogen! Is there any around? We could immerse the marble bust in that.'

'Probably in the Chemistry building.'

'All right, let's hurry then.' He rushed out of the lab.

She sighed, suddenly feeling her age. So much for the long day of fruitless research.

Cleaning the windows, Claudio noticed *dottoressa* Shaw and her assistant leaving the building and crossing the courtyard in a hurry. Weren't they supposed to be assessing the damage to the marble bust? He'd only left them a short while ago, he thought. Was that madman on the loose again?

He dropped the spray cleaner and paper towel on the cart and pushed it to *la dottoressa*'s office. Once there, he listened closely for footsteps and checked around the corner. The hallway was empty. He quietly unlocked the door. Inside, he closed the door behind him and crossed the room to the lab. Light shone through the door's translucent window. Claudio put his ear to the door just in case and listened intently for a minute or two. A faint hum, that was all.

Maybe they had taken the marble bust somewhere – perhaps to be X-rayed? But he didn't recall either of the scientists carrying a bundle. He glanced back at the office door before unlocking the lab. Edging open the door, he peeked inside.

'What the hell?'

The bust was on the table where he'd left it, but the scientists had stuck electrodes all over the head. Wires trailed from it to the electronic equipment at the table's edge. Paper slid out of a printer and piled in a nest on the floor. Memories of his brother hooked up to similar equipment at the hospital flashed through Claudio's mind.

'Look at how they're treating you!' he told the bust. 'What kind of freak experiment is this?'

He unfastened the electrodes and, with gloved hands, tipped the bust to remove the wire tucked in its base. Water trickled onto the towel.

The read-out pens twitched.

Claudio stared into Nero's eyes. They don't appreciate you, not like I do, he thought. They think of you as a scientific curiosity. A curio requiring endless tests. He suddenly shivered, the room feeling colder than usual. He turned off the air conditioning and knelt down to turn on the baseboard heater. About time this room felt some heat.

Sitting on a stool, he ran his gloved fingers over the damaged face, tracing ridges and brittle edges. He eyed the miniature quarry of marble in the dustpan.

This will take weeks to repair, he thought, maybe months. How could he be sure if *dottoressa* Shaw and her assistant would even bother? Rather than put it back on display, they might store the marble bust away in some warehouse, with thousands of other artefacts and antiques.

You must keep me close.

'I wish I could, but they'll come looking for you. And there are only so many places I can hide you here.'

Then take me away. But keep me close.

Claudio thought it over. Where could he go? Hiding the bust in his flat was too obvious. Somewhere outside the city... His sister's place in Siciliy, that could work. Store it in her cellar with his other belongings. He could travel there at the weekends to repair it.

The caretaker looked around the room. He needed something to hide the sculpture in, in case he passed someone in the hallway. He walked into the office and noticed *dottoressa* Shaw's green jacket. It would have to do. He slipped it off the desk chair and returned to the lab. He retrieved a garbage bag from his pocket and emptied the contents of the dustpan inside. Bundling up Nero in the jacket, he cradled it against his chest and hurried to the office door.

Claudio halted at the sound of footsteps in the hallway. Nero's blank eyes met his through an opening in the jacket.

I am the spark that sets the flame.

He held a finger to his lips.

The footsteps neared the office, then turned a corner in the other direction, fading down the hallway.

'That was close,' he whispered, sighing with relief. He glanced back at the lab door, which remained unlocked. How clumsy! I can't leave behind too many clues, Claudio thought. He crossed the office and fumbled for the key with his gloved hand. His hand trembled as he tried to insert the key into the lock. Removing the glove, he tried again.

Suddenly the footsteps returned, quickly growing louder as they approached the office.

Claudio flung open the door and closed it behind him, being careful not to slam it. He turned the lock then crouched beneath the door window. He heard the office door creak open. The footsteps crossed the room and stopped.

'*Dottoressa?*' said a light female voice.

Sweat trickled down Claudio's brow.

The stranger knocked on the window. '*Dottoressa* Shaw? I have a phone message from someone at UNIT.'

The air rippled above the heater as the warmth of the lab became uncomfortable. Claudio's knees began to ache. As he adjusted to a sitting position, he felt the sculpture slip from the jacket. He caught it before it could hit the floor.

The footsteps crossed the office into the hallway and faded away once again.

Claudio took a long, deep breath. He tried to stand up, but his aching knees wouldn't support the weight. He relaxed his muscles, feeling very tired. The room began to spin, Nero's gleaming white face its focal point.

I feel your inner fire. Sleep. Sleep now.

The room darkened as Claudio tried to stay awake, but his eyelids were made of lead. He clutched the marble bust against his chest with his bare hand. His head slumped forward, pressing into the chiselled hair.

Glorious warmth.

Claudio had read about out-of-body experiences, but seeing his slumped form at the base of the lab door – and realising it wasn't a reflection – was truly frightening.

Inner fire, coursing through the body. Glorious warmth.

The voice filled the room and hung in the air like smoke.

He sensed a presence reaching out from the marble bust to his body. He heard his pulse speed up as the presence drew forth on his body heat like a leech. The skin of his face and hands began to swell and redden. The presence intensified and burn blisters soon formed on the skin.

Claudio wanted to warn his body, but he had no voice, no corporeal form. He couldn't even look away.

The inner fire is invigorating.

He saw his body twitch and his face wince in pain, then suddenly relax. His hair began to singe and the skin blacken. Smoke rose from his coveralls as they smouldered.

The presence filled his body and the clothes burst into flame. The fire consumed his form and then, as if doused with petrol, became a roaring blaze. The nest of graph paper caught fire and flames spread to the table.

I shall consume all.

The presence intensified further, and the entire lab was soon blanketed with fire.

Liz brought up the rear as Smythe dragged a trolley down the hallway. She made sure its cargo, a round refrigeration unit filled with liquid nitrogen, remained as upright as possible. They both jumped as alarm bells rang through the Science building.

'Fate is determined to keep me out of this building today,' Liz said.

'Think you can transport this liquid nitrogen back outside on your own?' Smythe asked. 'I'm going to check your lab.'

'Worried about that creature?'

He backed down the hallway. 'I'm worried about what it's up to.'

'I'm coming with you then.' She left the trolley behind and followed after him.'

'Dr Shaw –'

'Save your breath. I was the one given this assignment, after all.'

They passed professors and students hurrying to the exits, some carrying bundles of notes. Rounding a corner, Liz and Smythe began coughing as they ran headlong into thick smoke. Wiping the tears from her eyes, Liz made out flames at the end of the hallway. They covered their mouths with their coat lapels.

'It's my lab!' she yelled over the alarm bells.

'There's nothing we can do: the blaze is too big.'

Liz pointed out the abandoned cleaning cart silhouetted in flames. 'Where's Claudio?' She saw Smythe's quizzical look. 'The caretaker!'

'Quick,' he said. 'Let's check his room and then get that refrigeration unit out of the building!'

They doubled back and joined the crowd of people making for the exits. They peeked in the cleaning supply room, but the caretaker wasn't there. Smythe picked up a sketch of Nero, with a Polaroid of the marble bust clipped to the page.

'Secret admirer.'

They returned to the trolley and dragged it out the nearest exit. Sirens wailed as fire engines arrived and screeched to a halt before the Science building. Liz and Smythe joined the crowd assembled in the courtyard. She noticed his eyes were distant.

'We don't have much time,' he whispered.

The fire chief, a burly man with a raspy voice, escorted Liz and Smythe to the scene of the fire.

'What exactly is this critical experiment you need to check on?' the chief asked Liz. 'Is it a danger to my men?'

'If they approach it, yes,' Smythe cut in, dragging the trolley.

'And what's inside that container?'

'A way to suppress the danger,' Smythe replied.

They rounded the corner, passing a firefighter standing guard at the end of the hallway, a charged hose in hand. The office was blackened by smoke; the one dividing the lab had been reduced to a charred heap. Adjoining rooms were visible through gaping holes in the walls.

The fire chief stopped them from proceeding further. 'The contents of the lab are on the floor below. It's safer if we view them there.'

They descended the stairs and spotted another firefighter aiming a charged hose at an open office. Inside lay a pile of charred wood, flooring and concrete fragments lying within a circle of warped, dented filing cabinets. Liz noticed pieces of circuitry from the EEG equipment.

Come closer. Closer.

That voice again, Liz thought. She looked at Smythe.

'It's in there,' he whispered. 'And it's become more powerful.'

'Most of this could have been prevented if they'd installed a sprinkler system. Tight budget, I guess,' the fire chief said. 'But I'm hard pressed to find a cause. No signs of an electrical fire or the use of an accelerant.'

'Have you sorted through the rubble yet?' Liz asked.

'Just a quick sweep.' The fire chief led them inside and crouched by the pile. He picked up something and held it up to them. A charred, broken jaw with a few teeth intact. 'I've only found a couple of bone fragments. The rest were incinerated, it seems.'

Liz's heart sank. 'Claudio.'

Smythe's expression was grim. 'He must have entered the lab after we left.'

Come closer. I shall consume you all.

Images intruded into Liz's mind: a fiery blaze, spreading through her lab, enveloping Claudio's slumped form. She winced.

'Do either of you know what could have caused this?' the fire chief asked. 'That blaze was intense enough to burn through a concrete floor! Yet the damage was relatively localised. I've never seen anything like it. It almost looks like spontaneous combustion. Though you scientists will quickly dispel that theory.'

'No, I think you're right,' Liz told him.

'It caused all this by drawing upon the body heat of one man,' Smythe whispered to her. 'Just imagine what it could do using the heat at the heart of a volcano...'

'Is it just me, or is there a radio on nearby?' the fire chief asked, standing between them. 'I keep hearing this muffled voice... What's going on?'

'Our experiment's buried somewhere in that pile,' Liz said.

The fire chief passed a small shovel to Smythe. 'Try not to disturb things too much.'

'I'll get the refrigeration unit ready,' Liz said as Smythe carefully cleared small piles from the rubble. She unfastened the metal clasps around the lid.

Smythe took another stab at the rubble and the blade clanged. He remained still. 'Your gloves please, chief. Your helmet, too. Quickly.'

The fire chief unfastened his red helmet and passed it to Smythe with his gloves. Smythe put them on and flipped down the visor.

'Open the refrigeration unit, please.'

A cloud of vapour escaped the unit as Liz removed the lid, exposing bubbling liquid nitrogen.

Smythe carefully set down the shovel and swept away debris with his gloved hand. Blackened eyes peered up at him. Further clearing revealed a soot-stained, marble head with a web of cracks across its face. Liz feared the slightest touch would shatter it. She suddenly felt much warmer.

Inner fire, coursing through you. I can feel it.

'What is that? A mask, a sculpture?' the fire chief asked, approaching Smythe.

'Stand back!' Smythe gripped the shovel and gently lifted the bust, watching it carefully as if it were a mine that might explode with any sudden movement. 'Stand back, all of you!'

The fire chief and Liz backed into the hallway. She noticed the hose nozzle trembling in the hands of the young firefighter.

Smythe poised the shovel over the bubbling liquid. 'If it breaks loose,' he told the firefighter, 'be ready to put me out.'

The young man exchanged a nervous glance with his chief.

With a flick of the shovel, the marble bust dropped into the liquid with a small splash. There was a muffled crunch, and Liz spotted something thrashing in the freezing liquid. Smythe dropped the shovel and slammed on the lid. Liz rushed over and helped him fasten the clamps. She winced as a scream pierced her mind. Smythe held the refrigeration unit still as the creature splashed about inside. After a few seconds, the movement slowed to the odd spasm, then stopped.

The fire chief gulped. 'What the hell was that?' he muttered.

Smythe passed him back his helmet and gloves. 'An experiment that went wrong.' He smiled at Liz. 'But it appears we've contained the problem.'

Liz smiled back. Gripping the trolley handle, she dragged it towards the exit. Smythe followed.

'Wait a moment!' the fire chief called after them. 'If you know what caused this, I require your testimony for my report!'

'Sorry, but this matter is classified,' Liz called over her shoulder. 'If you have any questions or concerns, contact the United Nations Intelligence Taskforce.'

'So what happens now?' Liz asked, coming to a stop at the Science building front entrance. The late afternoon sun cast her and Smythe's shadows into the traffic.

'I need to get this creature to UNIT HQ.'

'For further study?'

'No, too dangerous. If it accidentally got loose or fell into the wrong hands...'

Liz remembered UNIT's previous dealings with alien life. 'You wouldn't let them destroy it, would you?'

'Of course not, it's a sentient being after all.' He patted the refrigeration unit. 'As long as it remains in hibernation, it won't bother anyone during the trip.'

A small car pulled up to the pavement. The driver, a young red-haired man, stepped out of the car and left the engine running. He and Smythe loaded the refrigeration unit into the boot before getting into the car.

Smythe poked his head out the window. 'We'll take it from here, Dr Shaw. Looks like your work here's done. Enjoy the rest of your stay in Rome.'

Liz approached the passenger side of the car. 'UNIT HQ is just a stopover, isn't it? Where are you really taking the creature?'

Wise, disarming eyes looked into hers. 'Return to sender.'

The car sped away into traffic. Liz shook her head in disbelief. He was right though: her work here was done. Her lab was destroyed, her research notes were reduced to ash, and the focus of her assignment was bobbing in liquid nitrogen.

Of course, UNIT would remain tight-lipped about the whole matter, she thought, and turn a deaf ear to her unanswered questions. And she would be left standing around with nothing to do, feeling frustrated. Typical. No wonder she'd left the organisation.

Another car pulled up. It was her driver. He stepped out of the car and looked at her anxiously.

'*Buona sera, signora*. I came as soon as I heard about the fire. Are you all right?'

'Yes, I'm fine... tired though. It's been a long day.'

'Why don't I drive you to a nice café so you can relax.'

'I'd appreciate that.' Liz dragged the trolley to the front steps before getting into the car. Taking off her lab coat, something crinkled in the pocket. She reached in and pulled out a message scribbled on a piece of graph paper: 'Thank you for your help, Liz. Good luck with your research at Cambridge. Tell Lethbridge-Stewart the Doctor said hello.'

The Doctor? What did he have to do with this? Liz lay back in her seat. She felt a headache coming on.

'Mind if we take a drive through the countryside instead?' she suggested.

> A marble bust of Nero, thought to have been destroyed in a fire at the University of Rome last month, was returned today to the Palermo Museum.
>
> Other than a broken nose, the sculpture is none the worse for wear. Recent X-rays have proven the bust to be hollow. According to top scientists, the mysterious inner heat source and leaking condensation were an elaborate hoax perpetrated by Dr Orlando Dirossi to appease his archaeological survey project investors.
>
> Dirossi could not be reached for comment.
>
> *Giornale di Sicilia*
> 24 May 1999

These Things Take Time

Samantha Baker

The TARDIS door opens and the Doctor steps outside.

'Glorious day!' he says. Ace and Hex follow him out.

'Blimey, Doctor,' says Hex, 'you're not wrong. It's so hot!'

'Yeah,' says Ace. 'Humid or what? Well, we ain't in Britain, that's for sure.'

'It *looks* like Cumbria,' laughs Hex.

'Here!' says the Doctor.

'What's this?'

'This, Hex, is a tracker – if you should get lost it will lead you back to the TARDIS. Don't lose it!'

'I won't, Doctor. Thanks.'

'Now, I'll see you both later. I have some business to attend to. Don't wander too far!' The Doctor's voice trails off into the distance.

'I'll look after that, thank you very much,' says Ace.

'Eh?'

'The tracker. I can put it in my bag.'

'Is that the usual order of things, then?' asks Hex. 'We land, the Doctor goes off head-first into a situation we know nothing about and we just look around?'

'Pretty much! Come on, I'll race you.'

A busy market square. People are bustling about everywhere, going about their business – selling, buying, chatting. The clucks and squawks of animals mingle with carts being drawn across stone and mud being squelched by feet.

'How much?!' says Hex. 'You must be joking, mate! I know it's the fifteenth century and all, but that's taking the piss!'

'Aye, well,' says an older man. 'You can take it or leave it, can't you? I happens to know that you can't get better than this anywhere in this town.' Another customer's muffled 'I'll take this' distracts the market trader and Hex is left alone.

'I've seen better than this down Camden market,' he says to himself.

'It's not the fifteenth century,' says Ace, who's sidled up to join him.

'Well, whatever – fifteenth, sixteenth, twentieth. I'm no good on history.'

'I mean, it's not Earth, so it can't be the Middle Ages. This is Armstrong's Colony, a place where our descendants come far into our future when the Earth is no longer habitable.'

'The Doctor tells you a lot, you know.'

'Well, we've been travelling for a long time.'

'That's cool, but I still feel like the new boy. Like you two don't trust me.'

'You've got to earn your spurs, cowboy.'

'Oh, right.' Hex laughs. 'It's going to take me a while to get used to this time-travel lark.'

'You will. Get used to it, I mean.'

Hex is running – breathlessness is now his main concern. 'Wait, slow down.' He stops and sucks in lungfuls of air.

'What's the matter?' says Ace – she's panting, but she's not as inert as Hex. 'Are you okay? You look spooked.'

'I'm going dizzy.'

'What's the matter, Hex? You're scaring me.'

'Oh, it's nothing; I've just got a headache. And... and, don't laugh, but I seriously can't remember why we were running!'

'The Irisians of the planet Gamma XIII once realised they'd been patrolling their galactic borders for centuries –' it's the Doctor, who's snuck up on them – 'and no one could recall why they'd started: they'd never come into contact with an alien race, let alone come under threat from one. So, they stopped. Less than a solar day later, their entire culture was wiped from existence by a raiding party of Daleks.'

'Doctor?' says Hex. 'Where did you get to?'

'Here and there. Anyway, why *were* you running?'

'Oh,' says Ace. 'Just youthful exuberance, Doctor.'

'Come along,' he says. 'I want you to meet someone. You see across the valley? Down there? That manor house? That's where we're going.'

'Doctor, that's miles away!'

'Oh, Hex, don't be so... urban. It'll take no more than an hour.'

The Doctor is whistling to himself with a certain gusto. He seems happy.

'Further than it looks, ain't it?' says Hex, opening a gate. 'After you, Miss McShane.'

'Why, thank you, kind sir,' says Ace.

'Good morning!' the Doctor calls out, suddenly. 'Might you be Lord Denton?'

'I am so.' The stranger's voice is far away. 'Before I ask who you are –'

he's approached them now, and his volume has decreased – 'might I ask what you're doing on my estate?'

'Well, call me a rebel, but I'm going to answer those questions in the wrong order. I am the Doctor, and I am here to see you, m'lord.'

'Doctor!' Denton's whole demeanour is now more jovial. 'Of course! But I wasn't expecting you for days yet.'

'Really? I must see to the temporal decrystalisers. These are my friends, Ace and Hex.'

'Come inside, all of you, out of the heat,' says Denton. 'We can sit on the porch and drink to our agreement. Come, come, sit down. I'll order some refreshment from the girl.'

'Thank you, thank you.'

'He's a bit over the top, isn't he?' whispers Ace, an aside to Hex.

'He reminds me of a game-show host!'

'Venetia?' shouts Denton. 'Venetia! Oh, where has she got to?'

'It's a wonderful estate you have here, m'lord,' says the Doctor.

'Jaymes, please.'

'Jaymes.'

'Over a thousand acres, stetching from here to the next village. It's my little paradise. Or at least it was until last year. And that is why I need your help, Doctor.'

'Go on.'

'Bandits. Raiding parties are constantly attacking. At first it was isolated attacks – a sheep farmer was beaten and his herd stolen, our mill was burnt to the ground – but the attacks have increased. They're not just on my manor, you understand, but here there's no local authority to speak of. For some reason, the locals look to *me* to protect them.'

'Perhaps it's because of the tax they pay you.'

Denton laughs. 'Most probably.'

'Hang on,' says Hex. 'What's that noise?'

The tranquil countryside ambience – cattle gently mooing, crickets making their presence felt – is quite suddenly replaced; a sound flash of white noise marks the switch to a chaotic situation. A large crowd is shouting, baying for blood by the sound of it. Above it all is the noise of a woman struggling. It's Ace.

'Whoa!' says Hex, real panic in his voice. 'What's going on?'

'Now's not the time to flip out,' calls Ace from about twenty metres away. She is calm, which only panics Hex more.

'McShane! Get her down from there! What are they doing to you?' Hex is now screaming – confusion and bewilderment taking over. 'How did I get here?'

'What are you talking about? It was the girl, remember. It was Venetia.'

'I don't understand. Oof!' Hex is jostled by the crowd. 'McShane! McShane!' He is being pushed away from his friend – her voice, telling him not to worry, reassuring him, is getting distant.

Hex realises what's going on. 'No!'

He hears the drop of a heavy axe.

'Perhaps it's because of the tax they pay you.'

Denton laughs. 'Most probably.'

'Hang on,' says Hex. 'What's that noise?'

The others are silent for a moment, straining their ears, no doubt. The Doctor is the first to speak. 'What noise is that, Mr Hex?'

'Hang on,' says Hex. 'Something really weird is going on. I was just somewhere else.'

The Doctor, incredulously: 'You were somewhere else?'

Ace, sarcastically: 'Of course you were.'

'I'm serious.' Hex now has their attention.

'My dear boy,' says Denton. 'You're as white as a newborn lamb.'

'What's going on, Hex?' says the Doctor.

'Er... can we talk privately, Doctor?'

'Of course.' He turns to Ace and Denton. 'Excuse us. Mr Hex and I are just going for a little walk.'

As Ace and Denton's chatter – concerning tea, and the fact that Denton's maid hasn't brought them any yet – fades out of Hex's earshot, he begins to talk to the Doctor.

'We were just talking and I don't understand what happened, it was so odd and I still can't believe –'

'Shh, calm down.' The Doctor speaks slowly and reassuringly. 'Talk me through it.'

Hex composes himself. 'We were talking. About the bandits that are attacking... what's his name?'

'Baron Denton de Kay Leigh.'

'Yeah, well. He and you were talking, when I suddenly heard this noise. It was like static, the kind of noise you get when you turn the volume up – I mean, really up – on a telly that's not tuned in.'

'Go on.'

'And then... I moved, I was somewhere else. In an instant, I was somewhere else.'

'Describe it.'

'Oh, it was horrible, Doctor. There were some guards – soldiers or something. They were forcing McShane up some steps. She shouted out to me. She said, "It was the girl, remember. It was Venetia." Then, the crowd all around me started to move. I think people were trying to get nearer, get a better view.'

The Doctor, serious and sombre. 'I see.'

'Then,' continues Hex, 'I didn't see it, but they... they... I heard an axe come down and the crowd cheer.'

'But you didn't see it?'

'No, but I heard what I heard.'

'But you didn't see it.'

'This is a disgrace.' Denton stands, his chair scraping along the decking. 'Excuse me, my dear, whilst I go and find the girl.' He walks away.

'Don't worry,' says Ace. 'She'll turn up.' As Hex and the Doctor approach, the pair's voices are getting louder.

'Now, Ace,' says the Doctor. 'I want you and Mr Hex here to go back to the TARDIS.' His voice has a false security to it; he's trying to reassure her. 'I have to stay and assist Lord Denton with his little problem. You'll be safe until I'm finished.'

'Er...' Ace is reticent.

'Oh, what is it?' – the Doctor, iritated. 'You can use the tracker to find your way back.'

'Well, I wasn't going to mention it, but we lost it.'

'Oh, Mr Hex,' says the Doctor, headmaster-like frustration in his voice.

'What? When did we lose the tracker? McShane? I gave it to you.'

'Look, Doctor, it wasn't our fault...'

'It wasn't *my* fault at all.' Hex is now quite angry. 'I didn't even know you'd lost it.'

'What are you on about, you muppet? You were with me –'

'Okay, okay,' says the Doctor. 'It's easily replaced. The main thing is that you two get back to the TARDIS.'

'Yes, Doctor, it is,' says Hex.

A nearby door swings open, violently. 'I say!' It was Denton. 'The bleeding girl's gone missing!'

'The girl?' asks Hex.

'My housemaid. I told her when I employed her – without so much as a reference, I hasten to add – that I would not tolerate absenteeism. She gets an afternoon off every other week, that's very generous for a master of my standing.'

'Do you think she's in danger?' asks Hex.

'She will be when I catch up with her. Yes, Venetia Dalborough will be in most serious –'

'Venetia?' Hex turns to the Doctor. 'Do you remember, Doctor, what I said –'

'Yes, I do.' The Doctor is contemplative. 'I think we need to find this young girl, and quickly.'

'We can spread out...' says Ace.

'No, I want you and Hex to go back to the TARDIS.'

'Oh, Professor, don't be –'

'I will not argue, Ace.' He turns to Hex. 'Take Miss McShane back. Do you think you can find the way without the tracker?'

'We'll find it, Doctor.'

Ace's protests fade into the distance as she and Hex make their way.

'Now, Lord Denton. Let's see where this Venetia has got to.'

Hex and Ace are walking through countryside.

'There's something going on,' Ace says, bitterly, 'and you and the Doctor don't trust me enough to tell me.'

'Look, let's just get back to the TARDIS,' says Hex. 'I'll explain when we're safe.'

'Hmm.'

They're approaching the market square. The montage of people and animals surrounds them – almost deafingly so.

'It's not the fifteenth century,' says Ace, laughing.

'What?' says Hex.

'I mean, it's not Earth, so it can't be the Middle Ages. This is Armstrong's Colony, a place where our descendants come far into our future when the Earth is no longer habitable.'

'Oh, God, what's going on? McShane, you're not even looking at me.' Hex is freaked.

'You will,' says Ace. 'Get used to it, I mean. It may take some time –'

'Argh!' says a young girl. 'Please forgive me, miss. I didn't mean to knock into you like that.'

'That's okay,' says Ace. 'No harm done.'

'Let me guess: you're Venetia,' says Hex.

'I'm sorry, sir, I truly am.' Her accent is English, rural and soft. 'But if I don't get back to the master as soon as possible, he'll have my guts for garters.'

As she runs off into the distance, Hex says, 'That's Denton's maid. She's mixed up in this – she may be in as much trouble as we are.'

'Who –?' says Ace, who then suddenly realises something. 'Oh, don't worry, Hex, she'll get in trouble. She will.'

'What do you mean?'

'She pickpocketed me. She took the TARDIS tracker.'

'Hang on, hang on.' Hex is losing it. 'You mean the tracker you told the Doctor that you'd already lost?!'

'What are you talking about, Hex?'

'Look, not ten minutes ago, you told the Doctor that we'd lost the tracker.'

'Are you having a laugh? We haven't seen the Doctor since we left the TARDIS.'

'Let's keep moving,' he says. 'We need to get to the Doctor's ship. I've no idea what's going on, but I think we'll be safer there.'

'Oh, forget that,' says Ace, running off back the way they came. 'I'm going to find that girl!'

'McShane! McShane!'

'Calm down, Hex.' The Doctor's voice is reassuring, authoritative. 'I think I know what's going on.'

'Now, wait,' says Hex. 'It happened again.'

'You've jumped about in time again?'

'Er, yeah, I suppose. I was just chasing after McShane...' His voice tails off – worry taking over. 'McShane? It's happened, hasn't it? She's –'

'You must remember, Mr Hex: the tracker. Remember, the tracker. *It's* the problem. Remember that and you'll remember *everything*.'

'Come on, slowcoach!' McShane is still ahead.

'No,' shouts Hex. 'I'm serious. We've got to get out of here, back to the TAR–'

'Hey!' McShane isn't shouting at Hex. 'You there!'

'Oh, God,' says Hex to himself. 'That's the girl. That's Venetia!'

He runs, panting as he goes. Suddenly, he stops, gasps, as a sound builds – the same static as before, even louder, even more piercing. Hex cries out. The static becomes all-consuming; no other sound audible.

And then silence. Hex breathes out. A slow rise of noise begins. 'Wha...?' he manages before he realises where he is. 'Oh, no, not again.' It is as before: the savage crowd, shouting, chanting, cheering: the sound of a struggle.

'McShane? McShane, where are you?' He has to shout to make himself heard. 'I can hear you – I've been here before – but I can't see –' He stops dead.

'Let me go!' comes the shout from afar. It's the Doctor.

'Doctor?! What's happening? You too? Where's McShane?'

'Mr Hex!' shouts the Doctor. 'You must concentrate! This is only a possible future.' The Doctor's voice – for the first time, as far as Hex can remember – is panicked. 'You must find Venetia and destroy the tracker. It wasn't Denton, it was *her*!'

The axe thuds down.

The static returns. 'Argh,' says Hex. 'It's deafening!' He falls to the ground, still screaming. 'I can't stand it, I don't understand!'

'What's the matter?' It's Ace's voice. The static drops out, instantly.

'McShane! God, what *is* going on?'

'Are you okay, Hex? I turned round to see where you were and you'd fallen.' She pauses, then helps him to his feet. 'Okay, hint taken. Let's get back to the TARDIS.'

'Eh?'

'As you seem so determined that we hide away out of trouble...'

'What are you talking about? We've got to find that servant girl!'

Ace chases after Hex as he sprints on.

'There! Quick!' he shouts after a few moments.

In the distance, Venetia yelps.

'She's fallen,' shouts Ace. 'Get her.'

Hex grabs Venetia before she can get away. She struggles, but he's too strong.

'Where is it?' shouts Hex. 'Come on, where's the tracker?'

'I don't know what you mean, sir,' she says, all innocently.

'Hex, you're hurting her.' Ace is worried.

'There!' Hex has found something. 'I told you – what's this? Eh? This is ours – what's it doing in your pocket?'

'Okay,' says Ace. 'You can let her go now.' He does so. 'Now, do you want to tell us what's going on? You're Venetia, aren't you? His Lordship's maid? Why did you –' She suddenly breaks off. 'Hex, what are you doing with that rock?'

'Calm down, McShane. I wouldn't waste it on her. This is for the tracker.'

He smashes the rock down on the electronic equipment...

'I see,' said the Doctor. All three friends were now back inside the TARDIS's console room. Hex had told them all he'd experienced since they'd landed on Armstrong's Colony.

'But you don't remember?' he asked.

'Remember what, birdbrain?' said Ace, trying to lighten Hex's mood. 'We haven't been to that planet; how could we remember it?'

'But I remember it.'

The Doctor considered this for a moment, his fingers tapping rhythmically on the TARDIS's control banks. 'It would seem you've retained memories from a defunct timeline...'

'How about saying that with the subtitles switched on?' asked Ace.

'We *did* land on Armstrong's Colony – but in a timeline that no longer exists. From what you say, it seems that Denton's servant, the girl Venetia, stole the TARDIS tracker –' even though that event hadn't technically happened, the Doctor shot a look of disapproval at the pair – 'and tried to use it. The tracker is a time-sensitive scanner. Used incorrectly, it can have disastrous consequences. Because you, Hex, caught up with her and came into physical contact with it, it was you who suffered.'

Hex leaned on the console, his thoughts dominated by the sights of his friends on the gallows.

'It created a shockwave of possible realities,' continued the Doctor. 'But they were all yours, Hex. Ace and myself, Denton and Venetia, would only have experienced one possibility...'

'But, Doctor,' said Hex, his head spinning. 'You said it was me catching Venetia with the tracker that started all this. But, all the stuff I saw – meeting Denton, seeing you and McShane... in trouble – all that happened *after* I'd caught her.'

'In one possible reality, yes. In another, you destroyed the tracker, put time back on its course and found yourself here.'

'But why did everything happen in the wrong order?'

'Time.' The Doctor smiled. 'It doesn't always run smoothly. The main thing is that we're all safe and sound. Now!' He dramatically pulled at a couple of levers on the console. 'I think it's probably best if we leave poor Lord Denton to deal with his bandits on his own, hmm?'

'So, as far as he and Venetia are concerned,' asked Ace, 'we didn't show up?'

'Yes, quite.' The Doctor winked at Hex. 'Between us, let's just call it an adventure we never had.'

Categorical Imperative

Simon Guerrier

The Doctor had just said to find something 'for a christening', so Sarah had picked out an innocuous blouse and skirt. He hadn't got changed himself. As a result, they were almost the only ones here not dolled up like royalty. There could have been as many as a thousand people in the chamber, and she and the Doctor were easily the scruffiest. Sarah tried to ignore the disgusted glances thrown their way. She pretended not to hear what they said about his scarf.

The chamber had once been home to some kind of parliament, the Doctor had told her when they arrived. Now it was used for parties. He usually liked parties, she thought. But he was in one of his glowering moods now.

At first, Sarah had tried to pick out the scandals, pointing out to the Doctor who was cold-shouldering who, where the allegiances were, who she would bully for gossip. But the Doctor had shown no interest in her journalistic instincts, her efforts to provoke at least a smile. He just wanted to brood. So much for his promise to take her somewhere different, to get away from...

She didn't want to think about that. If the Doctor just wanted to watch these people in their pretty clothes and hats, then fine. She could sit here, behave herself, not show him up.

So they had sat for hours, some way towards the back of the room, looking down on the queue of great and good that snaked towards the crib. Tall, fearsome guards in black armour watched over the baby and those waiting their turn to see him. The guards didn't just look ceremonial, thought Sarah. In the far corner of the room, there was a buffet for those who had already done the queue. Over glasses of pink fizz, they could schmooze with each other and with the baby's family. The Doctor pointed out one sour-faced woman, probably not yet twenty-five, flanked by a pair of younger, prettier girls in far less formal dress. She was the mother, the Doctor said. The poor baby, thought Sarah.

It was this group that Sarah had been watching with most interest for the past hour. She couldn't quite work out the dynamics. The girls were not servants, and yet they weren't part of this aristocracy either. Perhaps they had not yet come of age or something. The baby's mother didn't seem to share any intimacies with them, which might mean she was playing to the rest of the room. Or that she didn't know them. As soon as Sarah realised this, it became obvious the girls didn't know each other, either. So who were they?

She nudged the Doctor, and whispered, 'Hey!'

'I *know*,' said the Doctor, tight-lipped. 'Don't let him see you.'

Sarah looked at him. What was he talking about? He could be so cryptic. Anything to make things difficult.

She followed his gaze down to the queue. Who was she going to recognise, anyway? This was years after her time, surely. And then she slapped her fingers over her mouth to stop the squeak of surprise. There in the queue, about thirty people from the front, was the Doctor. The *old* Doctor, the one she had first met, before he had changed into this one. The old Doctor fitted just fine into a room like this – which was probably why she'd not spotted him sooner. He sported a scarlet smoking jacket, and stood tall and regally. In his hands he cradled a slender box, tied with ribbon. It was an elegant, pretty little present. He held it like it was a bomb.

'What's *he* doing here?' she said. 'You knew he'd be here, didn't you? You'd have to. He's what you've been watching for.'

'Just don't let him see you with me,' said the Doctor, levelly.

'Why not? We probably haven't even met yet.'

'Exactly,' said the Doctor. 'If he sees you with me now, think what will happen when you do bump into him for the first time. He'll sit there nodding at you like he's known all along.'

Sarah bit her lip. He was right, of course. Then a thought struck her.

'That's what he – what *you* did do, remember?' she said.

The Doctor shook his head despairingly. 'He's an incorrigible show-off.'

'So why are *we* here if you've already been?' said Sarah.

But all the Doctor said was, 'Watch.'

She was in no mood for a lesson from him, not after what they had seen. And then she realised who the baby was.

She had no idea where or when it had been. As ever, they had arrived by accident, and it took the Doctor a bit of exploring to get his bearings. When he finally sussed it out, he wasn't happy. He had told her the name of the city, but it meant nothing to her. Somewhere on Earth, anyway. The only name that sunk in was the one on all the posters, the name of a man who promised everything.

The stench of the place had threatened to overpower them when they arrived; a mouldy, damp stink of things rotting away. Sarah had had a flat with blocked drains once, and been forced to move out because of the smell. This place was a million times worse. It made her eyes water and her nose run. The Doctor had looked grave. 'It's the dead,' he told her.

He had still wanted to investigate. It was all right for him in those clothes, she thought. She was hardly dressed for it. Rather than let her waste time going back to the TARDIS, the Doctor had tugged off his coat and draped it round her shoulders. It was far too big for her, and far too heavy. The contents of the pockets bashed against her knees as she walked. But he was deaf to her complaints.

The city would once have been bigger than London, he had said. In a tone that suggested he knew more than he was letting on, he said he couldn't imagine what had happened to it. He prompted her to make sense of it. Sarah did her best, but the skeletal remains of buildings afforded no clues. The wreckage told of cataclysmic disaster, not just decay.

They crossed the great river via the only bridge still intact. Buildings on both banks had collapsed into the water, the riverside streets on the far side had flooded. The Doctor found it fascinating. He explained how water couldn't carry shockwaves as fast as air, so the riverbank had had whiplash all along it. Hence the more serious damage done.

'Shockwaves from what?' asked Sarah. 'Do you think the place was bombed?' The Doctor looked around, sticking out his bottom lip while he considered. He didn't seem bothered by all this destruction – it was just another conundrum to puzzle out, no trickier than a crossword.

'It might have been an accident,' he mused. 'A power station melting down, or an experiment going wrong.' He scratched the back of his head. 'But who knows?'

'It reminds me of Hiroshima,' said Sarah. 'Documentaries about the bombing.'

The Doctor frowned, helped himself to the pockets she was wearing and produced a Geiger counter. He waved it around a bit, glibly, then looked at the readings. He obviously didn't like what he read. Then he pointed the counter at her. They had encountered radiation poisoning before, on Skaro. That had been miserable and, after everything they had suffered, he hadn't had the heart to go through with his mission there.

The Doctor kept the Geiger counter on her for an awfully long time. His expression grew steadily bleaker. She was just about to say something when he suddenly smacked the display with the palm of his hand. Then he pointed it at her again. When he checked the reading this time, he broke into a grin.

'See?' he said, showing her the needle well in the safety zone. 'Worry over nothing!'

They continued on. A few hundred yards later, the Doctor had – subtly –

told her what the first symptoms of radiation poisoning were. They joked about it. He said it took time to do real damage, that at the first sign of anything amiss, they could run back to the TARDIS and get it all seen to. Even if the worst happened, he said, everything would be okay.

He had tried to reassure her, that was all. In his typically morbid manner. He couldn't just come out and say it, he had to be different, had to take the circuitous route. But it didn't make things better.

When they did meet survivors, Sarah knew there was nothing to be done for them.

Her first thought was to try the hospitals, but they had been raided already. Sarah spent whole days trooping from one gutted building to another, but where things hadn't been looted, they had been smashed. She looked for shops, supplies, anything that might ease the suffering. Just to prove the Doctor wrong. He stayed with the dying, made them soup, asked them about the man whose picture was all over town.

Clear-eyed and handsome in a dangerous way, there were images of him everywhere, pledging himself to victory. Whatever the cost. The survivors – if you could call them that – had placed their faith in him and made all the sacrifices he asked for. Sarah listened to accounts of rationing, of medical experiments, of things done to children. Increasingly desperate measures on a population too afraid to argue. The man in the posters had said it was necessary. The Doctor had heard of him before, of course, of what he had done. He told them how he had died. It was comfort to some of them.

After nearly a week, Sarah couldn't cope any more and the Doctor had let her go back to the TARDIS. He stayed. She didn't know for how long – time was different inside the ship. He had stayed to the end, tending them, feeding them, doing what doctors do when there isn't any hope. He had buried them, too, he told her. That had been their worry – that the last of them to go wouldn't get buried. They were worried they'd get picked over by dogs or other scavengers. Not that Sarah and the Doctor had even glimpsed such things. Everything was dead.

'Take me away from here,' said Sarah. She had promised herself she wouldn't cry, and being cross with the Doctor helped with that. 'Somewhere we *can* make a difference. Somewhere we can stop things like this ever happening...'

So they had left. Perhaps, the Doctor said, other cities had been less badly hit, and one day their people would turn up and reclaim this place. But for now, the TARDIS fading away from the ruin of the city, took with it the last living things.

* * *

The Doctor clutched the box, trying to seem natural, trying not to look up at Jo, stood with the baby's mother and the other girls. He didn't want people to see they were together. And he wasn't sure he could look Jo in the eye.

There were less than twenty people ahead of him now. Casually, very casually, he removed the top of the box. Inside, elegantly presented, was a silver knife. Hardly a children's present. More like a surgical instrument. The Doctor had seen the multitude of silver spoons the child had already received. He hoped the others in the queue didn't notice. They might comment on his originality, draw attention to him, *remember* him...

If so, he would never get away.

Jo's job was distracting the baby's mother, Ann. She needn't have bothered: there were two other girls vying for attention, offering to help out, to fetch things, to let her have a break. Ann was exhausted just from dealing with them.

So, instead, Jo had been talking to her. She asked her questions – and not about the baby, not about the day. Things Ann never got the chance to talk about any more, Jo realised. How long had anybody thought of her as anything more than 'the mother'? Now Ann was telling her everything.

Jo, nodding rather than listening, felt sorry for her. Not because of the things she was saying, more because of what she left out. And because, for all the shocking things she came out with, no one else in the room seemed to care. She reminded Jo of some of her own mother's 'friends' – the catty ones whose important husbands were always away from home. The women had money and friends and hobbies, but they knew they were trapped. That's what made them so competitive and cruel. And they knew they were on borrowed time. They hadn't been married for their conversation, and who knew what their husbands got up to without them. Jo had seen what the old letches could be like, but she couldn't blame them for deserting their miserable wives...

Ann's story was just the same. She thought her marriage would free her. She had never wanted her son, knowing her husband would transfer what little affection he had to the baby. She hardly knew any of the people in the room. She hated them all.

'It's the worst day of my life,' Ann continued. She must have said the same thing four or five times in the last twenty minutes. And then she stopped, dead. Jo looked up. Something had happened in the queue. She instinctively grabbed Ann's arm, worried that the Doctor had started early, that she might have to improvise. But it wasn't him.

At the front of the queue, a bent-backed old man had dropped his present. The pretty little box had split open on hitting the ground and the contents clattered across the floor. It looked like the old man had brought the same small, silver knife as the Doctor's, thought Jo.

Those near the old man tried to help, but he didn't want his present back. He was agitated, cross – probably just embarrassed. It must be terrible at that age, she thought, getting all clumsy.

'I won't do it!' he exclaimed. 'I can't!' For such an old man, he was making a good job of pushing the courtiers and guards away. Good on him.

A teenage girl ran over to him, and on seeing her he settled down. His granddaughter, apparently. The girl – Jo hadn't caught her name – had been one of the pair earlier, the ones pestering Ann. She'd kept bringing her drinks, faster than Ann could offload them onto other people. Maybe the old man had said to make herself useful, but she'd ended up just getting in the way.

Taking her grandfather by the arm, the girl carefully pocketed the knife before leading the old man out.

'Silly old duffer,' said Ann, loudly and before they were out of earshot. 'Who was he anyway?' Nobody knew.

Watching all this from the far end of the room, the Doctor had been troubled. But not enough to get involved, as he normally would. Instead of bounding in to assist, he and Sarah had sat where they were, not even commenting on what happened.

The old Doctor hadn't got involved either. He had done worse in fact, and turned his head away as the old man and the girl walked past. Now he was just a dozen people from the front of the queue, and Sarah could see him gingerly stroking the knife he carried. The guards hadn't noticed, but then it hardly looked like a weapon. It was all too agonising to watch.

Sarah leaned in to the Doctor so no one else would hear what she said. 'But you can't kill a child!' she whispered. 'Remember? You said!' He raised an eyebrow.

'In *all* circumstances, Sarah?' he said, gravel-voiced. 'You saw what he'll grow up to do. Everyone in this room faces a gruesome end.'

'But it doesn't make it right!'

'You'd get on with Kant,' smiled the Doctor, thinly. 'He didn't believe in exceptions. Stealing sweets is wrong, he'd say, because if *everyone* stole sweets, there wouldn't be any sweetshops...'

'I don't want another lecture,' Sarah snapped, loud enough that people nearby turned round. She smiled at them until they looked away, and then said, 'You're going to kill him, aren't you?'

'In fifty-two years' time, he's murdered by his aides,' said the Doctor, slowly. 'They're so appalled at all he's done, they torture him first. For days. Acting now, it's preventing that from happening. Think of it as a surgical procedure.'

They continued to watch.

'I'm just saying,' said Ann, and again too loudly, 'that we're paying for all these people's drinks, and I don't even know who half of them are.'

The girl she was tearing strips off had only been trying to help, thought Jo. But Ann had taken against her as soon as she'd opened her mouth. Probably the accent. It was one of those brash American ones that got right up the noses of well-to-do sorts like Ann. Jo had seen the same thing before, at embassy dos.

She let the other girls intercede, though. One of them had got Ann another drink, which she knocked back in one gulp and handed back. The girl went to refill it and, though Ann continued her tirade, she now only spoke to the girls around her – not to the whole of the room.

'They've all got plans for him, you know,' she told them. 'What he is, what he'll grow up to be. And it all means nothing. I should know, I used to be the star. I was the one they came to see.'

While the girls attempted to soothe her, Jo watched the queue. The Doctor was one from the front now. He was holding the knife. He wouldn't look at her.

The archbishop in front of him finally moved off to the buffet. The Doctor had reached the crib. The usher asked his name, seemed not to notice that it had been given before, and let him step forward. The Doctor tore the knife from the box, and held it up above the baby.

The baby looked up at him and giggled.

The Doctor hesitated. He glanced round, quickly, at the room. The line of well-wishers to his right all gazed at him, willing him to get a move on. He had to do this. He gripped the knife and –

He looked back at the queue. Surely not...

About halfway down the queue stood a portly, blond-haired man in a striking blue cape. He held the Doctor's gaze, and his nostrils flared. He knew exactly what the Doctor was going to do. But how? The man's beady little eyes twitched, downwards. The Doctor followed them.

In one hand, the man in the cape was holding a small, silver knife. Exactly the same one as the Doctor held aloft. He looked up at the man again. The man nodded. The Doctor almost choked. He lowered the knife, tucked it away into a pocket, and leant forward over the child.

'Sorry old boy,' he said, aware of the relief in his own voice. 'Until next time.'

'He didn't do it!' said Sarah, watching the old Doctor collect a girl from the mother's entourage and escort her quickly out.

'No,' said the Doctor. 'But it's not over yet.'

'They've all got something to prove,' said Peri, sourly.

She had closed in on Ann again when the skinny girl had gone off with the weirdo in the red jacket. She had to press her advantage, determined not to let the Doctor down. She'd never hear the end of it if she did.

Ann didn't look round, but nor did she disagree.

'I always hated these family things,' Peri continued. 'Everyone's so nauseating.'

'They're some of the most powerful people in the world,' Ann replied, but her tone lacked conviction.

'Oh, don't get me wrong,' said Peri. 'They probably all mean well. But they want to take something away with them, don't they? It's the worst kind of social climbing.'

'So why do we do it?' asked Ann, quietly. Peri had to be careful. Push her too far, she thought, and she'll break.

'For love,' she said.

Ann spun round on her, eyes wide.

'Or duty,' said Peri, quickly.

'Go on,' said Ann, suspiciously.

'You do it because it's important to him,' Peri said, nodding towards Ann's husband, a fat man in uniform. Around him, important persons hung on his every word. 'You do it because it's easier than fighting him,' Peri went on, 'because, to him, it all *means* something.'

After a moment, Ann asked, 'You grew up in an embassy, too?'

She didn't seem half as intimidating any more.

Sarah had spotted the man with the knife. He took up a lot of room – though less round than some of the others in the queue, he had presence they lacked. His huge bow-tie, his expansive cape, here was a man who needed to be seen. He had a certain flair though, a style of his own. Kind of like the Doctor... Oh, come on.

'Is that you as well?' she asked, stonily.

'Which one?' he said, not caring at all.

'In the cape.'

'Probably.'

Sarah sighed. He was being difficult again. Who else could she have meant, anyway? That little guy in the straw hat? Actually, she thought, he could be a Doctor as well. She looked up and down the queue again. Quite a lot of them weren't dressed like royalty. Every five or six places in the line was some dandy or eccentric. A young man in a beige coat, a sprig of greenery in the lapel. A Byronic sort with a flashy silver cravat.

They all had that same steely look about them, that righteous determination.

And they were all carrying exactly the same knife.

There were catacombs and alcoves beneath the chamber in which the party was going on. There had once been a library kept here, but the books had long since been burnt. The place was kept locked, and except for the keepers who checked it each night and set traps for vermin, no one was ever admitted.

Except today, when there had been no end of people passing through.

The Doctor rolled up his hat and put it away inside his coat, then dipped into a trouser pocket for his key. Behind him, Tegan was not happy.

'Such a waste of time,' she muttered. 'What did any of that achieve? You said he was a monster...'

The Doctor didn't answer. He went over to the police box stood in one corner of the room and unlocked it. He held the door open, rolling his eyes as Tegan went in, still rabbiting on about what he hadn't done and how rude that woman had been. Tegan had *tried* to be nice...

He followed her into the TARDIS, the door slammed shut and – after a moment – the light on top flashed on and off and a raucous groaning noise echoed out through the catacombs. The box seemed to warp slightly, but stayed exactly where it was. The strange sound faded away to nothing, and the light went out.

Moments later, another Doctor marched up to the door. He swished his cape up over one shoulder, and rummaged around for his key. Behind him, Peri was simply exasperated.

'It was the right thing!' she chided. 'You couldn't murder a baby, it wouldn't be you!'

The Doctor held the door open for her, but she stood where she was, hands on hips, waiting for an answer. He gave her a moment, then shrugged and went inside.

'Don't just walk away from me!' she yelled, chasing after him. The door of the police box slammed behind her, the light flashed on and again the catacombs were filled with the strange wheezing sounds. The TARDIS stayed exactly where she was.

Shortly after the sounds had faded, another Doctor hurried in, pulling the key from his breast pocket.

'Professor...' whined the girl right behind him. 'You didn't *do* anything!'

Ann didn't know what to do with all the girls around her. She found she actually missed the American girl, wished the abrasive man in the cape had let her stay longer. These others were much more pushy, eager to make their mark. Did they think she could grant favours? They'd not done their homework. She no longer had any influence.

The girl with all the badges had made coffee. To help sober Ann up, she said. The impudence. But before Ann could say anything, Charley, the girl with the blonde bob, had stepped in and asked about Ann's shoes. Almost despite herself, Ann had started explaining all about where she'd got them and what an ordeal it had been.

It had been one of her more successful stories, recently. The bit when the shop manager got taken away for sedition usually brought the house down. At least, those around her would make every effort to show they thought it hilarious. The girls around her now weren't laughing, not one of them. They were staring at her. Ann hadn't been stared at like that before. Not properly. Sometimes by the mucky people who tried to mob her carriage before the police moved them on. But never by people in the same room, never so close.

She had sent that man in the shop to his death, she realised, and on a whim. He had only tried to help her. Ann couldn't remember what she was saying, and her words trailed off mid-sentence.

Blushing – which she never did – she took one of the cups of coffee. It calmed her, and she wanted to thank the girl who'd made it. But the girl had gone. She hadn't even said goodbye.

People always let you know when they were leaving. It was when they finally got to the point, told you what they expected in exchange for turning up. Which was funny – not one of the girls hassling Ann today had done that. Nor that boy in the kilt. They must all know there was little she could give them anyway. Why else? She finished her coffee.

Charley stepped forward, on cue. 'Top-up?' she asked politely.

The afternoon was nearly over, and the room had emptied out. Sarah had seen the Doctors, one-by-one, reach the baby, look down, pause, then grab their companions and scurry away. Whatever lesson her own Doctor was trying to impress on her, she really had no idea.

'Isn't it cheating to be here more than once?' asked Sarah. The Doctor, still watching intently, looked sly.

'There are exceptions to the rule,' he said.

'But none of you have done anything!' said Sarah. 'Why keep coming if you *know* you're not going to go through with it?'

There were only a dozen people left in the queue now, and all but one of them looked like aristocracy. The one who didn't, the Byron man, was next to see the baby.

'Of course!' said her Doctor, leaping to his feet. There was a mischievous look in his eye, and he was grinning, ear-to-ear. 'You keep the mother talking, I'll be back in a bit,' he said, and dashed off before she could argue.

Ann and Charley had just started to like each other when the competent-looking girl in a prim skirt and blouse came over. She didn't offer Ann anything, or to get her anything, and she didn't say anything, either. Of all the young people who had come and gone today, this one looked most out of her depth. She clearly had no idea what was expected of her, and stood awkwardly and terrified, praying for inspiration to come. Ann would normally have preyed on that weakness.

'I'm not that fearsome, am I?' she said. But the girl didn't smile.

Ann handed the new girl a drink. 'You'd better have this,' she said. 'Calm the nerves.' It was what one of those other girls had said to her, earlier.

The girl took the glass but didn't drink from it. Ann decided to give her space. She looked over at the crib. They were nearly done, just the last handful to pay their respects. The least important ones at the back, as ever.

The man at the front was taking his time, she noticed. They should have been told to keep it quick. But there was something about the way he stood over the crib. Something about the sad look on his face. And the way he held that knife...

'Stop!' someone shouted, and Ann realised it had been her.

The people left in the room all turned, and for an instant she thought she'd die of shame. But the man with the knife had reacted differently. He had tensed, like an animal caught in a trap. And the guards knew exactly what that meant. Two of them leapt on top of him, bashing him down to the ground. A third guard grabbed up the crib, turning away, shielding the baby with its own body.

Though Charley tried to hold her back, Ann pushed her away, not caring about decorum or what people thought. She reached the guard with the baby before her husband had even moved. The guard didn't resist when she took the baby from him, but he sidestepped so that he was between her and the man with the knife, now being beaten by his colleagues. They said later they couldn't stand the smug look on his face.

Ann was hardly aware of any of that. All she knew was what she'd almost lost. She looked over at her husband. Having not moved an inch towards them, he had returned to whatever discussion he had been having before the attack. He obviously felt the danger had passed. Ann couldn't quite believe it. He didn't care about the baby, not in the way he should. The boy was just an object to him, an artefact, something to show off, to be used. As long as it hadn't been damaged, why worry?

Ann gazed down into her baby's beautiful face. The last time she had held him, when she'd put him down in the crib at the start of the day, she hadn't even looked at him.

'You helped that other Doctor get away, didn't you?' said Sarah, coldly. She had waited for the Doctor in the catacombs, assuming he would come back to the TARDIS when he had finished his games.

'They think the guards killed him,' he said. He was struggling with the chain round his neck, trying to find the key. 'They needed a calm head and I just offered to sign all the forms for them. "Natural causes", of course.'

'He and the girl have been and gone,' said Sarah. 'They were parked in the same place, on top of us.'

'They saw you?' asked the Doctor.

'Does it matter? He's a later one than you, isn't he?'

'It's the principle of the thing, Sarah,' he said, seriously. 'Remember? No exceptions.'

'He spoke to me, you know,' she said. The Doctor turned back to her.

'Had a pearl of wisdom for you, did he?' he said as he opened the TARDIS door. 'Something frustratingly vague?'

'He said things would be different now. The way he'll grow up has been changed.'

'Just a little affection can make a lot of difference,' agreed the Doctor, eager to be getting on. 'You fancy a cup of tea? Maybe a buttered scone?'

Sarah would not be put off. 'Different, he said. But what if we've made things worse?'

'Ah,' said the Doctor, 'that's a good point. Or it would be, if I wasn't quite so brilliant.' He grinned, winningly, and draped an arm round her shoulder. 'And if I didn't keep such brilliant company!' he said, and led her into the ship.

This time, when the eerie cacophony faded away, so did the police box.

Trapped!

Joseph Lidster

Please don't be chicken paste.

Mr Thompson looked down into the perfectly disinfected lunch box, at the perfectly cut sandwiches, prepared by the perfectly nice Mrs Thompson. He removed the sandwiches from the cling film and cautiously inspected one.

Chicken paste. Well, of course, it was chicken paste. After all, it was Wednesday. He dropped the sandwiches, uneaten, into the bin and stared at his computer screen. The unfinished monthly report stared right back at him. He'd completed one column of figures and had two more to go. Mr Knowles had already reminded him that the report was due by the end of the day. It had been an unnecessary reminder as Mr Thompson had never once been late with a report. Mr Knowles knew this, of course, but it was part of his job description to remind people about things. In fact, he had never once had reason to discipline Mr Thompson as Mr Thompson was perfectly satisfactory in all elements of his work. Mr Thompson was a perfectly satisfactory employee all round – it said so each year on his perfectly satisfactory appraisal.

The problem was that Mr Thompson was bored. He was bored with his satisfactory job. He was bored with his satisfactory family. He was bored with the satisfactory Mrs Thompson and their satisfactory, fortnightly lovemaking. He was bored with chicken paste Wednesday and peanut butter Thursday. He was bored with weekly reports that merged into monthly reports, which then, with complete predictability, merged into quarterly reports.

He was bored with being Mr Thompson.

There was only one element of his life that did not bore him and that was Joanne from Human Resources. Young, beautiful and energetic, she had a vibrancy that distinguished her from Mr Thompson, Mr Knowles and all the other grey-suited drones. She was alive. Mr Thompson had fallen in love with her from the moment he had first seen her. Her body was slim and smooth and her burgundy business suit accentuated all her curves.

She was the reason he now wore novelty ties.

She was also the reason he was about to take up smoking. He knew that four times a day she would leave the office and go outside for a cigarette. And today he would join her. Perhaps he would even talk to her.

The change in Mr Thompson's behaviour had not gone unnoticed by Mrs Thompson. A week before, as she microwaved their Marks and Spencer's lasagnes, she had enquired if he was having a mid-life crisis. Her friend, the perfectly dull Mrs Herbert, had told her that Mr Herbert had taken to mowing the lawn each day – a sure sign of a mental breakdown according to that lovely Asian doctor on TV. Mr Thompson had dismissed his wife's fears and told her that he had just fancied a change. She had hugged him and he had found himself gagging at her putrid, lavender smell. That night, he had excused himself from her glassy-eyed presence and had gone to sit in his car. That night, he had gone for a drive.

Mr Thompson snapped out of his reverie as he noticed Joanne sashaying down the office towards the exit, her hips hypnotically swaying from side to side. He jumped up and half ran towards the door. Then he slowed down. He didn't want to look too eager. He strolled casually into the pot-planted corridor and approached her.

'Going for a smoke?' he asked.

She turned to him, with a slightly cruel but wonderfully lovely smile and waved a packet of Silk Cut.

'Ah. Me too.'

He remembered that night when he'd driven to her house. It hadn't taken Mr Thompson long to find where she lived as it was part of his job to ensure that the firm's staff (or 'family' as Mr Knowles liked to call them) records were kept up to date. He had parked across the street and watched her through the window. Like Mrs Thompson, Joanne had been watching television. Unlike Mrs Thompson, she was probably not watching *Animal Hospital*. It was more likely she favoured one of those lewd programmes on Channel 5 that he had once reprimanded his son for watching. Mr Thompson had watched Joanne watching television for an hour. Then, she had stood up and left her living room. He had watched as an upstairs light had flickered on. He remembered how she had looked as she had entered the bedroom and started to undo her blouse. Then, her pale breasts partially revealed through the unbuttoned silk, she had moved towards the window and shut the curtains.

He looked over at her and smiled once more.

The girl's face stared blankly out from the missing person flyer. It was a solid and stark reminder of the dangers of modern society and sent a chill through Sacha as she waited for the bus. Well, it would have done had someone not crudely drawn a moustache and glasses onto the girl's face. Sacha shivered as the wind picked up and breezed through her completely unsuitable jacket. She had been waiting for the early-morning bus for what had seemed like years and was contemplating walking home. Was that a good idea though? It had been all very well joking about the missing girls at the party. However, with dawn still only threatening to break, it didn't seem so funny standing at a poorly lit bus stop. She hugged herself tightly and looked down the road. Was that the bus turning the corner? Of course it wasn't. Cold and tired, she cursed the fact that Daddy's taxes weren't being invested in a decent public transport system. She looked back in front of her, just in time to notice a shadowy figure duck back into a shop doorway across the road. She shivered once more.

She had been in the shower for over thirty minutes but still it wouldn't wash out. The shampoo frothed down her face, the bubbly foam pink with blood. She didn't notice the burning sting as she unconsciously rubbed it into her eyes. She didn't hear the footsteps approaching.

She just saw the Doctor's face. No matter how hard she tried not to, all she could see was his face.

So absorbed was he by Joanne's beauty, Mr Thompson had completely failed to grasp why she was standing in the corridor.

'You're taking the lift?' he asked.

'I'm not going to walk down nine flights of stairs just to go for a cig.'

Mr Thompson did not like lifts. Actually, Mr Thompson was bloody terrified of lifts. Every day, he would arrive at work fifteen minutes early to give himself plenty of time to use the stairs. His phobia had gotten so bad that Mrs Thompson had insisted that he visit her hypnotherapist friend, Ms Hyslop. The surprisingly sane Ms Hyslop had suggested that Mr Thompson's fear stemmed from a childhood incident. Had he ever been trapped in a lift? No, he had not. Ms Hyslop had told him that he needed to 'personalise' his trigger. She explained that he needed to isolate what it was that scared him – was it the feeling of being enclosed or was it the fear of being in close contact with so many people? Mr Thompson had explained to her, in words of one syllable, that it was a fear of death. At that point, Ms Hyslop had given up and Mrs Thompson had dragged her husband away, apologising for his rudeness. Mr Thompson had not used a lift in fifteen years. His friends and family had ridiculed his fear but he remembered. He remembered the news reports. The two young men who had been fighting in a Southampton tower block and had fallen against some lift doors. The doors had opened and they had hurtled fifteen storeys, face-down, to their deaths. He remembered reading about the old woman in a care home, who had been caught in between the closing doors of a lift and had fallen and died. He remembered reading about a shop-owner in India. The lift had only been on the second floor when the cable snapped. Broke both his legs. Mr Thompson wasn't much of a fighter, an old woman or (thank God) an Indian but this didn't stop him realising the dangers associated with travelling in a cramped, confined box suspended by a metal cable. He started to panic as the fears he had kept buried started to resurface.

'Doors opening.'

He told himself that he would be fine. He knew that nothing would happen. It was quite simple really. Every possible lift-related death was rushing through his mind, so for one of them to come true would have meant that he was psychic. It was the same whenever he got onto an aeroplane. He would visualise the explosion, the pretty blonde stewardess being sucked to her death, the plane starting to fall and he would then know that this would not happen. It would be too much of a coincidence.

'You getting in?' asked Joanne from inside the lift.

The respectable Mr Thompson laughed to himself. He wasn't scared. It was just a lift. Then, panicking, he realised that if he wasn't scared then the cable might just snap or the lift might just stop between floors or that a plane might just crash into the building while they were between floors and that they might just burn and suffocate in a metal coffin suspended by a fraying cable. Then he stopped. If he wanted to be with her he needed to overcome his fear. This wasn't just about him escaping his perfectly satisfactory life; it was about him overcoming his perfectly normal phobia. With one small step, Mr Thompson entered the lift and changed the entire course of his life.

He had to be with Joanne.

Sacha wondered whether to put on her headphones and listen to some music. It would make her feel better but would also leave her more exposed. She could still make out the figure across the road. He was large, she could see that. Should she text a friend? She would feel less alone but it could also encourage a mugger. Her friend, Jacinta, had once been threatened with a needle. She would tell anyone who would listen how it had been the most terrifying moment of her life. Sacha didn't want to go through something similar. Why were there so few streetlights here? And why were there no buses? She looked to her left and then towards the right, glancing subtly at the figure across the road. He was definitely looking over at her. Then, on her right, she saw a taxi. It was parked, but the headlights were on. She considered her options. Empty street. No bus. Her. The man in the shop doorway. A silent taxi. Was she just scaring herself? Should she waste the money on a taxi when a bus was bound to show up eventually?

'Doors closing.'

The doors closed, trapping Mr Thompson in the tiny, metal box. He looked at Joanne and tried to block out all images of them plummeting to their messy deaths by focusing on her youthful beauty. Suddenly, his stomach lurched as the lift began to move. The sudden loss of gravity reminded Mr Thompson of a plane taking off. He forced himself to look at Joanne's reflection in the metal doors. He wanted to reach out and touch it. He wanted to touch her before he died. Before they both died. Then he realised that he should have taken the stairs. Stairs don't kill you. Lifts do. He looked around the lift, noticing how small and airtight it was. The metal walls and ceiling... the reflective doors... was there a world outside of this? Again, he looked at Joanne's reflection. She really was beautiful. That's it. Don't think about the lift. What are the chances of anything happening? Mr Thompson realised that they only had eight floors to go. He would be fine, as the time would pass quite quickly. Not too quickly, he hoped. Although, what would happen if the cable snapped? Obviously, the lift would start to fall. But then what? Would they suddenly fly up to the ceiling or would they be flattened against the floor? Was there any way out? Could he climb through that vent in time? How quickly would it be before the lift and its occupants were smashed into the concrete basement? Mr Thompson became aware of his heart beating faster and faster. Then he remembered someone telling him that the sudden increase in the speed of a lift dropping could detach your heart. The arteries would just snap under the pressure. Oh God! He could still feel it beating though. Faster and faster. Could Joanne hear it? Was he having a heart attack? What would that be like? Was it his imagination or could he feel a pain in his arm? Was this it? He realised that he was sweating and turned to Joanne. His mouth was dry.

'Shouldn't take too long, should it?' he asked, definitely not nervously.

Then, with a sudden clanking sound, the lift stopped.

For a second there was silence.

'Eighth floor.'

Joanne looked at him and shrugged.

'Typical. We're going to stop at every floor,' she muttered.

'Doors opening.'

Mr Thompson considered making a run for it as the real world began to gradually reveal itself through the opening doors. Then he saw them all waiting and staring and grinning. Their eyes bore into his own as they began to move forward as one. He drew back as they entered. Surely, there wouldn't be room for them all? He felt himself pushed back against the wall as what seemed like a thousand chattering people swarmed in and crushed themselves into the tiny amount of breathing space. Mr Thompson gripped the handrail tightly and closed his eyes. He wouldn't panic. He would not panic. He tried to force his heartbeat to slow down as he cautiously opened his eyes. He wished he hadn't. One of the new passengers had dark skin and was carrying a rucksack.

Mr Thompson's heart beat even faster.

The water was now cold. It had been for a while but she hadn't noticed. She stepped out of the shower, wrapped herself in a towel and sat down on her bed. She stared at the walls. She stared at the never-ending circular pattern that surrounded her like the bars of a cage. And, again, she began to cry.

Sacha remembered the news reports. Always stay in a group. Well, it was too late for that. She decided that it would be safer to get the taxi. Mummy could pay for it when she got home. Glancing again across at the man, she very carefully and very slowly began to walk towards the waiting cab. Everything would be fine. She had nothing to worry about. She would soon be at home and in bed. Just a few more steps. So close to the –

The man jumped out of the doorway and began to run across the road. Sacha stopped and stood, screaming as he got closer, then ran the remaining few steps, yanked open the car door and bounced onto the back seat.

'Quickly!' she screamed to the taxi driver as the man got closer. As the driver started the engine, she suddenly felt something tightly grip around her leg. She'd forgotten to shut the door! The man had his hand around her ankle and was pulling at her, shouting at her to get out of the taxi. She screamed again and tears began to fall down her face. She swore at the man and at the taxi driver and at anyone else who could hear when –

'Doors closing.'

'Going down.'

Mr Thompson wasn't racist. He even had black friends. But an Indian? With a rucksack? He listened intently for a ticking. Did modern bombs tick? It didn't matter. He couldn't hear anything over his own heartbeat. God, why had he got into the lift? He looked over at Joanne. He could hardly see her as a courier now stood between them. The courier stank of sweat and was nearly a foot taller than Mr Thompson. Suddenly, his radio burst into life and Mr Thompson jumped. The courier looked down at him with a smirk and Mr Thompson suddenly felt very small and very helpless. He tried to think about anything other than the suicide bomber or the huge courier or the fraying cables... he thought of Joanne's bedroom and of how, one day, he would be inside it. Perhaps she would have had a little too much to drink at a work do and Mr Thompson, being the gentleman that he was, would drive her home. His thoughts were interrupted by two of his fellow cell-mates having a conversation. She had apparently just returned from holiday and he had apparently been promoted in her absence. Their voices were shrill and sliced into his brain.

He. Had. To. Get. Out.

Sacha kicked at the hand as the taxi pulled away and the man was left lying in the road. She struggled over and managed to close the door, as the taxi sped off. Sobbing, she screamed at the driver.

'What took you so long?'

He apologised and asked if she was OK.

'Of course I'm not!'

The taxi pulled up at a set of traffic lights. The driver turned to face her.

'Ssh. It's all right. You're going to be fine.'

He had a slight Scottish accent and a kind smile although Sacha noticed that his eyes seemed sad. The lights changed to green and he asked her for her address.

Calming down, Sacha told him. Already, the fear was beginning to leave her and she wondered whether she would be on the news.

Mr Thompson could still feel his heart beating. He could actually feel it hitting the inside of his ribs. The smell of the other people was making him sick. He pushed himself into the corner believing that if the lift suddenly fell he would be safer there. How long? How long had he been in there?

He nearly screamed when, seemingly without warning, the lift stopped again.

'Doors opening.'

'Seventh floor.'

The doors opened revealing a man, calmly waiting.

'Room for a little one?' he asked with a cheery grin.

Mr Thompson wanted to kill him. He wanted to wrap his hands around the man's neck and crush the life out of him for prolonging his agony and for being so bloody cheerful about it. The man squeezed into the lift and looked directly at him. With a shiver, Mr Thompson realised that the man wasn't looking at him. He was looking right into him.

* * *

As the empty streets and yellow streetlights shot past the taxi, Sacha began to feel drowsy. Struggling to keep her eyes open, she asked the driver whether he'd had a busy night. Considering what had just happened, she realised that this was a stupid question. Perhaps she was in shock. She wondered if people in shock knew that they were in shock. The taxi driver said that she should just rest. He would get her home. He would make sure she was safe. That was his job. Sacha sat back into the seat and was only half aware of the doors locking. For her own safety, of course.

'Doors closing.'

'Going down.'

Mr Thompson looked at the closing doors and wondered why the manufacturer had thought that mirrored metallic doors were a good idea. He presumed they were meant to make the lift seem bigger. They were meant to be a calming measure. To Mr Thompson, though, they just made it seem more claustrophobic. There seemed to be thousands of people trapped in there with him. A row of grinning tinted ghosts stared at him. He looked at his own reflection. He was there. He was real. This was real. He tried to focus into his own eyes, willing himself to stay calm. Then he glanced over at Joanne's reflection. God, she was beautiful. He watched as she rubbed the back of her neck, pulling her blouse further open. Then he saw the courier's reflection, tall and arrogant, looking down at her. The man was looking at his Joanne! Mr Thompson looked away and tried desperately to ignore the suicide bomber's reflection. It would soon be too late for him to explode the bomb. They would be at the ground floor and everything would be fine.

Then, as the lift continued to descend, Mr Thompson noticed something that meant that everything was quite far from being fine.

'Do you mind if I put some music on?'

The taxi driver's words startled Sacha back into life.

'Er... yeah. Fine.'

The driver reached down and switched off the taxi radio. He pushed a tape into the machine and with a click it began to play.

Sacha smiled as Ol' Blue Eyes started to spread the news.

The taxi driver looked back across his shoulder and, again, winked cheerfully at her.

'Shouldn't you be, like, watching the road?' asked Sacha.

She began to feel a little uncomfortable with the way he was looking at her.

'And...' She tried to shout over the music. Why did he have it on so loud? 'And could you turn it down?'

Frank Sinatra was now at full volume. The song was deafening.

Sacha started to panic. The taxi was flying through the streets but the driver just looked at her, singing along to the music.

He began to smile, revealing...

And Mr Thompson screamed. The little man turned to him and put a finger to his lips.

'Ssh!'

'But you've... you've no reflection!'

The little man merely smiled. Then, to the complete disbelief of the various office workers, his face... changed. He stood still, smiling, and for a second everything in the lift was also still. Then, with a sudden burst of energy, the man's arm shot out, into and through the metal wall and with a terrible scraping sound the lift juddered to a halt and the lights went out.

And Sacha screamed as the friendly, little Scottish taxi driver belted out the chorus one last time. He seemed to appreciate his captive audience.

The Doctor walked, slowly and mechanically, like a man heading towards the gallows. The corridors grew darker, lit only by the dull orange glow emanating from the circular indentations in the walls. As he walked, he thought about what he could say. He thought about what she might say. He turned a corner, saw a mirror and stopped, staring at his own reflection. His mop of blond hair now seemed grey. His eyes, which usually sparkled with life, now seemed dead. His coat, once multi-coloured and vibrant, was now just red. He looked and felt old. He turned away and continued to walk.

In the distance, he could hear her quietly sobbing.

An emergency light flickered on, bathing everyone in the lift with an unnatural yellow glow.

Mr Thompson looked around the silent, cramped metal cage.

He looked at Joanne, her eyes wide and terrified. He looked at the courier, his face revealing an inability to comprehend what was happening. The Indian man looked close to tears. The couple who had been talking now had their mouths open, silent, as if someone had hit a pause button on their conversation.

Now he would never know if she had enjoyed her fortnight in Majorca. The only sound was that of twelve people breathing. In unison. Breathe in. Breathe out. Breathe in. Breathe –

Oh, and his own heart beating.

The little man looked around them, still smiling, as he slowly drew his uninjured arm back into the lift.

Mr Thompson looked in every direction except at *him*.

The Doctor knocked on the door.

'It's me.'

Her crying suddenly stopped.

'Can I come in?'

There was a pause then the door slowly began to open. She appeared in the gap and they looked at each other.

The Doctor knew what state he was in but that hadn't prepared him for how she would look.

Her eyes were red and sore from crying. Her hair was matted with sweat and tears. She was wearing a grey, shapeless t-shirt and she looked terrified. He had been expecting, hoping for, a sarcastic 'what do you want?' He had been expecting, hoping for, some sign of life. Instead, she simply opened the door and then walked over to her bed.

'Come in.' Her voice, like the look in her eyes, was dead.

'Peri?'

'Please don't be just office workers.'

The man looked around the lift.

'No offence, it's just that you all tend to taste the same.'

Mr Thompson could not move. The others had backed into him, trapping him against the cold metal wall. The Indian's rucksack was pressed against his chest, pushing his ribs further into his heart.

'I do like these modern lifts,' continued the man. 'It's the air-conditioning. Can you feel it?'

Nobody answered. Nobody dared to. They just concentrated on breathing and not on the *godhe'savampireandhestoppedtheliftandwe'retrapped-withhim*.

Suddenly, he lunged at a middle-aged cleaning woman, his face pressed right up against hers. She tried to pull back but there was nowhere to go. Nowhere for any of them to go.

'Can you feel it?' he screamed at her.

'Ye... yes,' she whispered.

'It's like a fridge in here,' he smiled.

Mr Thompson watched as the Indian slowly began to reach towards the *Press here in case of emergency* button.

Sacha screamed as the taxi continued to speed through the traffic. She hammered her bleeding fists against the window. As she pushed against one door, she stretched out and kicked against the other. She pulled at the handle, trying to force the door open. She tried to block out Sinatra's singing and the taxi driver's laughing by thinking, thinking of anything. How to get out? There's always a way out. Always. Then, as she screamed and pushed and hammered and cried, she glanced down at the floor.

There, discarded amongst the rubbish of previous passengers, was a tattered missing person flyer. She stared into the girl's face. The dead eyes stared back.

The Doctor walked slowly towards Peri; it felt as if he was walking for hours. She was sat in complete darkness – the only light was that coming through the open door. He didn't want to scare her. Not again. He wondered how... how he could make things right between them. How could he apologise? How could he make up for all the things that he had done? For all the things that she had seen.

Then, he too was swallowed up by the darkness. He tried to speak.

'I'm sorry,' said a voice. 'Oh, Doctor, I'm so sorry.'

When he had been a young boy, Mr Thompson had always wondered whether coloured peoples' bones were a different colour. White people had white bones so it made sense to his dull and logical mind that brown people had brown bones and yellow people had yellow bones.

He could see now that, in fact, coloured people did have white bones. Also, if you grabbed their arm and snapped it open, they would scream just like any white person. Mr Thompson found this oddly comforting. The man, the vampire, had grabbed hold of the Indian man's arm as he had reached for the emergency button. He had grabbed it, squeezed it and out had popped the bone! The Indian man was on his knees now, screaming in agony. Well, he was nearly on his knees. There wasn't really room so he looked decidedly uncomfortable as he half stood, half knelt, and pleaded for the man to let him go. Mr Thompson hoped he would let him go. But he didn't. Instead, he pulled the young, probably-not-a-terrorist up and towards him. The young man struggled but, in slow-motion, found himself being pulled to his feet. No one moved as the vampire suddenly thrust his teeth into the man's neck, tore out a chunk of skin and began to suck the blood out of the screaming, agonised, terrified, young man. The courier suddenly lurched forward and threw up over the people in front of him. The contents of his stomach mixed with the rapidly growing pool of blood on the lift floor.

Mr Thompson noticed, with some irritation, that some of the sick had fallen on his left shoe. Mrs Thompson wouldn't be happy if she had to clean his shoes again this week. She polished them every Tuesday night, while watching *The Bill*. She liked to have a system.

Frank had long finished singing and, for a while, all Sacha had been able to hear was her own hoarse screaming. Then she realised that even that had stopped. All her energy was gone and she had lain down on the back seat of the car, almost accepting her fate. Perhaps, when he eventually stopped the car, she could escape. It would be quite simple. He would stop and would have to unlock the doors to let her out. He would then open the door and she could run away. She'd always been good at running. She'd been the fastest in her year at school. School...

Hello Sacha and welcome to St Luke's. This is your teacher, Miss Appleton. Double Maths! Toby! I kissed Toby Hunter! And we did tongues! I'm not ready. What results did you get? Three 'A's!!! You jammy cow! Sacha, you haven't just let the school down. You've let yourself down. It's OK, all the others are doing it. But Miss! I got lines! Can you believe it? Me, sir? Me, in the school play? Fantastic! Do you want to skive Geography and go to McDonalds? Toby! I love you too. Is love treated as merely laughable folly in A Midsummer Night's Dream*? And it's the last day for you all. We're proud of you and wish you all the best at university... I hear what I dream...*

Her first day, her first lessons, her first detention, her first kiss. The memories tumbled through her mind as she bounced up and down on the seat of the car. She felt as if the memories were trying to tell her something. Trying to remind her of something, of some thing.

Then, she realised what it was. She was who she was. She was the living, breathing –

'My name is Sacha Mary Palmer.'

She wasn't going to be a victim. She wasn't just going to be another –

Her mother's tear-stained face on the news:

'My daughter, Sacha, was a wonderful girl. She was well liked by everyone. She was captain of the gymnastics team and had got a place at university. She...' Her mother breaking down into rasping sobs.

'So?' The taxi driver turned to face her.

'So! So, you can't do this. I'm not one of them. I'm not one of your list. I'm me. Don't you understand? This isn't meant to happen.'

'Ssh, girl. You're in shock.'

'No. No, I'm not.'

But, of course, she was. So in shock that it wasn't until the third dee-dee-do-da-dee-dee-do-da-dee-dee-doo-da-dah that she realised her mobile was ringing.

Her mobile.

She sat up realising. She wasn't trapped! She could call for –

The thought stopped as the taxi suddenly slammed to a stop and she found herself flying towards the windscreen.

'What?'

'I said I'm sorry.'

'Peri? What do you have to be sorry for?'

He heard her shift uncomfortably.

'It's me, isn't it? It's my fault you... Doctor! It's my fault you're what – I mean, you're who you are.'

'Oh Peri,' he said quietly. 'Am I really that bad?'

The glass exploded as Sacha's face smashed through it. She screamed in pain as she felt the shards tear into her neck and shoulders.

Mr Thompson wanted to giggle. He couldn't help himself. The Indian man was now completely dead! But dead people are meant to lie down on the floor! There was no room for that here, though. Not in their little cell. His body, drained of life, was lolloping around the lift. His little white eyes stared aimlessly as he bounced from person to person, sloshing around in his own blood. Mr Thompson didn't dare laugh though. He wished he'd stayed and eaten the lovingly prepared chicken paste sandwich. He could taste it now. But, the smell of the blood that now reached their ankles in their little private room clouded all other senses. Then, gradually, he became aware of a noise. It was like a fire alarm or something. Then, he realised it was Joanne screaming. He'd quite forgotten about her and her breasts. She was lovely but he wished she would stop screaming. The Indian man had fallen against her and his head was resting on her shoulder. Mrs Thompson wouldn't have screamed. She'd have done something constructive like wrapping the man in cling film. To keep his corpse fresh. Corpse. That's what actors do when they can't stop laughing. Mr Thompson had wanted to be an actor once. He really wished Joanne would stop screaming. He hoped the *ohmygodhe'savampire* would take her next. He didn't want to have to be the one to stop her screaming. Not when she was otherwise so lovely.

A stone was pointing into the small of her back, which Sacha was finding quite uncomfortable. She started to panic as she realised that she'd lost her bag. It had her phone and purse in! She was feeling terrible and the thought of ringing her bank and cancelling her cards... well, she couldn't face it. She was trying to think of a new PIN number when she realised that dark blood was gushing out of her arm. There was a big piece of glass sticking out of it. No, *protruding* was the word. It was *protruding* out of her arm.

Oh yeah! She'd been in a taxi! She'd forgotten about that. Then she remembered the accident. Then she remembered the taxi driver.

Then she heard that very same taxi driver stepping out of his car and shivering to himself in the cold early-morning air. Come to think of it, she was fairly cold herself. Soon be time for sleep.

Then she heard him walking towards her, humming an old Frank Sinatra tune.

'It's not your fault.'

Peri was quiet. 'Doctor, you sacrificed yourself to save me. You became what you are now, because of me.'

'It was my choice.'

For a moment, there was silence again.

'What have I become?'

Mr Thompson was surrounded by thousands of corpses. They stared into his face, grinning. Again, he cursed the designers who had thought that reflective, metallic doors were in any way a good idea. Hadn't it crossed their minds that this sort of thing could happen?

'Please! I'm begging you! I've got kids!'

The cleaner was screaming and shrieking and crying. The noise was like fingernails on a blackboard and Mr Thompson wished it would stop. His headache was getting worse.

'I'll be sure to look them up,' smiled the vampire before tearing her throat out. Mr Thompson was pleased that the noise had stopped. He knew that soon, all the noise would stop.

Then, with a loud crash that sent the corpses splashing about in the blood, something fell onto the lift.

Sacha started to crawl. Surely, she couldn't be that far from home? She looked forward to seeing Mummy again then being able to climb into bed and curl up under the duvet. She would be warm and safe.

'It's like the real me is inside here –' Peri heard the Doctor thump his chest.

She didn't know what to say.

'He's inside but trapped. He can't get out and I can feel him...'

'Doctor...' she began. She felt the Doctor move closer to her and tried not to flinch.

'It never used to be like this!' he interrupted. 'I used to... I used to use my wits. My intelligence. I used to be... I used to be a good man, Peri!' He began to shout.

'Doctor, you're scaring me.'

He laughed. 'You think you're scared? Imagine what it's like for me! I killed those people. My stupidity, my arrogance – me!'

'No, Doctor. The vampire killed them. Listen to me! Saric Warder killed them!'

He jumped up from the bed.

'But it was my fault!'

Mr Thompson, pushing the courier's corpse off him, looked up at the ceiling.

'Doctor? Doctor, is that you?' laughed the vampire.

Mr Thompson hoped it would be a doctor. He had realised with horror that his headache was turning into a migraine. Probably caused by the flickering yellow emergency light.

'Saric! Saric, stop this now!'

The man's voice shouted through the ventilation grill with no consideration for the pain in Mr Thompson's head.

'Oh, but I'm having so much fun. Here, Doctor,' he grabbed the hysterical Joanne. 'This one's for you!'

'Ssh, it's OK. I'm here now.'

Sacha relaxed. She was starting to feel numb to the cold now.

'I just want to sleep,' she mumbled.

'I know.' The man's voice was comforting.

He pulled his weight on top of her and whispered into her ear.

'It's because you have a huge piece of glass sticking out of your skull. You've gone into shock, which is good for me as it means you'll struggle less.'

The words didn't make much sense to Sacha. She just wanted to sleep in the man's embrace.

'Saric, no!' The man's voice shouted across the wasteland.

He stalked around the room as Peri cowered.

'I blundered in, unthinking. It was my fault he was there.'

Mr Thompson could see down Joanne's blouse. The blood, from the gaping hole in her neck, was trickling down her cleavage. Red on white. Finally, he started to giggle.

The vampire looked surprised.

'You find this funny?'

Mr Thompson explained that he always laughed when he was nervous.

'Am I next?' he asked.

Then he noticed that there was still screaming. Only now it was from the man above them.

Sacha looked up into the taxi driver's face then tried to turn to see who the other man was. It was the man who had tried to pull her out of the taxi. He had a girl with him. She was pretty.

'Saric Warder! I won't let you do this.'

The taxi driver gently turned Sacha's face back towards him and looked into her eyes.

'Oh dear! That's the Doctor. I'm done for.'

Sacha struggled to speak then fell silent as the man, Saric, suddenly lurched forward and bit into her neck.

She was vaguely aware of the girl screaming.

He was standing still now.

'Listen to me now! Shouting, arrogant, self-obsessed. People died and all I can do is selfishly whinge about my own state of mind!'

Peri had never seen him this bad before. In the darkness, she could make out that he was looking at her.

'I've become the monster, haven't I?'

Suddenly, a man fell through the ceiling of the lift. He tumbled onto the heads of the swaying, stood-up corpses and then fell, splashing, into the blood. Mr Thompson backed himself further into the corner.

'Thanks for dropping in, Doctor.'

Mr Thompson laughed at the dodgy pun. The new man – the Doctor – jumped to his feet and lunged at the vampire.

Sacha could feel the darkness drawing in around her.

Then, a light exploded in her face as the taxi driver's face disappeared. She looked on drowsily as the man dragged the taxi driver away from her. The other girl screamed as the taxi driver managed to escape from her rescuer. He ran off, laughing into the night.

'Stay here, Peri.'

The girl, Peri, cried out as the man chased after the taxi driver.

'Doctor! Wait! Don't just leave me here. Think about what you're doing.'

* * *

'I chased him into that building. It was my fault he was in the lift.'

'You're going to be OK.' Peri tried to embrace Sacha, but... her face. She must have been pretty before. Sacha could tell that something was wrong but didn't ask. She heard a siren in the distance.

'I have to go after him. Are you going to be OK?'

Sacha nodded. She felt her head gently lower towards the ground as Peri stood up and left her. Then she heard the ambulance arrive with its noisy sirens. Then she heard it swerve and brake. Then she heard the ambulance doors opening. Then she heard the nice ambulance man approaching her. Then she fell asleep.

And never heard anything ever again.

'I'll destroy you, Saric.'

The man, the Doctor, had his hands wrapped around the vampire's throat.

Mr Thompson wasn't sure what to do. Should he try and help?

The vampire looked at him, his eyes pleading.

'He did this, you know. He chased me here and trapped me in this building. It's the Doctor's fault you're here!'

The words cut through Mr Thompson's shock and he suddenly became very aware of where he was.

Now, it was his turn to scream.

Peri stood up and slowly walked towards the Doctor.

'It wasn't your fault. You were trying to help. You were trying to –'

He interrupted her. '– be the Doctor.'

'It was a mistake. You made a mistake.'

He looked down at her.

'But, I can't make mistakes, Peri. When I make mistakes, people die.'

She didn't know what to say to that.

Saric and the Doctor continued to fight. The Doctor had the upper hand when, suddenly, Saric pushed him away knocking him into the courier's corpse, who fell against Joanne's corpse who fell into Mr Thompson. He fell, heavily against the wall and *something* moved.

'The lift! It's falling!'

Mr Thompson screamed as he felt the sudden loss of gravity. He coughed and spluttered and choked as the blood poured over his face. He was vaguely aware of Saric clambering over the corpses towards him as the lift continued to fall. That's when he felt his heart finally explode.

* * *

'And then there's everything I put you through. The things I've said to you. The way I've treated you.'

'Saric! No!'

Before Mr Thompson succumbed to the darkness, he watched the Doctor struggle to force open the lift doors. The last thing he saw was the lift shaft flying past and the blood and the bodies beginning to gush out. Then he gave in to the blackness.

Perpugilliam Brown ran into the building's reception area. She stood, helpless, watching the lift's numerical display as it counted down the floors too quickly. 'Doctor!' she screamed.

The Doctor, his face twisted into a violent snarl, made one final lunge at Saric. He screamed out as he wrapped his hands around the laughing vampire's throat and dragged him over to the open doorway.

Perpugilliam Brown. Peri to her friends. A typical nineteen-year-old American student with a normal life. Well, normal until she had met *him*. The man who would become her greatest friend. The man who would then change beyond all recognition.

She listened as the lift crashed violently into the walls above her.

Please, let him be OK.

'Goodbye, Saric!'

The Doctor screamed as the next floor approached. The vampire was decapitated, his grinning face bouncing up into the lift shaft. Then, with a terrible, buckling sound, the lift crashed into the ground floor.

'The things I've made you see.'

'Doors opening'

Despite everything, she still cared so much for him. The man, the Doctor, who had been so sweet and wonderful and who had sacrificed his life for her. Who now seemed so *distorted*. She would not give up on him.

He was her best friend.

'Doors opening'

And the lift doors exploded out, as with a terrifying crash, the lift hit the ground floor. The remaining blood and bodies splashed out into the foyer, drenching her. The blood was everywhere. In her hair, in her eyes, over her clothes.

But she didn't even notice.

Her best friend was screaming in rage, his face twisted in anger and hatred. His hands wrapped around the throat of the headless vampire.

Unable to talk or cry or even scream, Peri ran outside and threw up.

'Why do you put up with it? Why do you put up with me?'

Peri paused before answering. She wasn't sure that she knew the answer. Then she realised. Despite the arguments, despite the violence they seemed to continually face, despite the deaths, he cared. He was still trying his best to do the right thing. He was still the Doctor. He was still a good man. He was still the man who had saved her life. And she...

'Because I'm your friend.'

He looked down at her, astonished. Then he leaned forward and kissed her gently on her forehead.

'Thank you,' he whispered.

To the surprise of the hospital doctors, Mr Thompson had survived his heart attack. Physically survived it, anyway.

He lay in the bed, his eyes staring up at the white ceiling.

The nurse showed his wife in.

'Hello, dear.'

Mrs Thompson sat down next to the bed, kissing her husband on the cheek.

'How are you?'

'I'm fine.'

She could tell that he wasn't, but she knew not to push him. So, instead she told him about the TV programmes she had watched that day and about how she had met Mrs Gilmore and the twins in Sainsburys.

'Oh, and she was telling me about how terrible the food was here so...'

Mr Thompson weakly turned to his wife as she rummaged around in her bag.

'I brought you some sandwiches. They're chicken paste. Hope that's OK?'

Mr Thompson sat up, wrapped his arms around her and, tears pouring uncontrollably down his face, told his wife that he loved her.

Not So Much a Programme, More a Way of Life

Anthony Keetch

The air, fragile in its stillness, was perturbingly shattered by a raucous sound, akin to a million elephants having a boisterous argument. A tall blue box, a lamp flickering on its roof, shimmered into existence, wobbled a bit then, with a thumping noise, settled down nicely, as though it had been there for donkey's years and had no intention of moving, thank you very much.

The door – only clinging to its hinges by the skin of its teeth – creaked open, and a blond head that defied carbon-dating peered out of the blue box. A broad grin split the face into two and, accompanied by the body to which it belonged, stepped out into the open air.

Nyssa stared round her in horror. In all her travels with the Doctor she had encountered many alien environments, some astonishingly beautiful, others less so, although her Trakenite upbringing had educated her in an awareness of the different perceptions of beauty. But this! This was... how would Tegan have described it?

A hellhole.

'Where are we?' she gasped.

The Doctor screwed up his eyes and peered into the distance. 'Well, according to that sign over there,' he pointed, 'it's Greenford Broadway.'

He went into his annoying 'teacher' mode. 'At least three unsuccessful invasions of Earth have originated here, or hereabouts. A combination of ley-lines and localised and minor temporal anomalies has always made Greenford a target for phenomena of a cosmic nature.' He spun slowly on his heels, a full 360 degrees. 'It shouldn't be this quiet, though.'

'Surely, no one would actually be here unless they had to?'

The Doctor examined the empty street, devoid of people and moving cars. 'Admittedly, it was never the most populated place in England, but there should at least be cars driving through, if only by mistake.'

Nyssa shuddered. 'Much as I disapprove of behaviour influenced by irrational impulses, I think I'd like to leave.'

The Doctor didn't move. She wasn't even sure if he had heard her.

'Please, Doctor.'

The Doctor shrugged and reluctantly turned back towards the direction of the TARDIS. But before he reached the door, the deafening silence was scarred by a distant noise. An arrhythmic clacking, accompanied by a synchronised rasping.

Nyssa stared at the Doctor, unnerved, but he held a finger to his lips, in the recognised galactic sign for schtum.

Around the corner staggered a man, middle-aged and almost podgy. Hair awry, eyes popping, lungs clawing in oxygen, but otherwise the man seemed nothing out of the ordinary, dressed in the smart casuals affected by Rotarians at charity barbecues.

Blindly, the man lurched on, chest heaving, unaware of anything in his vicinity. He crashed into a rubbish can, stubbing his toe quite badly, but he didn't seem to notice. He just stumbled on, without even smoothing down the strands of hair that normally lay plastered firmly down on his flushed pate.

'It's on!' the man shouted at the Doctor and Nyssa as he careened through them, almost knocking Nyssa over. The Doctor grabbed hold of the man, who stared wildly around without really seeing anything. 'It's on,' he repeated, this time in a breathless whisper. 'It's on.'

'What is?' the Doctor asked him.

Abruptly the man wrenched himself out of the Doctor's grip.

'No!' he roared, with a strength neither of the travellers would have guessed he possessed. 'I'm missing it!' he shrieked, and staggered away as fast he could manage.

'Extraordinary,' the Doctor muttered to himself. 'Come on, Nyssa.'

And with that, he chased off after the man. Nyssa gazed wistfully back at the TARDIS, then she reluctantly followed the Doctor.

They didn't have far to go in order to find the man. He was crouched outside a TV rental showroom, clinging to the window, almost as though he had been licked and flung at the glass. All the TVs in the window were switched to the same channel, and the man slavishly watched all four screens simultaneously, mouth agape. His tongue lolled lazily out of one corner of his mouth, and a tendril of drool languidly ambled groundward.

The Doctor squatted onto his haunches and looked into the man's eyes. The man ignored everything except the TV screens.

'Ah, excuse me?' ahem-ed the Doctor. The man betrayed no signs of hearing him. The Doctor blew into the man's ear. Still no reaction. So the Doctor waved his hand in front of the man's face. Angrily, the man pushed the hand out of his line of vision.

Nyssa peered into the window to see what the man found so fascinating.

Two-dimensional visual entertainments had never really caught on back home, not even amongst the children of her society, and she had always been bewildered when Tegan and Adric had rushed to the TARDIS TV lounge on returning from some bowel-shattering adventure just to watch some dramatic representation of an event. As if any of the TARDIS crew needed improbable fiction in their lives.

The action on the TVs was depicting a lurid, violent spectacle. Unconvincing soldiers with longish hair were pretending to fight what seemed to be some kind of alien species, although one unfamiliar to Nyssa. Not surprisingly, she thought, as they were obviously invented. They were basically humanoid in shape; tall, but not so tall that they needed more than one actor inside to manipulate them. Their skin appeared to be of a nylon-like texture, made up of various different shades of purple. Huge heads dominated the bodies, threatening to topple them over. Wide mouths, almost as wide as the head, with large uneven blubbery lips, out of which protruded triple-layered tongues. Two large eyes could be found at the ends of enormously long, but muscular and sinewy stalks. These swirled around like snakes under the rhythmic sway of a pipe-playing charmer.

The aliens stomped around on trunk-like legs that ended in large suckers, while their upper limbs, in which they clutched their weaponry, were little more than vestigial stumps with black rubbery gloves at the end.

All in all, they looked exactly like the sort of alien life form that only someone with no knowledge of real alien life forms could dream up.

On a small budget.

But no money had been skimped on the gruesome special effects. As each soldier was gunned down, so their insides made a vivid appearance, convincing entrails splattering across the picture, until the cast were knee-deep in fluorescent gore.

Nyssa watched in horror. What sort of intelligent beings would want to watch such a monstrously vicious display as this? For entertainment? It made her feel sick. She turned to the Doctor to ask him why humans revelled in such degrading barbarism, but was horrified by what she saw.

The Doctor's eyes, normally such deep pools of intelligence and compassion, were locked onto the screens, an expression of excitement – no, not excitement, relish – gripping his face. Quickly, so fast she wasn't sure if she imagined it, he licked his lips.

Nyssa glanced at the other man. He was still crouched on the ground, fingers suckered onto the glass. His expression was of that of a starving man watching a feast being prepared.

When she thought it couldn't become any more obscene, a flash of light dragged her attention back to the TV screens. An explosion was dominating the picture, dense clouds of smoke and ferocious flames, out of which lurched a woman clutching a bundled-up baby. As the woman ran, limping, from the inferno, so she was confronted by one of the alien creatures. The woman froze, a look of terror jamming her face into inaction. The alien smirked, a masterpiece of animatronic manipulation. The woman instinctively hugged the baby tightly to her chest. The alien raised its ferocious-looking gun. Cut to a close-up of the trigger. The alien's finger squeezed...

And the end credits rolled.

'Oh, what?' shouted the Doctor, thumping the glass with frustration.

The man groaned and slumped down to the ground, rolling into a fetal position, oblivious to the small pools of stale phlegm that puddled the pavement.

The Doctor swung away from the window, hands in trouser pockets.

'That was brilliant!' he exclaimed, to no one in particular.

Nyssa stared nervously at him. 'Doctor, you are being ironic, aren't you?'

The Doctor looked up, startled, and seemed to notice Nyssa for the first time. He smiled and grabbed her by the shoulders. 'Oh, Nyssa,' he said breathlessly, 'wasn't that exciting?' He stared around wildly. 'But where can we find out when the next episode is on? I simply can't miss it.' An idea seemed to strike him and he smiled heavenward in triumph. 'Of course, a newsagent. We must find a newsagent.'

'But, Doctor,' Nyssa protested, 'everywhere's deserted.'

'Oh no, it isn't,' the Doctor said, and pointed behind her.

Nyssa looked around. Greenford was transformed. It was still a dump, but now a reasonably populated dump. Cars sped along the Broadway, shoppers bustled about, mothers pushed kiddies along in pushchairs, and a general air of normality had returned.

Or had it?

Nyssa tugged at the Doctor's sleeve. 'What country is this?'

'England.'

'I thought so. But look,' She pointed at the newly emerged people. 'They are all talking to each other.'

The Doctor examined the crowds keenly. It was true. An excited buzz filled the air, and not just of conversation. Mothers talked to their children, traffic wardens chatted to shoppers, while drivers rolled down their car windows and leaned out to discuss something animatedly with lollipop ladies.

'The English never talk to each other, not in public,' Nyssa said. 'Tegan told me so. "Surly buggers," she said, whatever that means.'

'Well,' the Doctor began, but he was interrupted by a voice from somewhere near the ground.

'It's the programme.'

The man stood up, the hysteria so evident earlier, seemingly gone. He ran his fingers through his hair and steadied himself. 'The programme. *Surrender, Earthlings!* That's what they're talking about. It's what everyone's talking about.'

'Of course!' the Doctor exclaimed. 'And what better topic of conversation than that masterpiece of televisual genius. At last something has brought mankind together, and it's a television programme.'

'Are you all right, Doctor?' Nyssa asked him. 'You don't sound like yourself.'

'No, but I could get to like being like this. Hmm, *Surrender, Earthlings!* Snappy title. So tell me,' he addressed the man, 'when's the next episode?'

'In about half an hour.'

'Really, as soon as that?' The Doctor was pleased. 'They don't keep you hanging about, do they?'

'Oh yes, it's on every hour on the hour and it runs thirty minutes. Then at midnight there is an omnibus edition. Which most people record. Except some extremists who like to keep all the cliffhangers. Then the next new episode is at seven o'clock.'

'In the evening?'

'No, 7 a.m.'

'Really?' The Doctor stuck out his hand. 'I'm the Doctor, by the way, and this is my friend Nyssa. How do you do?'

The man warily took the outstretched hand and shook it. 'The name's Norman Atkinson.'

'So, Norman, tell me all about *Surrender, Earthlings!*'

The Doctor and Norman strolled along Greenford Broadway, Nyssa trudging reluctantly behind. Norman had kindly invited them back to his house to watch the next episode, an invitation the Doctor, to Nyssa's annoyance, had accepted with alacrity. She had contemplated saying that she would return to the TARDIS and wait for him there, but this whole business worried her. The Doctor was behaving strangely. Suppose he didn't return? He might become so hooked on this programme that he would insist on staying and watching every episode. Twice. He might become so familiar with it that he might start – she shuddered – quoting it at her, as Adric had done with those old comedy broadcasts which Nyssa hadn't found the least bit funny. What was it, something about dead cheeses? No, that wasn't right. Not that it mattered now. No, much as she wanted to return to the relative sanity and dimensions of the TARDIS, Nyssa knew that it was her duty to stay with the Doctor and keep an eye on his behaviour.

The Doctor and Norman were chatting away, nineteen to the dozen, as if they had known each other all their lives. Of course, they had only one topic of conversation. How long had the series been running? Who directed it? How long did the make-up take to apply? Who was the scariest alien? Was there a fan club? Was it as good as it used to be? Norman expressed surprise that the Doctor had missed so many episodes. It had been running about a month, and by the fourth episode it had become the top-rated programme in Britain. So much so that the other channels had given up even trying to compete. Channel 4 had gone out of business, Five had become exclusively pornography, while ITV1 had tried to start up its own rival sci-fi *Invasion of Earth* series, which had flopped so badly that it had almost bankrupted the network.

Nyssa was taking in all that was going on around her. The incessant prattle of passers-by struck her as hysteria-fuelled. Every conversation was about that programme, that much was clear from the snippets that she could hear. But none of the chatter seemed to be joyful, of people delighting in sharing something wonderful. Quite the opposite, it reminded her of the obsessive babble of people in shock, desperate to evacuate something horrendous out of their system. Verbal diarrhoea, that was another apt Teganism. Nyssa wished Tegan were here. She knew these people, this world, she might understand more of what was going on. Earthlings, in Nyssa's eyes, always seemed to behave oddly. Perhaps she was worrying about something that was quite normal for the occupants of this planet?

As she passed an overflowing rubbish can, a notice proclaiming 'Property of Ealing Council Do Not Remove' on the side, Nyssa noticed a newspaper – a picture of one of the TV aliens emblazoned on its front page – protruding from the top. She grabbed the newspaper and opened it out, wrinkling her nose at an oily stain that had only partially dried.

The main story was some gossip about one of the leading aliens. One of the aliens had been 'done for dangerous driving'. A statement from the alien's representative claimed that his client had been desperate to get home from the studio to catch his performance in the next episode because it was 'artistically the best thing I've ever done'. He was let off with a caution, provided he signed a photo for the judge.

Something strange was very apparent to Nyssa. The alien was referred to only as his character's name, not as the actor who played him, even by the PR person. Nyssa always admired dedication, but she felt this was going a bit too far, indeed was positively unhealthy.

She flicked through the rest of the paper; it was all the same, stuffed with news, gossip and quizzes about the alien stars of the programme. There was even a photograph of one of the aliens, pouting with all its lips at the camera, without its battle armour on. Nyssa screwed the paper up, ready to lob it into the next rubbish bin. But before she did so, something odd occurred to her, so she speedily scanned the paper again. Yes, she was right. While the newspaper was saturated with frothy nonsense about the alien stars of the programme, there was absolutely nothing about the actors who played the human characters.

'Chop chop, Nyssa, we'll miss the beginning of the episode!'

Nyssa rarely got in a strop, but she was contemplating one right now. Was this how Tegan felt all the time? No wonder she was so grouchy. She scrunched up the paper again, threw it with more force than was necessary into the bin, and, with a face like thunder, was on the verge of giving the Doctor what she believed was called a 'mouthful'. But her mouth opened and instead of a stream of invective crossing it, her jaw locked into place and little more than a squeak erupted.

'Doctor,' she tried to say. Her open-mindedness regarding the multi-faceted nature of the fauna of the cosmos fled, leaving her with just one word in her vocabulary.

'Monsters!'

Marching in formation up Greenford Broadway was the largest collection of alien creatures Nyssa had ever seen. And not just any alien creatures, but the ones off the telly.

The most Nyssa could manage was to point. All other brain activity had shut down, with the exception of boggling. The Doctor had turned around again to chivvy her along, and seeing her face, had spun back to see what she was gawping at. The Doctor's eyes opened as wide as they could go – and then, with a broad smile, he bounded up to the first alien, hand outstretched.

'Hello, I'm the Doctor and I'm your number one fan.'

A chorus of safety catches clicked, and countless gun muzzles pointed in his direction.

Nyssa gasped, and she gazed wildly around, hoping someone would help. But all the people around, instead of fleeing for their lives, screaming and arms flailing, were watching the events with excitement, nudging each other and whispering, broad, almost embarrassed grins on their flushed faces.

Even the Doctor didn't seem perturbed. On the contrary, he reacted like a child whose favourite uncle has just produced a Cadbury's Creme Egg from his ear. He clapped his hands in appreciative applause and then grabbed the alien's upper limb to shake it, but a minor electric shock from the nylon texture of its skin caused him to drop the limb pronto.

The TV in the shop window started screaming.

'Who do you want to die a horrible death at the hands of the marauding aliens? Well, now's your chance to choose! For the first time ever, *Surrender, Earthlings!* is going interactive – and you can decide the outcome. A major character of your choice will die a gruesome death. Will it be Sister Immaculata? Little Tommy Jones? Mrs Brewster? Or Old Ned? The manner of their death is top secret – but rest easy, it won't be something you'll forget in a hurry!

'Don't forget – telephone lines close in 45 minutes. All calls will be charged at national rates. Check with whoever pays the bill before ringing. Calls may be monitored for training purposes. And get voting!'

'I don't suppose I could have your autographs. They're not for me, they're for my friend...' He gestured at Nyssa, but on hearing no reaction from her, glanced back in her direction – he couldn't see any sight of her. Where was she, he briefly wondered. Perhaps she'd gone to the TARDIS? She'll be livid that she's missed out on this, he truly believed.

The alien leader crawled towards the Doctor, its eye-stalks swirling all over him, head to toe, inputting every facet of his appearance.

'We know you,' it hissed.

The Doctor blushed. 'No, not me. Surely?'

The alien's eye-stalks stared at each other, as though in consultation, and with its triple-layered tongue it licked its lips. 'You are the Doctor.'

The Doctor didn't know how to respond to this. He was extremely flattered that his heroes had heard of him, but he was quite aware that a lot of alien races didn't hold him in such great esteem, because of his habit of stuffing up their plans.

'Erm, yes,' he admitted.

The alien turned its back on the Doctor, and with a chorus of hisses and grunts and unpleasant abdominal noises, convened with its fellows. The Doctor flashed a sheepish smile at all the Greenford residents who, mobile phones clamped to their ears, were watching this from the sidelines, the mixture of excitement and envy apparent.

The alien leader turned to face the Doctor again. 'Fancy a drink?' it rasped.

Nyssa didn't know where her kidnapper's hand had been, but she knew where it was now; stuffed in her mouth.

She had been rooted to the spot when the aliens had arrived in Greenford Broadway, unable to do anything, even if she had known exactly what to do. No one around her had seemed upset by their arrival. No, that wasn't quite true. There had been a reaction, but it was a positive one; excitement rather than fear and panic.

Normally she would applaud such a rational and humane reaction from one species to another, but this time it just didn't feel right.

Now she was being bustled along an alleyway filled with dustbins to who knows where. Of the identity of her kidnapper she hadn't a clue. He was a man, of medium build and well-done body odour.

They reached a wooden gate through which the man led Nyssa, across a cramped muddy garden bordered with bluebells, past a washing line on which hung a row of pale blue Y-fronts with once-white trimming, and into a small house via a red back door.

Once inside, the man let go of Nyssa, and she took a deep breath, hoping to rid herself of the taste of the man's nicotine-stained hand. Unfortunately the house smelt even worse than the hand, of an aroma unfamiliar to Nyssa, although the chemist in her surmised that it was evocative of some kind of green vegetation, albeit in a dampened, maybe heated state. She examined her surroundings. It was a kitchen, not very clean, in some state of disarray. Soiled crockery was piled up totteringly high beside a basin, wallpaper of a floral nature threatened to peel away from the wall any minute now, while the tiled ceiling was a peculiar shade of dirty orange.

All in all, it was exactly what Nyssa expected a Greenford habitation to be.

An old lady, blue of hair, ornately rimmed spectacles roosting defiantly on the bridge of her nose, was tackling the washing-up, sleeves rolled up, a peach-coloured fuzzy hat pinned to her head. When she saw Nyssa, she put down the gravy boat she was scrubbing and approached, curiously.

'Hello, dear. Would you like a cuppa?'

The Doctor sat on the floor of his cell and wondered what had gone wrong.

Again.

It had all started out so amicably. He couldn't remember the last time an encounter with a new species had begun so promisingly. The aliens (whom he had learned were called the Xyz) had bundled him into their anti-grav skimmer, and, silent in the face of the Doctor's endless babble about their series, had flown him to Central London. They had landed in South Moulton Street, and had led the Doctor into a pink-façaded townhouse, admittance only by video entryphone. 'Our club,' they had revealed, the solitary utterance they had made since leaving Greenford.

The Doctor had, unusually for him, barely taken any notice of his surroundings. He had asked incessant (some might say impertinent) questions, and in the face of their taciturnity, had answered himself with a stream of excited speculation. In fact, he had carried on pretty much as usual.

It had all started to go horribly wrong when they reached the Xyz's club. Instead of the comfy chair, drink, crudités and sophisticated media chat the Doctor had expected, he had been clubbed from behind and, dazed, pushed downstairs into the wine cellar (empty, sadly) and locked in.

They hadn't even left him a TV. But how was he to watch...?

'I'll miss it,' he groaned, and shifted unhappily in the dust.

Nyssa now had her first chance to look at the man who had kidnapped her, and the sight made her jaw drop.

'Norman?' she gasped.

The man shook his head, unleashing a gentle downfall of dandruff. 'No,' he replied, 'Norman is my twin brother. I'm Reg.'

He was identical, Nyssa marvelled, even to his voice and taste in cardigans. The only difference was that while Norman parted his remnants of hair from left to right over his increasing scalp, Reg parted his from right to left. A true mirror image.

There were three other people in the purple-papered sitting room. A young boy, about Adric's age, with a pudding bowl haircut and an unpleasant skin condition around his mouth. He looked so cowed by life that Nyssa felt sorry for him, but not much.

'Who got chosen?' Reg asked him.

'The Nun,' the boy replied.

'How do you know?' Reg demanded suspiciously.

'Heard next door cheering.'

The older woman with blue hair and an expression on her face as though there was a permanent bad smell within the vicinity of her nose sat primly, knees brusquely clenched together. Every thirty seconds she tugged her skirt further down over her knees. Guzzling from a teacup was a middle-aged black man, dressed in black with a white collar around his neck. It rang bells with Nyssa that this signified some sort of professional religious operative.

They all introduced themselves. The boy's name was Tim and he was Reg's son. The lady referred to herself as Mrs Cooper, while the black man was known as the Very Reverend Vincent N'kabe. Nyssa was offered the chance to call him Vince, which she felt it would be churlish to refuse.

Nyssa asked Reg why he had kidnapped her.

'Mr Atkinson would never do anything as vulgar as kidnapping a young lady, young lady,' Mrs Cooper told her.

'I'm sorry,' Nyssa responded tartly, 'but grabbing me from behind...' – Mrs Cooper winced at the word 'behind' – 'and dragging me here with his hand over my mouth would be considered kidnapping where I come from. That is, if we had such a dreadful thing.'

Reg apologised, something which Nyssa felt he wasn't accustomed to doing. 'But I could see that you weren't affected by the corruption that is currently afflicting the country and we need as many recruits as we can get.'

'Recruits?'

'We are the Provisional Wing of the National Viewers and Listeners Association.'

'Oh. And what is this "corruption", as you call it?' Nyssa asked. 'It appears to have affected my friend.'

'It has affected everyone in the country who watches television.'

'I always said that disgusting box would lead to our downfall,' sniffed Mrs Cooper.

'The devil's instrument,' agreed the Reverand Vince.

'I've been watching my foolish brother,' explained Reg, 'and I had earlier tried to prevent him reaching a TV screen. Unfortunately he escaped from me. I followed him, and that was when you and your friend became involved.'

'But when did it all start?' asked Nyssa.

The Doctor shivered on his cell's floor, teeth grinding, sweat streaming down his face in torrents. It was three hours since they had shoved him in here, and there had been no communication since.

He had survived missing the first episode with great forbearance – by shooting his own version in his head – but missing the second had been painful and, by the third, hot flushes had set in and the walls had started crowding in. Now, time had lost all meaning for him (had it ever had any?) and who knew how many episodes he had missed? Why wouldn't they let him watch them? They could at least come in and tell him what had happened. They must know, they were in them. Perhaps they had a script? Perhaps they'd let him have some old scripts? Or videos, although DVDs would be preferable. When he got out of here, the Doctor decided, he'd go straight to the TARDIS and travel back in time and record all the episodes he'd missed. Right from the beginning. That would show them...

The Doctor crawled to the door, dust and grime seeping up his nose, every limb shaking. Feebly, he tried to knock on the door, but it was no good, he had little strength. No one could possibly hear the pathetic taps he was producing.

They must be on location. Or were the programmes live? That was something he hadn't considered. Oh, for an episode guide!

'Let me out!' he gasped, then slumped back into unconsciousness.

Reg Atkinson, to a hush from the others, related how one day the TV news had been replaced, no announcement and no reason, with the first episode of *Surrender, Earthlings!* Because of the surprise nature of its appearance in the schedules, few saw it, but it was repeated the next day and from then on its dominance of the schedules began. The nation was quickly hooked, and the country had ground to a halt as watching the latest episode had become the be-all and end-all of everyone's life. Everyone, that is, except those that didn't actually own a TV.

'If it weren't for the half-hour breaks between episodes,' continued Reg, 'I don't think anyone would eat or wash themselves or even go to the lavatory.'

'So none of you owned a TV?' asked Nyssa.

'Certainly not,' answered Reg. 'I'm more of a Radio 4 nut myself. The box is a shocking time-waster. Eh, Tim?'

Tim agreed, half-heartedly.

'Sex and violence, that's all you get from TV,' Mrs Cooper admitted, her pulse racing.

'It has been my crusade,' explained the Reverend Vince, 'inspired by the Lord God Almighty, to rid the world of TV.'

'Whereas, it looks as if the TV is going to be rid of the world,' said Nyssa, grimly.

The Doctor's eyes snapped open. He peered around, his head throbbing and his mouth tasting like he'd just licked out the inside of a Dalek. Where was he? A cell, obviously, but a comfortable one, all things considered. A wine cellar. Unstocked, sadly. He shook his head, hoping to loosen up his brain. No, not a thing. The last thing he remembered was ... well, actually he didn't remember anything. Except ... shouldn't there be someone with him? He always had someone in tow. Who was it nowadays. Hang on? A posh girl. Bit prim. Nice, though.

Then it all flooded back. Greenford, the man – Norman, wasn't it? – and the TV programme. The Xyz! What on earth had got into him? The Xyz weren't celebrities, they were parasites!

So this was how they did it. The Xyz were famous throughout the multiverse for dominating wherever they spread, but no one knew how or why, especially as their military capabilities were deemed utter rubbish, even by the Dulcians.

But now he did. The Xyz used ubiquitous serial drama. Omnipresent and addictive.

He had to get out of here and save the world.

'Don't even think about it.'

The Doctor glanced at the source of this. A corpulent Xyz stood at the door, eyeballs quivering in his direction.

'So how are we going to stop them?' asked Nyssa. 'Normally I'd leave it up to the Doctor, but as he is currently their biggest fan, I don't think we can rely on him this time.'

'I think we should all write letters to the Director-General of the BBC and demand they take *Surrender, Earthlings!* off the air,' said Reg Atkinson firmly.

'What, all five of us?' asked his son.

'Certainly.'

'Millions of people watch this programme,' Nyssa pointed out. 'I don't think the TV bosses will react just because of the angry views of five people.'

'I think we should get down on our knees and pray to the Saviour, then I'm sure everything will be just fine,' suggested the Reverand Vince.

Everyone ignored him.

'Well, I think we should blow up the BBC,' said Mrs Cooper.

The Doctor sipped his double decaffeinated cappuccino with sprinkled organic nutmeg, and listened patiently to the Xyz's tale. He had been led upstairs, and now sat on a comfortable sofa, situated in a brown-panelled reading room, cloistered by thousands of unread first editions.

'We are, as you know, not the most accomplished of military tacticians.' The leader of the Xyz ('*Executive Producer* is my official title,' he had informed the Doctor) spoke beautifully, with modulated tones more suited to a newsreader than an alien. The Doctor marvelled that such a cumbersome mouth could produce such pleasing sounds. 'So we have to find alternative methods. The media seemed the most effective and one for which we had a...' the Producer struggled for a word, using the opportunity to gulp down some Nigerian espresso, '... knack.'

'So the battles on TV are fake?' the Doctor asked.

The Producer considered. 'Sort of.'

'And what does that mean exactly?'

'Well,' the Producer said, 'they are as far as we are concerned.'

'And as far as the humans are concerned?'

'Not humans, actors – professional, only the best. The auditions are very rigorous.' The Producer smiled, its triple-layered tongue vibrating gently, making a slight humming sound. 'And you know actors, they do like to go for authenticity.'

The Doctor was outraged. 'You kill the actors?'

'There are plenty of them,' said the Producer, 'far more than they need.'

'But you kill them. For the entertainment of their fellow human beings.'

'Their fellow human beings like to watch each other being killed. Always have done. Giving them the real thing seems more honest somehow. Besides, suppose we didn't really kill them and then accidentally used the same actor twice? It would break the suspension of disbelief.'

'The only disbelief around here is that I am actually listening to all this.' Something occurred to the Doctor. 'Just a moment, I thought that you said you were incapable of taking part in military activity?'

'Oh we are, we are. Utterly hopeless.'

'But what about the battle scenes on the TV?'

'Oh, we don't mind wars when they're *pretend*.'

'But it's not pretend for the actors.'

'I don't see what the problem is,' the Producer said. 'No one gets hurt – except a few Equity members – we get a new home and the humans get something to bring a little excitement into their drab, short lives. After all, we don't make them slaves or do anything they don't want to do. Most of them sit slouched in front of their televisions anyway. We just give them something of quality to watch. And by supplying their actors with work, we have halved the rate of unemployment in one fell swoop.'

'But you kill them,' the Doctor shouted.

The Producer shrugged with his eye-stalks. 'At least they don't have to worry about where the next job is coming from.'

Nyssa looked at her. 'I thought you were against violence, Mrs Cooper?'

'Only on TV, dear,' Mrs Cooper informed her. 'I don't mind it in real life.'

'It's an idea,' said Reg, thoughtfully.

'But, Dad, where are we going to find explosives?' asked Tim.

'Just you trust your old dad, son,' Reg replied, winking. 'You'd be amazed what you can rustle up in a well-stocked garden shed.'

'What about the people who haven't succumbed?'

'Hmm,' said the Producer. 'They are regrettable.'

'And what will happen to them?'

'Eventually we are going to run out of professional actors.'

The Doctor suddenly twigged what it was that was puzzling him. 'But why did you leave me here to dry out? Surely I would have been more useful to you under the influence?'

'You mean... you were genuine when you asked for our autograph?

'Oh, yes, you had me hook, line and sinker.'

'We thought you were pulling our legs.'

'I must say, you've taken to the local lingo beautifully.'

'Do you think so? Thank you very much.'

'So what happens to me now?'

'Hmm!' The Producer leaned back and his two eye-stalks reflected inquiringly at each other, as though he were consulting with himself. Why not, thought the Doctor, sometimes yourself is the only person who seems to have a grain of sense.

'My Lieutenant-Script-Editor made a creatively tactical suggestion which I think – sadly – is the only solution.'

The Doctor wasn't too wild about that 'sadly'.

'The series has been running for nearly a month now. I think some new blood is required.' The Producer leaned forward and touched the Doctor on the arm, surprisingly gently. 'Sorry, bad choice of word – blood.'

'So what do you suggest?' asked the Doctor. 'I recommend a change of location. How about Skaro?'

'Ha ha joke,' said the Producer, politely. 'No, a new character. A human traitor. Someone the audience can love to hate. Hate so much that the actor in question will not be able to walk down the street without being torn apart by outraged viewers. How about it, Doctor?' The Producer smiled, blubbery lips akimbo. 'The part's yours.'

Nyssa had tried to point out that as she was fully qualified in chemistry she would be the better choice to rustle up something from Reg's motley ingredients, but he had just looked at her with an amused smile, as though his goldfish had offered to map-read. She had not pressed the matter, but for the first time in her life, had snatched a glimpse of the attractions of ultra-violence. So, he gathered up a collection of stuff from his garden shed; paint and wallpaper stripper and weedkiller and who knows what else. Reg's idea of constructing a useful weapon had been to mix all the ingredients into a bucket. Then he had snipped off a few yards of string from a ball and taped one end to the inside of the bucket (the end actually dunked inside the gloop).

'A fuse,' he had explained to Nyssa's raised eyebrows.

'I was never a terribly good actor, you know,' the Doctor babbled. 'And dreadful stage fright. Ever since that first night of...'

'Oh don't worry,' the Producer said. 'You don't actually have to take part in the recording. We already have our Casters-in-Chief scouring *Spotlight* for a dead ringer. You just have to take the brunt of the public disapproval. It'll make a nice change for you – being the villain.'

The Producer opened the door of the club, and with a gentle yet insistent push, shoved the Doctor out into the street.

'Off you go, Doctor. Break a leg!' The Producer suppressed a giggle. 'At the very least.'

Nyssa sat in the back of Reg's lime-green Skoda, trying not to be sick. A smell reminiscent of nearly dead Terileptil permeated the car, and her nausea wasn't helped by Reg doing his step exercises on the clutch. The streets were deserted and they were making good time, even though Reg drove at a snail's pace. 'The end of the world is no excuse to break the law,' he had replied when Nyssa had asked if the car could go any faster.

When they had first left the house, there had been a mild argument between Reg and his son over who should drive. The decision had been made when Reg had pointed out that if he wasn't allowed to drive then they couldn't use his car or his bomb.

The Reverend Vince had then insisted that he had to sit in the front because he always felt sick otherwise. He didn't specify if he merely felt sick or if he actually was sick, a distinction Nyssa felt that he should have made clear, because if it was the latter then, fair enough, it was best for all that he should sit in the front, if not, then he should jolly well lump it.

This caused further havoc as Mrs Cooper had wanted to sit in the front next to Reg, for whom she obviously had a soft spot. Nyssa also had a soft spot for him, but it was the mallow marshes on the seventh moon of Gruntina 3.

Eventually all was sorted, and they were squeezed into the small vehicle. Reg and Mrs C. in the front, Nyssa, Tim and the Reverend Vince squashed in the back. Nyssa had made sure that she was sitting as far away from Vince as possible, just in case.

The next development was that it transpired that Mrs Cooper couldn't read a map if you put a gun to her head, which Reg seriously considered after they had got lost for the third time. Tim mumbled something about knowing the way perfectly well and he didn't even need a map actually, but no one listened to him.

'Oh, Doctor,' Nyssa wailed to herself, 'how am I supposed to save the world surrounded by this motley crew.' It then struck Nyssa with a pang of shame that the Doctor regularly saved the world – and occasionally the universe – surrounded by people so ragtag it made this lot look like well-drilled Sontarans.

The Doctor lurked in a doorway and pondered his next step. He had to get to the BBC and persuade them to take this series off the air. So, White City. How was he to get there? His dastardly alter ego wouldn't be making his debut on television until the next episode, which started in about 22 minutes time.

If they got their dramatic structure right, a brand new long-running character – and a villain to boot – wouldn't appear until the end of the episode, as a cliffhanger. So that gave him just over three-quarters of an hour to get to White City. Central Line, if he remembered rightly.

It was a long time since he had last been there. Now, were the trains running?

They had just driven past the Hanger Lane Underground Station. The roads had been deathly silent, a new episode having started about five minutes after they had set off from Greenford.

'Look, they're filming,' shouted Tim, pointing at the squad of arc lights.

After the emptiness of everywhere else, the sudden appearance of the film location was quite a jolt. A gaggle of lorries and coaches crouched around a group of brightly lit actors, alien and human, like campers around a fire. A catering van was dishing out bowls of something fluorescent to alien actors, while the humans huddled together, shivering, and clutching what looked like bacon butties in their hands. The aliens and the humans weren't mixing, that much was obvious. So much for the egalitarianism of the film indus...

Then Nyssa's blood ran cold. It was the Doctor! Standing with an alien, chatting cordially. Surely it was? What was he doing there? And why so friendly? Perhaps the aliens weren't so bad after all? Or maybe they had really got to him?

As the car approached, she could see that it wasn't the Doctor but, whoever it was, he not only looked unnervingly like him, he was dressed like him too; panama hat and celery and everything. So what was all that about? It was no coincidence, of that Nyssa was emphatic.

The car chugged on towards White City, wherever that was.

The Doctor stood in front of BBC TV Centre and regained his breath. It had been an uneventful journey. The trains were running, virtually automatically, as the driver's attention had been fully fixed on a portable TV in his cabin. The deserted train had stopped at every station, but more often than not, the doors hadn't opened, the driver unaware of anything that wasn't happening on the TV.

Even the stations had been empty and desolate. There had been no one to sell the Doctor a ticket, and he had no loose change on him, so he had leapt the ticket barrier and raced down the escalators. Of course, by the time he had reached White City, the programme had been off-air for a short while so station staff were milling about the place, bleary-eyed and blinking excessively.

Challenged about his lack of a ticket, the Doctor had offered a frantic excuse about being in such a hurry to get to home to see *Surrender, Earthlings!* that he had completely forgotten to buy one. The sympathy he had received was so touching that he felt momentarily guilty, until he reminded himself that he was trying to save their planet, after all.

The Doctor bounded across the traffic milling along Wood Lane, casually preventing a mobile phone being snatched from the driver of a passing Volkswagen Golf convertible by a scrawny youth with a pierced left frontal lobe – and ran to the barrier at the entrance to the TV Centre.

Luckily, the commissionaire was ensconced, not in the latest episode of *Surrender, Earthlings!* but in an item on *Blue Peter* about the making of the series (and how to make your own Xyz from toilet-roll holders, Blu-Tak and two boiled eggs). The next episode would start in just a few minutes: the one in which the Doctor's rascally twin would make his debut. He briefly wondered who would play him. Someone good he hoped, although he suspected that he was probably actor-proof. At least the poor thespian would be guaranteed a good run in the series. Until, that is, the Doctor was eliminated by some rampant member of the audience, and the actor was surplus to requirements.

The Doctor sneaked in to TV Centre; and not for the first time, very much uninvited.

The Director-General of the BBC was watching the TV. In fact, he had five sets in his office and all five were switched on and showing the same channel, not that there was anything on the other channels, all the rival station employees having given up and gone home to watch the *Surrender Earthlings!*

The DG was a man of about fifty-eight, short, and with unnaturally darkish hair with a would-be boyish floppy fringe; although many a time the DG thought ruefully of his shoulder-length ponytail, which he had forced himself to cut in order to look suitably Establishment material for his initial interview. His immaculate suit, despite being made to order, and for which he was personally measured by a ludicrously deified Italian designer, made him look like a sack of potatoes.

The Doctor silently entered the room without knocking. The DG barely looked up. 'Damn good, this programme thing,' he informed the Doctor. 'Just a few minutes and I'll be with you.' His eyes returned determinedly to the screen.

The Doctor kept his gaze firmly away from the TV. He had beaten the addiction, but he couldn't afford to have his interest in the story roused again. Not that there was a lot else to look at in the office; clean lines and uncomfortable chairs were the order of the day. No nice pictures on the wall, just a chart showing ratings, demographics, financial outlay. A solitary pot plant, admittedly a Triffid of shoulder height, was the only vestige of humanity in the room, unless you counted the DG himself and, sadly, not many did, least of all his colleagues.

A flicker of yellow from the screen caught the Doctor's eye and he couldn't resist grabbing a quick peep – and his blood ran cold at what he saw on the screen. A young couple, each carrying a child, had just been captured by three Xyz. The family, tattered and exhausted, had just, one gathered, been betrayed by a third party, at whom the father swore and shook his fist. It was obvious that they were being led in front of a firing squad. As the family were felled by a barrage of bullets, the Doctor glimpsed in the background a small orange car stall, stop, then hurriedly speed up and out of the picture. The guilty character, a tall blond chap dressed in a yellow frock coat with a sprig of celery in his lapel, merely threw his head back and laughed at the scene before him in a rather hammy fashion.

The Doctor stared worriedly at the DG. This could be tricky.

'It's more than my job's worth!'

The gorilla in the ill-fitting uniform, about to burst like an unforked sausage, held up his hand (or was it a bunch of purple bananas?) and prohibited the Skoda's further movement.

After the shock of the murders they had just witnessed (live, not Memorex), the rest of the journey here had been rapid and mundane – and silent. Now they were parked in the driveway leading to the BBC TV Centre. But the barrier remained relentlessly down, and the man with his finger on the *up* switch wasn't playing ball.

'Damn!' said Reg. After a pursed-lip face from Mrs Cooper, he apologised. 'A few minutes earlier and he would have been watching the programme.'

'Should have let me drive straight away then,' muttered Tim.

'I will pray to God to strike him down with a lightning bolt,' offered the Reverend Vince, generously.

'Perhaps Nyssa could seduce him,' suggested Mrs Cooper. 'Then we could slip in while...'

'Why,' asked Nyssa between clenched teeth, 'don't we wait until the programme starts up again?'

Reg shook his head. 'Every minute is crucial. We have to get in.' He tut-tutted. 'That bugger's – pardon my Swahili, Mrs Cooper – my employee, as a licence payer.'

'But you don't pay the licence, Dad, on principle,' chipped in Tim.

'That's not the point, son,' his father icily replied.

'If only we had a gun, we could kill him,' rued the Rev.

'I suppose we could run him over,' offered Mrs Cooper, 'if we backed up and drove at him really fast.'

'And play havoc with my paintwork? No, thank you very much.'

Nyssa was feeling very strange, a sensation with which she was quite unfamiliar. It had been building up ever since she had encountered this baffling group of humans. Was she ill, she wondered? Or was it something to do with whatever was going on here? Perhaps she was beginning to succumb to the strange force that was influencing so many lives. No, it wasn't that. It wasn't something physical, either, or at least nothing tangible. She couldn't really have explained it if anyone asked her to. The nearest way she could describe it was that...

She really *really* wanted to punch someone.

Reg abruptly came to a decision with a smack of his steering wheel, the decisiveness of the sound muffled by the brown woolly cover.

'I am going to talk to him.' He undid his seat belt, opened the car door and with a creaking noise from his left knee, disembarked.

'Take care, Mr Atkinson,' twittered Mrs Cooper. 'He looks a brute.' She dribbled slightly.

Reg rolled up his sleeves and approached the commissionaire.

Nyssa slumped back in her seat and closed her eyes. She really didn't want to watch this. Much as Reg annoyed her, she had no wish to see him pulverised.

Nothing happened for a while. Nyssa could almost feel sleep drifting over her when suddenly there was a cry from the front of the car.

'Where's he going?'

It was Tim. Nyssa opened her eyes and peered through the side window towards the gate of the BBC. Reg and the commissionaire were both entering the kiosk.

'I'm going to check what's going on,' said Tim, a trace of panic in his voice. He hopped out of the car.

'I'm coming too,' said Mrs Cooper, trying to scramble out from underneath her seat belt without undoing it. Vince politely slipped out of the rear passenger door, opened Mrs Cooper's door, then held the seat belt up in the air for her. She hauled herself out of the car, showing all her knees, and scurried after Tim.

Nyssa sighed very deeply and stared out of her window at Wood Lane. Was it worse than Greenford, she pondered, or was it just about the same? Whatever, it showed a fondness for ugliness that she hadn't realised humans possessed until now. Heathrow had been bad enough. What was it about concrete that they liked so much?

She realised that the others had been gone for quite some time now. Had they decided to break in and blow the place up without her? No, they wouldn't be so considerate. Besides, it was such a stupid idea she had to go with them and try and stop them, if possible. Although there was a stubbornness about Reg that might prove extremely hard to wear down.

Nyssa rolled down her window. Funny, there was no sign of them. She slipped out of the car and headed towards the barrier. They couldn't all be in the kiosk, not unless it was bigger on the inside than the out.

But they were, although Vince couldn't technically be described as being inside the kiosk, since ninety per cent of his body mass was wedged outside. What were they all doing in there?

Nyssa tried to peer over Vince's shoulder. He was too tall, so she tapped him on the shoulder. Angrily, he shrugged her off. She bounced up and down a bit. She then walked around to the other side of the kiosk to see if she could peep in through the window.

What she saw made her bite her lip in shock. All of her friends – well, the people she had got stuck with – were avidly watching the commissionaire's TV, avidly watching *Surrender, Earthlings!* Surely it shouldn't be starting for another ten minutes or so? Well, it didn't matter why it was on, it was on and that was what mattered. They all wore the same expression that she had seen on Norman's face at the beginning of this whole saga. In fact, Reg could have been Norman, the likeness was uncanny, what with the slack-jawed mouth and vacant expression.

Nyssa quickly averted her eyes. She didn't want to end up like that.

Oh well, Nyssa, she told herself, you're on your own.

And so she ducked gracefully under the barrier and plodded up to the BBC TV Centre.

The Doctor became aware of the theme music – not that he'd had a chance to hear it before, portentous little piece too, all oboe and drums and stylophone – and he turned expectantly to face the DG.

'By God, that's good stuff,' the DG said with a beaming smile. 'Rarely watch the box usually, but can't miss that.' He flicked a switch atop the telephone on his desk. 'Two teas, please, Miss Scammell.' He raised an eyebrow at the Doctor. 'Lapsong Doodah all right?' The Doctor nodded. He could murder a cup of tea, unlike his lookalike, who, it seemed, could murder anybody he liked.

'You know, you look familiar, old boy. Charterhouse?'

The Doctor shook his head. 'Gallifrey.'

'Ah, yes, we played you at rugby once. Got thrashed, I think.' The DG thought to himself for a bit. 'When wasn't one thrashed?' he said sadly. 'Can't remember the name. Or the face. Always had a terrible knack with faces. See one, forget it straight away.'

The Doctor emitted a huge puff of relief.

The door opened and the DG's miniature secretary – mid-fifties and mousy, definitely averse to boo/goose situations – made an appearance, laden with a tray bigger than herself, on which could be found a silver teapot steaming with Earl Grey, milk, sugar, biscuits and three different cakes, two of which were stuffed with cream.

'Ah, yummola,' said the DG. 'Perk of the job, Doctor.'

At the Doctor's name, the secretary stopped still and jerked her head in the Doctor's direction. He gave her a weak smile, knowing full well what was coming. Shame, he thought, that tea smelt delicious.

The secretary's face crunched up, her hands started quivering, and it was only a speedy reaction on the Doctor's part that prevented the Blytonesque spread from sailing through the air to land in someone's lap.

'The traitor!' she hissed.

'Oh, don't be ridiculous, Anita,' the DG said, a smile on his face. 'This is an old friend of mine, from donkey's years back.'

'Actually, we don't know each other from Adam,' the Doctor pointed out gently.

'Really? Are you sure? I could have sworn...'

'We must do something,' Anita the secretary screamed. 'People are dying because of him.'

'What is the ridiculous woman talking about?' the DG asked the Doctor.

The Doctor gestured at the TVs. '*Surrender, Earthlings!*' he explained. 'I think she thinks she's seen me in that. Being a cad.'

The Doctor stood up and faced Anita. She backed away fearfully. 'It's not me you know,' he tried to explain, 'it's only an actor who looks a bit like me.'

'It's you all right,' she spat. 'And I'm calling the police.'

'Anita, Anita, Anita,' the DG approached her, hands outstretched placatingly. 'Sit down and have a cup of tea and let's forget all about this nonsense.'

Anita shook her head. 'How can you sit here with a man like this, a traitor and a murderer of small children.' She stared accusingly at him. 'Unless you're a traitor too. Why isn't the programme on all the time? It's your doing, isn't it? You're a traitor too. You know that everybody wants the programme to be on twenty-four hours a day but you ... you won't let it. Yes, you're a traitor too. Why didn't I see it before? I'm calling the police.' She turned to leave, but as she got to the door. 'And not just the police,' she added. 'The army, too. And the Board of Governors. And Ofcom. Collaborating scum!' And with that, she swept out quivering in triumph.

The DG ran his fingers through his Grecian 2000-ed hair. 'I say,' he said weakly. He flopped down into his chair.

The Doctor grabbed the arms of the DG's swivel chair and swung him around so they were face to face. 'Now, listen, DG, this has got to stop. You saw how Anita behaved just now. Was that normal for her?' he asked, praying that it wasn't.

'Well, not really,' the DG admitted. 'At least, not since she started the HRT.'

'Exactly,' the Doctor said. 'It's the programme, it's doing terrible things to people's minds.' He debated whether to tell the DG about the Xyz, or was that pushing his luck? Bringing aliens into explanations was always such a lottery.

'Doctor, really, you sound just like that dreadful Whitehouse woman. And look where she ended up. Holloway was no place for a woman of that age. Look, old man, I really can't take the programme off air. It's been our biggest hit for years, since...' The DG struggled though his memory, 'since whatever the last big thing was.'

'But surely you've taken off programmes before that people have liked?'

'If I take this one off air now, I'll be lynched.'

'And if you don't take it off the air, we'll both be lynched. She wasn't joking, you know. I have been framed. The people behind this programme want me out of the way because I know too much and I'm the only one who can stop them. What better way to get rid of me than to put a lookalike in the programme so that the poor deluded people in the street who can't tell fact from fiction will tear me apart.'

'I don't believe it.' The DG shook his head doubtfully. 'Do I? Perhaps if I could consult a focus group...?' He reached for his telephone.

The Doctor grabbed the arms of his chair again and swivelled it around to face the TV. 'And there's your proof,' he shouted. 'Look!' The Doctor pointed at the screens, on each of which his doppelganger was swaggering, hands in pockets, and laughing while a pram was fire-bombed.

'Now can you imagine how the public is going to react to that? And Anita is going to tell them that you are my friend, after all, isn't that what you just told her? Everyone is going to be gunning for you just as much as me. You will never be safe in public again. You won't be able to walk the streets, go to supermarkets, even eat a happy meal in a McDonalds.'

The Doctor looked at the DG. Perhaps he was saying the wrong things here? But obviously he had struck a nerve. The DG's face had turned white, and a trickle of coloured sweat had dribbled down his forehead. He grabbed the phone on his desk and, after consulting a sheet of internal numbers, jabbed his finger on the dial.

'Transmission!' he barked. 'DG here. Cease transmissions of *Surrender, Earthlings!* immediately.'

'N'King I'Klee!' came the muffled response.

The DG pulled an embarrassed face at the Doctor. 'Erm, they say no, they'd rather not.'

The Doctor sat, apparently uncomfortably cross-legged, on the DG's desk, his fingers pressed against his temples.

The DG studied him, awe-struck, as he had never seen anyone think that hard before.

The DG clutched his nose suddenly. He waited. Nothing happened. He took a deep sniff. He had thought he was going to sneeze, but no, his nasal passages were beautifully clear. But he had a funny sensation in his head, and he had no idea what it could be. It didn't hurt, it just felt unfamiliar, as though something was going to explode in his brain.

'There is only one way that a programme can be taken off in this sort of emergency,' said the DG.

The Doctor's eyes snapped open and he stared at the DG in surprise, although not as surprised as the DG felt.

'And that is?' the Doctor probed cautiously.

‘World War Three.’
‘Hmm, a bit drastic, don’t you think?’
The DG, now he had started, was on a roll, although where it was flooding from he hadn’t the foggiest. He hadn’t been known to make a constructive suggestion since... well, ever, really.
‘No, it’s just that if the ratings ever fall to zero – or below, then the computer thing will assume that there has been a nuclear holocaust and will switch off all broadcasts.’
The Doctor’s eyes gleamed. ‘Like a snooze alarm, eh? So, where is your ratings processor?’
The DG shook his head, which was far too much trauma for his brain after its recent unaccustomed activity. ‘No idea.’

Nyssa crept along the deserted corridors of TV Centre, exhausted from pushing open the stiff heavy doors every few yards, and her shoulders ached. She had presumed that the boss of this place would be situated at the top of the building, so she had taken the lift up as far as it would go. Now she followed the circumference of the building, peering at the nameplates fixed to each door as she passed.
The thickly plumed carpet squashed any potential noise, so Nyssa was utterly unprepared for the hysterical woman who popped up unexpectedly in front of her, her face puce and her teeth clenched.
‘Hello,’ Nyssa said, once her heart had resumed beating after a brief hiatus. The woman just stared at her, chest heaving and eyes faintly crossed. ‘Are you all right?’ she asked, a syllable at a time.
The woman pointed back the way she had just come, her hands vibrating as though she were sitting on a spin-dryer. ‘He’s there.’
Why did human beings feel the need to be so *dramatic*, Nyssa wondered? Why couldn’t they just explain things simply and clearly without all this unnecessary – and frankly contrived – suspense?
‘Who is?’ Nyssa asked, quite patiently, she thought, in the circumstances.
The woman grabbed Nyssa’s shoulders, squeezing her fingers viciously into the Trakenite’s collarbone.
‘The Doctor!’ she rasped.

The Doctor wrenched the door of the DG’s office open, only to be confronted by a figure waiting outside, arm raised threateningly. He instantly leaped out of his skin, one heart hammering away while the other froze into inaction like a twin-drummer glam rock band doing a routine.

'Doctor?' asked a familiar voice. 'Have you stopped being insane yet?'

The Doctor controlled his breathing, and stared at the figure facing him. It was Nyssa, arm still upright and ready to knock on the office door.

'Well, that's a matter for debate,' he admitted.

The Doctor grimaced as he examined the Ratings Machine. It was a mess, a jerry-built collision of valves and bulbs and unnecessarily large knobs, all served on a tangled bed of wire spaghetti, and housed in an industrial-green Bakelite box, which even the in-house Special Effects Department would feel shamefaced about using.

'This is no good,' he groaned. 'No good at all.' He thrust a handful of leads at Nyssa, who grabbed them with as much distaste as if they had been freshly removed intestines.

The Doctor shoved his head inside the machine, pursed his lips and blew. He was enveloped in a mushroom cloud of dust, and he hastily withdrew his face, spluttering.

'Now what?' asked Nyssa.

It had been a brazen fluke that they had even found the Ratings Machine in the first place. After Nyssa had burst into the DG's office, the Doctor had grabbed her arm, still sore from the secretary's clasp, and the pair of them had scurried off into the bowels of the BBC, leaving the DG with strict instructions to lock himself in and admit no one. He riposted that admitting nothing was his usual occupation, and settled down to watch the Channel 4 test card.

The Doctor and Nyssa had wandered around the circular corridors, at a complete loss as to where to start looking, until, at an X-junction of passages, Nyssa pointed out a floor plan that read:

Ratings Department – Lower Ground Floor

'Well, that's handy,' muttered the Doctor, and they sought out a downward-bound lift.

But not everything was on their side. As they reached the parade of lifts, one opened its maw and disgorged an angry mob, shouting and shaking fists. They would probably have been clutching burning torches if it hadn't been for the stringent safety regulations regarding open flames. Nyssa was disturbed to notice the Reverend Vince among the crowd, a rictus snarl etched on his features. Mrs Cooper was present too, her fists clenched and a stream of foul-mouthed invective flowing from her mouth.

Fortunately, the charming specimens of humanity who comprised this rabid mob were all so caught up in their TV-fuelled hysteria that they failed utterly to notice the object of their wrath, and barged on past the Doctor and Nyssa, who had not had the time to hide themselves properly, but had merely pressed themselves up against the wall.

And after a short but leaving-your-stomach-several-storeys-behind trip down in a lift, here they were. The Ratings Machine was stored in a small boxroom, dusty, windowless and gloomy, with only a yellowing poster of Hope & Keen breaking up the drab greyness of the walls.

The DG sprawled in his executive chair, legs up on his desk, and waited patiently for the next episode of *Surrender, Earthlings!*, which was due on any moment now. He sipped delicately from a vodka and Red Bull, which he had had to make for himself, as Anita was still off on her strop somewhere. He just hoped that he had got the proportions correct.

The door from the corridor opened, and the DG glanced up in mid-swig. Anita stood there, hair awry and wild of eye, but nothing that drastically dissimilar to her little 'episode' a few months ago.

'Ah, Anita, could you be a perfect sweet and dig out the reduced fat bombay mix. Feel a bit peckish actually, and I haven't the foggiest where you keep it.' Anita didn't stir. 'Hurry up, there's a good girl, and then we can watch the next episode of *Surrender, Earthlings!* together.'

Then the DG noticed that Anita wasn't alone; she appeared to have about thirty people with her, all with matching bloodlust straining at the leash, judging from the taut veins on their collective necks.

'Hello everybody,' he said weakly.

The crowd surged forward to rip the DG to shreds, but then *Surrender, Earthlings!* started so they all sat down to watch that instead.

'Oh, this is hopeless,' the Doctor said angrily. 'A shoddy piece of work. Can't ever have worked properly. Look...' He pointed out a particularly worn connection inside the Ratings Machine. 'Completely defunct. They can't have received any accurate data from this junk for years. One sneeze and it'll just disintegrate.'

'Erm,' said Nyssa, 'isn't that what we want?'

The Doctor raised his eyebrows higher than should be possible on a humanoid face. 'Oh yes.' And with that the Doctor picked the Ratings Machine up off its stand and threw it against the wall.

And by one of those quirks of universal law, the number of pieces it shattered into was exactly the same as the ratings for *Surrender, Earthlings!* at that very moment.

The Doctor and Nyssa emerged from the concrete hell that was the BBC

TV Centre, blinking in discomfort as the sunlight surprised their retinas. Nyssa took a deep breath. She'd quite like a lie-down now, but there was a sense of unfinished business hanging over their heads.

'So,' she asked the Doctor, 'we've stopped the transmissions, but so what? The Xyz are still in control. Won't they simply start broadcasting their programmes again?'

'Hmm,' the Doctor was non-committal. 'Never overestimate bullies without their propaganda. Besides, by the time they can start broadcasting again, the humans – or at least the stronger-minded of them – will have started to break through the brainwashing.'

Nyssa didn't wish to query his use of the words 'strong' and 'mind' in relation to human beings, so instead she dragged him towards the kiosk where she had left Reg and company.

The sight she saw shocked her. Reg was curled in a fetal position, weeping. Tim sat on the ground, legs splayed, simply staring vacantly into the distance, while the commissionaire was wracked with silent sobs.

Nyssa felt awkward, she wanted to comfort these people but somehow she felt that she would be intruding. Added to which, she didn't understand this despair they were revealing. Lose your father, your step-mother, your world – then you might know what anguish is like.

'All this grief over a TV programme,' she said to the Doctor.

He shrugged. 'It's not really grief, they're suffering withdrawal symptoms, that's all.' He squatted down on his haunches, gently took Tim's face in his hand, and looked into the young man's eyes. They lolled in the Doctor's direction, but were focused on something much further away or nowhere at all. 'Added to which, the programme was the only time some of these people ever connected with anything emotionally. Mundane reality is going to be a bit of a shock.'

He stood up. 'Time will be the great healer, it usually is. Now, let's persuade the Xyz to pack up and leave.'

The chugging journey in Reg's Skoda, the Doctor at the wheel, would be forever etched in Nyssa's mind as the nearest she would ever come to experiencing Dante's *Inferno*. The streets were thronged with the hysteria of thousands; weeping and wailing, heads buried in hands, faces crunched up and soaked with tears. No one comforted anyone else, everyone seemed isolated in their desolation.

'Look!' The Doctor slammed on the brakes and pointed. Through the middle of the frenzied crowds – like Charlton Heston and chums crossing the Red Sea – a group of Xyz walked slowly, their heads wrapped in what resembled silk scarves, strange dark glass shields covering their stalked eyeballs. The Xyz were watching the humans warily, their movements delicate and furtive. Almost tiptoeing, Nyssa thought. They were all clutching large bags to their chests, their pathetic little claws wrapped delicately around the handles.

'What are they doing?'

'I think they are making their excuses and leaving,' the Doctor said, triumphantly.

A middle-aged woman, face blotchy with black mascara streaks, rubbed her eyes and moved away from the TV showroom outside which she had been paying vigil. As she caught a glimpse of the Xyz, she screamed. Everyone else in the street was instantly jolted out of their solitary misery and stared in curiosity, first at the woman, and then at the object of her terror: the Xyz.

The Xyz looked apprehensive and, still in furtive mode, began to shuffle forward noticeably faster. As all the people in the street actually acknowledged what their eyes were showing them, with one movement and voice they opened their mouths and emitted a yell.

The Xyz forgot all about any delicacy of motion. They metaphorically picked up their skirts and fled as fast as they could, the population of the street in hot pursuit.

'Are the humans chasing them because they know what the Xyz have done to them?' Nyssa asked. 'Or are they wanting...' she struggled for an unfamiliar word, '...autographs.'

'Both, probably,' the Doctor grinned. 'It's all right, I shouldn't think that the humans can harm them, just give them a bit of a scare. They won't be back here in a hurry.'

Nyssa breathed a sigh of relief.

'Unless, of course, they're invited back for a convention...'

Screamager

Jacqueline Rayner

It was late summer, and yet Victoria was cold.

She was wearing layer upon layer of thick cloth, too many layers for comfort, but a chill radiated from the stone walls of the house despite the slivers of sun struggling through the thin slit windows.

She wanted to run away, run far out into the fields and bask in the sunlight, but the Doctor had told her to wait here, wait in the house with Cormac and Sorcha where she would be safe, and she would do as the Doctor had said.

She hoped the Doctor – and her friend Jamie – would return soon. She wasn't entirely sure what they were doing, somewhere out there – something to do with robots, she thought – but surely the Doctor would soon solve the problem and defeat the menace so they could go back to the TARDIS. Oh, she liked Cormac, and Sorcha his wife, and Niall his brother, and she adored young Tadhg, eight-year-old son of the house – but as a pampered and fastidious Victorian she found it hard to bear the all-invasive stench of human waste, tainted in the evenings by the fatty smell of burning tallow – and worse still was the filthy bedding with its circuses of jumping insects, on which she was expected to sleep. But the Doctor had said that according to the lights of mid-fourteenth-century Ireland, this was perfectly acceptable, even luxurious, and by her own standards of courtesy, she could not complain – at least not within the hearing of her hosts.

But since the Doctor and Jamie had left, three days ago, Victoria had barely slept.

Tadhg ran in, wet-haired from playing in the stream with the village children. It should have been his bedtime an hour ago, but the bright evenings put paid to any ideas of forcing him to go to sleep.

'You must dry your hair or you'll catch cold!' Victoria scolded, looking around for something – anything – that resembled a towel. Tadhg grinned and shook his head like a dog, causing Victoria to shriek and jump out of the way of the spray. He ran out of the room, only to run back in a few moments later with Sorcha hot on his tail. Oatcake crumbs surrounded his mouth, and his cheeks looked stuffed full.

'You have eaten three full meals this day, when poor children get none!' shouted Sorcha, throwing her arms above her head in a gesture of disbelief. 'Yet still you are not satisfied.' But Victoria could tell she was not really cross with her skinny son, who easily worked off those three meals over the course of a hectic day.

Sorcha sank down on a wooden bench, and Victoria joined her. 'Who would have a son?' Sorcha asked rhetorically, as Tadhg ran off again. 'He eats food quicker than Martha can prepare it! Now, a little girl, who I could dress in ribbons and who would sew and bake, and stay in one place more than two minutes – she I could love.' There was a pause. 'But none of my girls lived to see a year.'

Victoria didn't know what to say. She grasped Sorcha's calloused brown hand in her smooth white one, and squeezed gently. But the moment passed in an instant, and Sorcha was back on the trials of being mother to Tadhg.

'He listens to no one but his father – but does his father tell him to mind Martha, or even me? No, he just ruffles his hair and tells him he is a fine lad.' She sighed.

The mention of hair gave Victoria an opening. 'I wish Tadhg would dry his hair properly after he has been in the stream,' she said, trying not to make it sound like a criticism of Sorcha's care of her son. 'A summer cold can be very nasty.'

'Oh, Tadhg is never sick,' said the boy's mother. 'He is as strong as an ox.' She grinned. 'A skinny ox!'

But, that very night, Tadhg became ill.

Tadhg had finally been made to go to bed when his father and uncle arrived home, and the rest of the household soon followed. Tadhg slept in his parents' room on the upper storey, a sheet hung from the ceiling to separate his bed from theirs. Martha slept in a corner of the kitchen, on a pallet of straw. It had seemed as though Victoria would have to sleep in a curtained-off partition of Niall's room, but all thoughts of politeness to her hosts had fled at the thought of such terrible impropriety, and in the face of her tears they had made a space in the tiny storeroom on the ground floor and set up a bed in there.

She was now in bed, on her straw mattress, lying on her side so as to keep as small a portion of her body in contact with the bug-ridden covers as possible. First she tried shutting her eyes, hoping that sleep would come. But she imagined she could feel the tiny creeping touches of insects all over, even though she knew they did not really cover her so densely. Her hands flew from her face to her arms to her legs, desperately brushing, brushing, dislodging both real and imaginary insects. Sleep was nowhere to be found.

Then she tried lying with her eyes open. But she still felt the insects. And now she could make out the shapes of the things hanging from the ceiling – just as bad in reality as in her imagination: pheasants and ducks and rabbits hanging lifeless from hooks, the moonlight occasionally glinting off a cold, dead eye, staring into Victoria's soul and asking why they should lose their lives just to provide a moment's sustenance...

And she saw monsters in every deep, shadowy corner of the room. By that broom – surely that was an Ice Warrior, leaning against the wall, ready to come to life any minute and stride towards her. And that was no pile of sacks heaped in the corner – that was a Yeti, one of the new, scary Yeti with fangs and glowing eyes, and it was about to pull itself up and smother her. And at the window, peering in through the narrow gap in the stones, that was... that was...

It seared itself on Victoria's mind: a face, an evil, eager face surrounded by billowing hair. A woman's face? But no woman alive could look so deathly white – almost green in the moonlight – or twist her face into the ecstasy of horror worn by this creature as it opened its mouth and shrieked, a chilling, unearthly screech. Victoria unconsciously mimicked the pose, her eyes wide and staring as she sat up in bed, screaming and screaming.

And then the face was gone. Victoria calmed, but only because the screams had drained her energy. She sobbed out as a footstep sounded overhead, but came to her senses long enough to realise it must be Cormac or Sorcha or Niall, awakened by her cries. She must warn them! She stumbled out of bed, and grabbed a cloak to go over the top of the daytime clothes she was still wearing. Martha was still asleep in her corner, an old woman determined to grab all the rest she could, whatever the distractions. Cormac was hurrying down the stairs, candlelight showing the concern on his face.

'Oh, Cormac! Cormac! There's something outside, a monster! I saw it! No!' The last was as Cormac turned to the main door, seemingly prepared to dash straight out and face whatever was there.

But whatever he was about to do went undone. For there was another anguished cry, this time in the direction from which he had just come.

Cormac turned and raced back up the stairs. Victoria followed. Niall, who had just been on the top stair, got there first and they joined him in Cormac and Sorcha's room. Sorcha was crouched over Tadhg's bed. 'I think he's sick,' she said.

Niall lit more candles as Cormac knelt by his wife. Tadhg was stretched out on his back, whimpering in pain. 'My head hurts,' he whispered hoarsely.

Sorcha placed her palm on his forehead. 'He has a fever,' she said. 'Oh, Victoria, you were right. I should have taken more care of him!'

Victoria was aghast. 'Oh, no, no! I didn't mean that at all! Sorcha, please don't worry. He's just caught a cold.'

But Victoria could see Sorcha's dead daughters staring out of her eyes.

There was nothing outside, no green-faced woman, no monster. Niall and Cormac went to search while Victoria fetched wet cloths to cool Tadhg's head. She apologised again and again for waking the household, her concern for Tadhg having driven the more abstract fear from her mind. But Sorcha was grateful: if it hadn't been for Victoria, they wouldn't have discovered Tadhg's fever till the next day; he would have suffered the night on his own.

For Tadhg was no better by the morning. Sorcha would not leave his side, gripping his limp, hot hand as if trying to anchor him to life.

Niall left at first light to fetch a doctor, but the sun was fully up by the time he returned. The doctor – how Victoria wished it was her own Doctor! – was a short, fat man who smelled faintly damp.

'He has a fever,' the doctor said, finally, huffing and puffing as he got up from beside Tadhg's bed. Victoria waited for the rest of the diagnosis – but there was nothing more to come. 'Got several like it this morning. Only thing to do: let out the hot blood, help him balance and cool down.'

He got out a knife and a cup, holding out the cup to Victoria, asking for her aid. She shook her head, turning to Sorcha. 'You can't let him do this! It's barbaric! It doesn't even work!'

But when they asked her what she suggested they do instead, she couldn't answer. 'Just... keep him warm,' she suggested.

'Keep him warm! He's hotter than the fires of Hell!' The doctor dismissed her. And she couldn't really argue. She knew very little about medicine, and she didn't possess the sort of authority that would make people listen to her, not like the Doctor. She left the room, unable to bring herself to watch, unable to stop it, unable to help.

Food. She could help by fetching food for the family; they needed to keep up their strength. In the kitchen Martha should have lit the fires and be already stirring a pot of porridge.

But there was no fire in the kitchen range. No porridge in the pot. Martha still lay in her corner, dead to the world. Dead.

Victoria bent down and shook her by the shoulder, already half knowing what she was going to find. Martha flopped on to her back, eyes milky and sightless. Victoria screamed.

* * *

The doctor didn't bother to look at Martha's body. He had enough work to do with the living, or so he said. Cormac and Niall laid it out in the front room until burial could be arranged. But Victoria could see that their minds weren't there as they carried out their grisly duty, they were upstairs with little Tadhg.

She wasn't happy being in the kitchen on her own – oh, by now she'd seen many deaths, so many more than one girl should ever see, but she wasn't yet inured to the horror. She didn't want to be. Sometimes Jamie and the Doctor could seem callous to her, and she knew they'd seen many more deaths than she had – the Doctor through his long, long life, Jamie from his days on the bloody battlefields of Scotland. She knew they weren't heartless, but they didn't feel it as she did. And she didn't want that to happen to her.

She stirred the porridge – it was going to be lumpy, she knew, she was no cook – and shook in some salt. She hoped it wasn't too much. Then she ladled it into five bowls. It was doubtful that Tadhg would be able to eat any, but she couldn't bring herself to leave him out. Then she carried the carefully balanced bowls upstairs.

Sorcha, still kneeling, was holding a long piece of knotted rope, fingering the knots as she muttered beneath her breath. She looked up as Victoria entered. 'Will you not take out your rosary, Victoria, and join me in prayer for Tadhg?'

Victoria took a step back. 'I – I'm sorry, Sorcha. I'm a Protestant. I don't have a rosary.'

Sorcha frowned and turned away. Victoria flinched inside. Sorcha wouldn't know what a Protestant was, of course. And neither would Niall, who entered behind Victoria, and who must have heard what she had said. Should she try to explain, convince them she was not ungodly? No, not now. She would attempt it another time. A better time.

Niall ate his porridge, and so did Cormac when he joined them a few minutes later. It took some persuading from Victoria to get Sorcha to eat. Victoria herself, fussing around, had not started her own porridge when there was a moan from Tadhg, a sudden movement as he flung out his arms.

'What's that?' gasped Sorcha. 'What is happening to my son?'

Victoria looked. There, in the tiny hairless armpit, was a swelling, a growth the size of an egg. 'I don't know,' she said. She went round the other side of the bed and gently lifted Tadhg's other arm. It was just the same.

Victoria no longer wanted to eat her porridge.

* * *

By the end of the day, Tadhg had swellings on his neck and legs. Angry, pus-filled lumps covered his face, arms and chest. He vomited and no longer knew his mother.

The doctor would not come again, saying he was too busy. He sent word to burn herbs to clear the atmosphere. Victoria gathered thyme from the kitchen garden; anything that might help.

That night, Victoria saw the face at the window again. She screamed. This time, no one came running. Upstairs, the family was weeping, because Tadhg was dead.

In the morning, Sorcha had the fever, and Victoria was scared.

Niall came back from the village to say that seven people had died in the night, including the doctor. He gave Victoria a look that scared her further.

'I know what is doing this,' she tried to tell them. 'I've seen the monster that comes in the night and kills people with its alien disease! We have to destroy the monster!'

But no one would listen to her.

She knew she had to be brave. She knew that she wasn't a brave person, she knew that she was scared, but she had to try. She had no Doctor, no Jamie. Her friends here in this house were not true friends – they didn't know her, didn't care about her, were just nice people who had offered her hospitality. Anyway, Sorcha was too ill to help, and Cormac too consumed with worry and grief, and Niall – well, had Niall ever been a friend to her then he wasn't any more.

She had only seen the creature at night, but perhaps it was hiding during the day. She would look for it. She crept from the house, ridiculously trying not to make a noise as if the creature might hear her from its hiding place and escape. She carried an axe that she had found in the storeroom. Whether she could use it if it came to it she didn't know, but having it made her feel just that tiny bit braver.

She walked down the path towards the stream. Perhaps the monster was hidden in the reeds, perhaps Tadhg had stumbled over the hiding place as he played and the monster had infected him to stop him coming too close.

There were a couple of peasant huts near the stream, and an old man sitting out in the sun, whittling a piece of wood. He looked up and saw Victoria in the distance, and hurried into the nearest hut. A few moments later, a younger man came out, carrying a scythe. Two women came out of the next hut, one wielding an iron skillet, the other a long lump of wood. The old man came back out again; he held an axe like Victoria's.

She was terrified, but kept going. They couldn't mean to hurt her. Perhaps they knew of the monster. If they were going after it she could help them. But as she got closer, saw the expressions on their faces, she knew that it was no monster they were after. The women were screeching at her, the men shouting. It took her a moment to work out what they were saying. 'Keep away! Keep away! Diseased! Diseased!'

They thought she was carrying the disease. They thought she would bring it to them. She stopped.

'No! No, I'm not sick! I'm looking for the monster that's doing this to your people. I'm trying to help!' She lifted her axe and pointed at it. 'I'm going to fight the monster!'

But as she tried to take another step forward, the scythe was waved threateningly in her direction, and she could see that her words meant nothing to these people. Frightened and disheartened, she stumbled back to Cormac's house.

Sorcha was worse. Victoria sat by her bedside. She told herself that she would stay up that night and watch for the monster. She had seen it only at night; night would be the time to catch it. And perhaps – she was being cowardly she knew, but she couldn't help but hope – perhaps the Doctor would be back by then. He would confront the monster, cure the illness, take her away from here, away to somewhere...

Somewhere where she would once again be surrounded by monsters, and death, and dying.

She never wanted to see death again.

Sorcha moaned and flailed on the bed. She was wearing a dress, but the underarms were not sewn up. Tricky to sew, and it let your armpits breathe, so Victoria had been told. There, standing out clearly, were the same sort of egg-shaped lumps that Tadhg had developed. And there, on Sorcha's neck – pustules were beginning to form. There could be no doubt that the same monster that had killed Tadhg had got Sorcha too.

Cormac came back later in the evening. He was distracted and brusque with Victoria. More people had died in the village. Many, many more were sick. He listed names of people she didn't know: Bryan and Donal and Diarmaid, their wives and children and parents.

'And now Sorcha will die,' he said, his face blank.

'No, no, she might recover,' Victoria said desperately, sounding almost as if she were pleading with him for his wife's life. 'I'm doing everything I can for her.'

'And what is that?' he sneered. 'You are doing nothing! No one can do anything to help! All around, people are dying!' He suddenly sank to his knees, an involuntary collapse. Victoria nervously inched towards him, and put out a trembling hand to touch his forehead. It was red hot. He had the fever.

She helped Cormac stagger to the bed, to lie beside his wife. Sorcha's eyes flew open. 'The devil! The devil has come for me!'

'No!' Victoria cried. 'It's your husband, it's Cormac.' But it seemed that Sorcha no longer recognised her spouse, certainly did not know who Victoria was. Limbs spasming, she shrieked and shouted about devils and demons and witches.

Niall came rushing in, his rosary in his hand. 'What is happening?'

Victoria had backed away into a corner and was trembling. 'Cormac is sick and Sorcha is delirious,' she stammered.

Niall turned on her, his eyes wide and bright. 'Not delirious,' he said. 'Perhaps she speaks the truth. This is a punishment from God.'

Victoria shook her head violently. 'No. No, it isn't! It's the work of a monster, I keep trying to tell you!'

He wasn't listening. 'God has looked down on us and judged us for our sins. This is a sign of His displeasure.'

Victoria darted forward and grabbed his arm. 'No! It's a monster! I've seen it, you must believe me!'

Niall turned to look at her then. 'A monster is making them sick?'

'Yes, the monster that I've been seeing at night. I told you!'

He stared off into the middle distance. 'Then we must kill the monster.'

It was out of the storeroom window that Victoria had seen the monster on the previous two nights, so that was where she looked for it again. She had no thought of even trying to sleep, and didn't dare lie down for a moment. She just sat perched on the edge of her straw mattress, gazing past the hanging game and shivering with fear. Outside, she knew, Niall was waiting with the axe, alert for any sound, waiting for the monster to appear.

Hours passed. Several times a creak came from above, making Victoria jump. But she knew it was Sorcha or Cormac tossing and turning on their sick bed.

And then she saw it. The same ghostly pale face, the same hungry expression. Although she'd told herself she would remain calm, there was not a thing on Earth that could have stopped the piercing scream ripping itself from her throat. She collapsed back on the bed, clutching her chest, gasping in shock. A moment later, Niall rushed in.

'What is it? Why did you scream?'

'The... the monster!' stammered Victoria, pointing to the window.

'What are you talking about? There was no monster there! I was watching the window the whole time, not a thing came near the house.'

'But – but – but –' Victoria couldn't speak. She had seen the monster, she had, she had!

Niall took a menacing step towards her, then seemed to think better of it and ran from the room. Victoria heard his footsteps hurry up the stairs and into Cormac and Sorcha's room. Then she heard a howl of anguish.

Terrified of what she would see, and remembering the way Niall had looked at her, it took all Victoria's courage to follow him upstairs. Niall was kneeling on the floor, arms and eyes raised to the ceiling, crooning in grief. Candlelight flickered over the motionless forms of Cormac and Sorcha. Both were dead.

A floorboard creaked beneath her foot, and Niall spun round towards her.

'I'm – I'm so sorry,' Victoria said, backing away. 'The – the monster...'

He hissed at her. 'Monster! There is no monster save you! You come here, witch, and bring the wrath of God upon us! Great we have suffered for opening our home to a Godless witch!'

'But there is a monster!' screamed Victoria. 'I saw it, I saw it!'

She turned to run, but Niall was on top of her, his hands around her neck. 'There is a monster, and I shall kill her! Die, witch, die!'

Victoria pushed at him, but his grip was so strong and she felt as weak as a kitten. Bright spots were dancing before her eyes as she gasped out 'No... No...' with her remaining breath. She thought of the axe, lying forgotten in the storeroom, and wondered if she could have wielded it even if she had it. But her thoughts as her head began to swim were of the blade falling on Niall's head, and the bright scarlet blood flying to give her freedom.

And then there was another voice in the room, a voice that soared above Niall's angry grunts, a voice that made Victoria's heart sing. 'Oh, no! Let go of her at once, you bully! Jamie! Jamie, come and help!'

And as Niall was dragged away, his hands still clutching for her neck, she flung herself into the Doctor's arms.

'Well, this is a pretty pickle, Victoria,' said the Doctor, sometime later.

She had sobbed out the whole story – the monster that no one else could see, the horrible deaths, even the unfriendly villagers and the flea-ridden beds and the horrid, horrid food – petty grievances that heaped on top of the major horrors to show how utterly wretched her time away from them had been. But when she had finished, the Doctor stood up from where he'd been examining the bodies of Sorcha and Cormac, and looked her in the eye. 'Oh, Victoria, I know it's been terrible for you – but I wonder if perhaps you did imagine the monster after all.'

Jamie frowned. 'Och, Doctor, Victoria wouldnae make up such a thing.'

'No, of course, she wouldn't, Jamie, but I wouldn't be at all surprised if she had had nightmares and, well, imagined a monster. I wouldn't blame her at all.'

Victoria shook off the Doctor's hand and stamped her foot. She couldn't believe it. 'I am telling the truth, I am!'

The Doctor smiled kindly at her. 'Of course you think you are, Victoria. But you see, these poor people aren't dying from an alien disease. They're dying from the Black Death. I should have realised the date; never left you here in the first place... But the point is, it's a terrible, terrible thing, but it's perfectly natural.'

Jamie jumped to his feet. 'The Black Death! Shouldnae we be getting out of here?'

The Doctor nodded. 'Yes, we should. In fact, we're very lucky that Victoria hasn't been infected already, with so many poor people in this house succumbing.'

But Victoria – desperate as she was to leave – had to make them believe her. 'I did see a monster. A woman with long hair, screaming at me.'

Jamie half grinned. 'Would it be a mirror that you were seeing?'

She didn't dignify that with a response. But the Doctor was actually looking interested. 'She was screaming, you say, Victoria.'

'Yes, but not because she was frightened. It was horrible. A sort of wailing and screeching.'

'I see,' the Doctor said, his eyes lighting up. 'I think I may have misjudged you, Victoria.'

She hmphed. 'So you believe me?'

'Yes, I do. And tonight, I think we will all watch for the monster.'

'Ah, now, Doctor...' began Jamie, the fear of remaining somewhere so diseased evident on his face.

'But what about Niall?' said Victoria, glancing towards the corner of the room where the cowed man sat glowering at them, keeping his eyes from the twisted bodies of his brother and sister-in-law.

The Doctor walked over and placed a hand on Niall's forehead. 'Burning hot,' he said. 'I don't think you're going to give us any trouble, are you, Niall?'

Niall's eyes slowly closed, and he sank onto the floor.

'No, I'm afraid he probably won't be troubling anyone again,' the Doctor continued. 'Which is why I'm almost certain we'll see Victoria's monster tonight.'

But all the same, putting his attack out of her mind, Victoria nursed Niall until nightfall.

The Doctor had insisted on checking Victoria from top to bottom, as much as her modesty would allow. He had even drawn her blood, saying he would have a look at it later, in the TARDIS. And he was the last to assemble in the storeroom that night, having been checking on Niall. For all that he occasionally got a bit flustered, it was so wonderful to have someone who was just taking charge.

In the middle of the night, the monster appeared. Victoria spotted it first and screamed, but it was a scream of shock, more than fear; the sudden shock almost greater because she had been tensed up, expecting the apparition. Somewhere inside she almost felt relief, too – because she hadn't been dreaming, she hadn't been imagining things, here was the monster, and the Doctor and Jamie could see it too.

The Doctor didn't flinch from Victoria's scream, but strode straight up to the window.

'Well?' he shouted. 'Don't just stand there, come on in. I want to talk to you!'

Victoria buried her face in Jamie's shoulder as the monster began to do what the Doctor asked. She didn't know if it somehow fitted itself through the tiny window, or if it walked through the wall, and she didn't want to know. But suddenly there was a deep chill in the room, worse than ever before, and she knew the creature was inside. Trembling, hands still grasping Jamie's arm, she lifted her head.

There was the monster in front of her. In the light of the Doctor's lamp its – her – skin was pale green, and she was dressed in floating black rags. If the lamplight hit her face, the skull could be seen beneath.

'Aha!' cried the Doctor, triumphantly. 'A Banshee, I presume!' He turned and whispered in an aside to Victoria and Jamie: 'An Irish spirit whose cry heralds death.'

The Banshee's voice rattled in her throat. 'I am.'

'Probably beginning to get a bit overworked at the moment, as well, what with the Black Death having just arrived on these shores...'

The Banshee inclined her head. 'Which is why we want her.' It held out a skeletal finger – which pointed straight at Victoria.

Victoria shrieked and buried her face in Jamie's shirt again. For his part, his arms encircled her, keeping the horror at bay.

The Doctor spoke out indignantly. 'You want Victoria? Oh, no no no no no. I can't allow that.'

'Have I got the Black Death, Doctor?' sobbed Victoria. She felt Jamie shrink away from her involuntarily for a second, but then resume his protective hold.

'I don't think that's what she means, is it?' the Doctor carried on. Victoria looked up again as the Banshee shook her skeletal head.

'We have watched her,' she said. 'She is already close to being one of us. Her screams have heralded a dozen deaths, two dozen.'

'No...' whispered Victoria, horrified, as images began to float unbidden in front of her mind's eye. Her scream, and a Cyberman killed a man. Her scream, and someone dropped to the ground as a Yeti's gun fired. Her scream, as the Daleks... 'No!' she cried, beginning to panic. 'Doctor, she's lying, she's lying!'

But the Doctor was also looking horrified as the Banshee again shook her head. 'It is not I who has heralded the deaths of this family,' she continued. 'They are not my charges; I came merely for the servant. But then I saw her.' Her bony finger stabbed again at Victoria. 'And I knew her. So I watched. Every night, her cries have heralded a death in this house. Now there is only one of the family left. When he dies, she will be free to come with me, to assume her rightful place.'

Victoria choked back a sob. 'Doctor, I want to go back to the TARDIS...'

'You have no choice,' hissed the Banshee. 'It is part of you. Every time your screams precede a death, you get closer to us. Don't fight it. Come with me now.'

Victoria felt herself yielding. The thought was horrific, it was against her will, but she found herself moving towards the monster. Somehow she knew that the Banshee was telling the truth. She had been too close to death, too many times. And she knew it had changed her. She just hadn't realised how.

'Victoria!' cried Jamie, trying to hold her back. But it was the Doctor who stepped out in front of her, barring her way.

'I don't think so,' he said calmly.

The Banshee hissed at him. 'It is inevitable.'

But the Doctor shook his head. 'There is still one member of this family alive. Victoria's cries have not heralded his death.'

'But they have,' said the Banshee. 'I have felt his death approaching.'

'But they haven't!' said the Doctor forcefully. 'Perhaps you should check again.'

There was silence. Victoria gazed at the Doctor's back, but the visions were still in her head. Her scream, and yet another death...

'No!' wailed the Banshee in anguish, causing Jamie to throw his hands over his ears. 'He lives still! Death has retreated from him! How can this be?'

'Ah, well,' said the Doctor, turning so Jamie and Victoria could see the little grin that meant he thought he had done something quite clever. 'You see, far from heralding his death, Victoria actually saved his life.'

'I did?' said Victoria, puzzled.

'You did,' said the Doctor. 'You see, you hadn't succumbed to the disease, for which I was very grateful. But then I thought, well, we've travelled all over the universe, haven't we? We're bound to have picked up all sort of antibodies, protections and so on. Maybe that's why you were safe. And so if I injected Niall with a little bit of your blood...'

Victoria struggled to understand. 'Then... he'd have the same protection in his blood, and he wouldn't die?'

The Doctor smiled at his bright pupil. 'That's it, Victoria.' And then the smile faded as he turned on the Banshee once more. 'So, your hold on Victoria is broken! The last of this family is not dying. And I give you my word, Victoria's screams will never herald death again. Never!'

And with a shriek, the Banshee was gone. The Doctor, Victoria and Jamie were alone.

They were back in the TARDIS again. Victoria knew that the Black Death lasted for years and killed thousands, and wanted the Doctor to stay and cure it all with her blood. The Doctor had shaken his head sadly. Niall hadn't died, it was true, but then some people did survive. Perhaps it was just a coincidence. And even if it wasn't – well, they couldn't interfere with history. Not on that scale.

And then there was the Doctor's promise. 'Wherever we go, there's always death,' she said to him. 'Always. And I can't help screaming, really I can't.'

The Doctor shushed her. 'Oh, I know that. But I gave my word, and I intend to keep it. Who knows, perhaps your screaming will save people instead next time!'

'I don't know if I want there to be a next time,' Victoria murmured. She didn't know if the Doctor had heard her. And she thought of all the deaths she'd seen, all the deaths that had surrounded her, every time and everywhere the TARDIS landed. 'I don't know if I want to do this any more.'

And she vowed in that moment that the Doctor's words would come true. She would never be a herald of death again. She would save herself from the fate the Banshee had promised. She would turn her back on death by turning away from this life.

And in that moment her fate was both saved and sealed.

The Colour of Monsters

Steve Lyons

It should have worked, this time.

The plan was perfect. The people of the target world had been observed, and found to be soft and weak. Their technology was primitive – they hadn't even the faculty to reach their nearest star. And the invaders? They had had the weapon, of course. The ultimate creation of the most fiendish minds of their galaxy.

The soldier had believed his leaders. They had claimed that victory was assured – that, although their prey numbered billions and they were only a few thousand, they could not be defeated. And the soldier's heart had swelled with such pride in his maligned race.

How could they have been so wrong?

The explosion had ripped through his carrier ship without warning. He had heard the invasion force was in rout, was preparing to join in a desperate rearguard action. One moment, his head was buzzing, trying to rationalise this turn of events, to understand how one man could have upset so much. The next, his world had burst into flames, and an eternal second of howling, searing agony.

And then, there was the rain, soothing his burnt hide in blissful patches of icy cold.

He was lucky, he knew, to have been thrown clear; to be lying here, face-down in the foul-smelling grass, dirt soaking up his blood and scratching inside his wounds. A million to one chance. Or perhaps his comrades had been the lucky ones. Their deaths had been quick, clean – while he was left, with no gun to protect him and no armour to hide behind. The lonely survivor, crippled and stranded on a hostile world. Exposed.

His enemies would find him soon. He could expect no mercy from them.

To them, he was a monster. A twisted horror from their nightmares. That had been his greatest strength, before: the fact that his very aspect paralysed their minds. Now, it was his weakness, because their fear would drive them to destroy him.

Perhaps he would just lie here and wait for them. Let them come, from the north, from the south, from the cloud-heavy sky. They would end his pain, his confusion.

But no, he had been taught better. Since his birthing, the soldier had been programmed to fight, to follow orders to the last breath. Never, ever to surrender. His race's pride rested on him alone, now.

And so, with blood pumping and battle cries ringing in his auditory organs, with green pus seeping from behind his eye, he lifted himself onto two of his appendages and began to crawl.

He crawled for a lifetime, before he saw it.

At first, he thought it might be a mirage, a cruel trick of the dying daylight. He braced himself, tried to stop himself from shaking, tried to focus on the dark, square construct through the slicing rain. It was sturdy; it did not creak or sway in the gusting winds. It was probably inhabited. But he had no choice. He needed shelter, before night fell. Not just to save himself from discovery now, but to save his life.

With an audible groan, he hoisted himself up again. And, not caring if he left a blood trail in his wake, the last monster dragged himself towards the primitive dwelling.

The barn was warm, but not warm enough to touch the chill in the monster's bones. The straw on which he lay was soft, but it prickled against his burns. The darkness made him feel a little safer, but not safe enough.

He had searched for something to prop against the door, scrabbling at rusted hunks of machinery but finding nothing of the required mass and lacking the strength to move what he did find. In the end, he had simply buried himself as best he could in the farthest corner. He had listened to the rain crashing down on wooden timbers, and watched the sky turn black through the half-wheel pattern of holes above the door.

He hadn't been able to sleep. His heart was a steady drumbeat, his chest rattling with each laboured breath. And there was one more thing: a sickly, fluttering sensation in his stomach, like nothing he had felt before. A sensation that kept his gaze rooted to that door, and made him see – in those quasi-real seconds when his dreams managed to steal up on him – his enemies, the people of this world, bursting through it with their primitive weapons raised.

He didn't see the girl at first.

She was a patch of dark against the greater darkness – and, even as the monster picked out her shape, he denied it to himself. A trick of the shadows, he thought. Too small to be an enemy – and anyway, the door hadn't opened, not in reality. He would have seen. And an enemy would have run, or screamed, or attacked, not sat with its legs drawn up to its chest and its back to one of the square pillars that supported the barn roof, staring.

It was the stare that gave her away. The glint of curiosity in her eyes provided him with pinpoints of light, around which the rest of her fell into place. And the monster realised that he had slept after all, or dozed at least, long enough for her to slip in here unnoticed.

His first thought, as the sickness in his stomach erupted with fresh intensity, was that she was toying with him. Why else hadn't she dispatched him when she had the chance? His muscles tightened involuntarily, shifting the straw around him – and the silent observer flinched, and drew in a sharp breath.

She was afraid, of course. The question was, what would she do with that fear? He remembered something his leaders had told him, in scornful voices: the people of this world were so weak, so stupid, that their offspring weren't taught to kill until they had reached adulthood, sometimes not even then. Perhaps he could deal with this youngling, even in his weakened state. If only he could lift his limbs; if she would move a little closer...

She had recovered her composure. She was crouching in the straw, one hand laid on the floor to push herself up if she had to run, and she cocked her head as if she might see him better from a different angle. And she spoke, in a breathy, flute-soft voice. She said, 'Don't be afraid.'

The monster almost choked on acidic bile. 'I... I am not afraid,' he protested, in his rasping whisper. 'Rather, it is you who should fear me.'

'Why?' the little girl asked, in all innocence.

'Why?' He groped for the words to answer her. He had never considered the question before. 'Look at me. Am I not the embodiment of your most dire imaginings? Am I not the fear that lurks in the corners of your mind?' He raised his voice, scouring his throat to produce his most intimidating bark. 'I am a monster!'

The girl put a hand to her mouth, and her body trembled – in horror, he thought. But the sound that burst through her fingers was light and playful, like the babbling of a mud pool.

'You're funny,' she giggled.

He could see her properly now, the haze of sleep falling from his sight. She had the typical bald, pink skin of her kind; he had touched it once, and found it cold and clammy. She was of slight stature, her skeletal structure evident beneath her flesh; one sharp twist would probably snap her in two. Yellow fur grew only on top of her head, and hung to her shoulders, baffling him as to its purpose. She was the female of her species; the monster had recognised that at once, recalling long-ago briefings. A breeder, then, not a warrior.

'I'm Amy,' said the little girl. 'What's your name?'

'We have no need of names!' Saliva dribbled out from between the monster's uneven teeth.

'You must have a name, silly. What do your mummy and daddy call you?'

It took him a moment to realise what she meant by that. Then, he shuddered with revulsion. 'You insult my people,' he snarled. 'We do not breed unchecked, as you do. We are birthed under controlled conditions, in laboratories where imperfections can be corrected and our population managed. We grow stronger with each generation. In comparison, you are a virus, mutating haphazardly.'

The girl was silent for a moment. Then, she said, 'I think that's sad. Everybody should have a mummy or a daddy.'

'Yes,' said the monster, elongating the 's' into a thoughtful hiss. 'Your kind are raised by your progenitors, are you not? A foolish custom. Their uncontrolled hormones lead them to coddle you, to shield you from the realities of life. It is little wonder, then, that your people are so squeamish, your armies ineffectual.'

She didn't seem to have heard him. Her thin, one-piece gown – sodden from the rain outside – had a drawstring around its waist, and she played idly with it. 'I think I'll call you... Misha,' she announced. 'That was my cat's name. She was pretty. She was black, with a white patch over her left eye, but she ran away. Oh, but Misha's a girl's name, isn't it? Are you a girl monster or a boy monster?'

'I am a unit in the glorious army of –' He let the words gurgle away, furious at himself for having been drawn into this futile exchange.

'Are you angry with me, Mr Monster?' asked the girl, quietly.

'Anger is for lesser beings,' he spat. 'You – your entire species – are no more than microbes to me, fit only to be farmed, enslaved or destroyed by your superiors!'

'You're mean,' she pouted. 'I thought you were a nice monster, but you're horrid. I ought to tell my daddy on you.'

She was edging away from him, beginning to see him as he was at last. He liked that. That was how it should be. But what would happen, he asked himself, if she were to leave? She would return, with adult reinforcements.

Much as he loathed the idea, he had to placate her. He had to keep her here, long enough for him to recover his strength. Only then could he be rid of her nuisance.

'No!' She started at the ferocity of his objection. He forced himself to soften his tone, and continued. 'Nobody must know of my presence here. Do you understand?'

She hesitated. 'You are the only one who can... help me,' the monster wheezed. He tried to reproduce the identity code she had given him. '...Ay-mee... Stay with me.'

The girl looked nervously over her shoulder, at the barn door. 'I'm not meant to be here. It's dark. My mummy and daddy don't like me to go outside on my own when it's dark.'

'They do not know your location?' asked the monster, eagerly.

'I tried to tell my mummy,' said the girl. 'I said I'd seen a monster from my window, but she thought I was being silly. Mummy says there's no such things as monsters.'

'Then she lied to you.'

'Did not!' the girl protested.

'She denies the existence of my kind, even as we lay siege to your planet. How did she explain the events of the past few days to you? Did she even tell you of the war being waged for your survival? Did she warn you, little girl, that you might die?'

The girl's face crumpled into a scowl. Then, she ventured, 'My best friend, Claire, she says grown-ups can't see monsters. She says that only boys and girls can see them.'

'You must have heard the... explosion,' said the monster – and even as he formed the word, he returned to that flame-filled instant, and winced.

The girl's eyes crossed with concentration. 'There was something. The man on the radio... He said there'd been an accident at the gasworks, but it was all right because no one was hurt. Only, then I saw you crawling into our barn, and I... I've never seen a real live monster before. I waited for my mummy and daddy to go to sleep, and then I got up and I snuck down here to see if... if you were...'

'You disobeyed your orders,' said the monster. The girl stared at him. 'You were instructed to remain in your shelter,' he elucidated, 'but you disobeyed.'

'I suppose,' said the girl. 'But –'

'You disobeyed, because... you feared I may have been injured? On my world, that would have been considered an act of treason, for which you would have been executed.'

The girl's eyes widened, and she gasped. 'Just for sneaking out of your room?'

'We are conditioned to obey. It is what makes us strong.' The monster's voice was building to a proud rant. 'We are disciplined, united, single-minded in our purpose.'

The girl stuck a finger in her mouth, and thought for a second. Then, with a knowledgeable air, she pronounced, 'I think you're a boy monster.'

He took a deep, shuddering breath.

'You are hurt, aren't you?' said the girl, alarmed.

'My body will... repair itself in time,' he grunted.

'M-maybe I should go and fetch my daddy.' She was clambering to her feet.

'Your "daddy" cannot help me,' he said quickly. He thought back to what the girl had said. He didn't understand her logic, but if it kept her here... 'You were correct, Ay-mee. Your progenitors are unable to see me. Only you can see me. Only you.'

'You're my secret monster, then,' she beamed. 'But... but I don't know what to do.'

'Come to me, Ay-mee,' said the monster. 'Talk to me. That is all I need.'

She took a hesitant step towards him. He tensed, preparing himself to rend her revolting flesh, to break her bones. Just a moment's effort, then he could rest again.

But she stopped, and lowered herself to the floor, her legs crossed beneath her. Close, but not quite close enough. The people of this world may have been weak; they were backward; but there was one skill at which they excelled. One area in which even the monster's leaders had acknowledged their superiority. They could run. Fear gave them speed. He needed the girl to come closer. Close enough to touch her.

'I used to come in here with Misha,' she said, wistfully. 'She liked the straw. She used to roll around in it, and then Daddy would complain because it got stuck to her fur and she got it all over the house. And... and one day, we went down to the park, and Misha got through the fence around the pond and scared the ducks.'

'Ah,' said the monster. 'Then this creature of which you speak – it was a superior being? The lesser animals feared it?'

The girl blinked. 'She was only playing – but Mummy told her she'd been very naughty, and we weren't allowed anywhere near the pond after that.'

The monster bristled. 'Clearly, it was in the animal's nature to hunt lesser species. What right had you to deny it?'

'Mummy said... she said Misha could have hurt the ducks.'

'The taste of first blood,' breathed the monster, feeling that iron tang on his tongue again. 'It would have strengthened her. This predator could have worked for you, as we make the predators of our world work for us. She could have protected you, killed for you. Instead, you made her weak. Is it because you are so weak yourself, little girl, that you seek to neuter the species with which you share your planet? Is it because you fear them?'

'It's not right to be cruel to dumb animals,' said the little girl, stubbornly.

'How else do you expect to gain power? How can any race evolve, but through glorious, bloody combat? Survival of the strongest? Have you no ambition?'

'I do so have an ambition! When I grow up, I'm going to be a nurse. I'm going to look after sick people, and make them better.'

The monster let out a harsh, bitter laugh. 'The sick should fend for themselves. The survivors are fortified by the experience, and the rest are no loss to us, for they were weak and useless.'

A short pause, then, as the hate-filled words died away into the rain. Then, her tone sympathetic again, the little girl asked, 'Is that what they did to you, Mr Monster? Did the other monsters leave you behind because you got hurt?'

Unexpectedly, her words brought a lump to his throat. He thought of his comrades. He remembered the security that being a part of the galaxy's most fearsome army had given him; the innocent certainty of success. He remembered that moment of fire, in which it had ended. And suddenly, the loneliness was too much for him, and the sickness in his stomach became a wrenching pain that made him shudder.

The pain coaxed a pitiful mewl from the monster's throat, and he burnt with shame.

Through a pale mist, he detected movement. He realised that the girl had reached out to him, tentatively. She had shivered, and snatched her hand away before it could make contact. He cursed himself for having missed his chance, for being so weak.

His proud boasts – now, they were all meaningless. So, what meaning remained?

'T-tell me about your world,' he rasped. 'Your parks, and your... your ponds.'

He wasn't interested in what she had to say. He just needed time. To think; to recover his resolve. In his mind, he was clinging to a cliff edge, and it was crumbling under his grasp. He remembered his leaders' words, their promises, and he recited them under his breath. He had believed them, once. He had to have faith. Pass this test. Don't let go.

And he realised that he was listening to the girl, after all – to her talk of trees and fields and streams and gardens – and a part of him despised her for the paucity of her imagination, scoffed at the sheer banality of her life. But as time passed, and her constant voice became a comfortable drone rather than a high-pitched irritant, he found himself drawn into the landscapes that her words painted.

It took him a moment to realise that she had stopped talking, her topics of conversation evidently exhausted. 'On my world,' he said woodenly, into the silence, 'the lakes are acid, and the ground mostly barren. Our few jungles are rich with flora that is deadly to us. We make our homes in the rock, and exist in darkness. We do not have a fraction of the natural resources available to you, and yet still our technology far outstrips yours.'

'Is that why you came here?' asked the little girl. 'Because our world is nicer than yours?'

'Of course not,' snapped the monster automatically. 'We plan... planned... to subjugate your species, because it would have given us power.'

'What for?'

'We would have been feared.'

'What for?'

'We would have been recognised, at last, as the superior beings of the universe.'

'But what for?'

'I... I do not know,' he confessed.

'My mummy,' said the little girl, after a moment's reflection, 'says all bullies are cowards. She says they pick on people weaker than they are so they'll look stronger, and then they won't get picked on themselves.'

'You dare question...?' the monster spluttered. 'There is no army braver or more dedicated than ours. You speak of the superficial beauty of your world – but it is the harsh environment of mine that has shaped me into a warrior, a survivor. Your environment only makes you soft. Perhaps, little girl, that is why you are afraid, while I... we... we fear nothing!'

'Are... are you crying, Mr Monster?'

'Do not be ridiculous!'

'You are,' said the girl, with infuriating conviction. 'You're crying!'

The monster choked on a retort; took a deep, controlled breath; opened his mouth; and found his words trapped in his throat as her fingers brushed his hide.

She had come to him, at last. Her touch was light, and her skin not at all clammy. He blinked until he could see her clearly again, crouching over him. Her fear was gone, nothing but concern in her delicate, pointed features.

'I think you are a nice monster,' said the little girl. 'I think it's the other monsters who made you do bad things. And I just bet, if you'd been born on a nice world instead of an ugly one – I bet, then, you wouldn't even be a monster.'

And something tightened in the monster's chest, with the knowledge that he had only to reach out... Silence her twittering voice. End her life. Hold on to that cliff edge.

He almost howled with the realisation that even this simple action was beyond him. His limbs were like dead weights. He must have been more badly injured than he had thought.

'I know!' said the little girl brightly. 'Since the other monsters have all gone, why don't you stay here? You could live with me, and my mummy and my daddy and my big brother.'

And the monster thought about it. Just for a moment.

He wondered what it would be like to live the little girl's life. To have no cares; to find joy in such small, insignificant events as she did. No longer to hate. For the first time, he wondered if he could be something else, and the idea turned his world-view upside down. He could let go of the precipice, he realised with giddy anticipation. He could let go, and the fall might not be so bad.

Then the girl continued, falling over her words in excitement. 'You... you could have Misha's old bowl, and her bed in the kitchen, and we could come in here and play, and... and maybe Mummy would let me take you to the park, if we promised to leave the ducks alone.'

And he realised that there was nothing beneath his feet, after all.

He cursed himself for his false hopes. He had no place here. He wasn't like the girl. He didn't have her soft skin, her symmetrical features, her ability to laugh. He was an outsider. Something to be feared at best, and pitied at worst. And this latter, he could only achieve by abandoning everything he had ever been. By playing the part of a pet to this insufferable child, becoming subservient to her. Her inferior.

The injustice of it boiled up inside him. What had her wretched kind ever done to deserve their riches? Why had fate given them this world, this peaceful existence, when others – when his people – had nothing? This girl had never had to fight. She would never know that desperate longing – for power, for fear, for respect, for simple survival. While, for such as he – those who had planned and trained and disciplined themselves, and worked to earn what so many others took for granted – for such misguided creatures, fate reserved an even more bitter reward. Against all odds, defying all reason, it had contrived to tip the scales of war against them. It had kept their prize from them.

It wasn't fair!

And the monster had the little girl by the throat, not sure where his newfound strength had come from but feeling it coursing through him, driven on by his heart's hammer beat.

It wasn't fair!

But hadn't it always been this way? Hadn't his people suffered defeat after defeat, even as their leaders boasted of superiority?

It wasn't fair. But maybe, he thought with a distant sense of clarity –

maybe there was no other way. After all, he was a monster. And, just as it was in the nature of monsters to breed and to scheme in dark places, maybe it was also in their nature to be destroyed by the light.

In which case, what else could this monster do but hold on to that cliff edge?

She was squirming, the little girl; clawing weakly at him. Her skin was pale, and a feeble rattle escaped her trembling lips. But, more satisfying than all this was the look in her bulging eyes: the fear that came to lesser beings with the prospect of death. Her body would be found here soon, and the fear would spread, and that would be his legacy.

Tomorrow, the rest of her kind would be that little bit more afraid of monsters.

The girl had ceased her struggles. She hung limply in his grasp, and the fear had drained from her, leaving him with an empty feeling. He resolved to taste that fear again, before he died, before his enemies overwhelmed him with their numbers. He wondered how many more he could kill before the end; how much more powerful he could become.

And then:

A resounding crash, and a burst of light, yanking the monster's attention back to the barn door. It had been thrown open, slamming into the wood behind it. At that same moment, lightning had illuminated a staunch silhouette, framed in the aperture. It was gone in an instant, but the image remained burnt into the monster's mind.

He knew that shape; knew it like a racial memory, a symbol of danger, without ever having seen it. The wild hair, the extravagant clothing, the haughty posture of a man used to getting his own way. The light's residue was still playing tricks with the monster's vision, and he couldn't tell if the newcomer was tall or short, fat or thin, but he knew him.

And that sick feeling was back.

The shape glided toward him through the shadows, accompanied by a light gust of rain and a receding roll of thunder. And, suddenly, he was there, close enough for the monster to see the disapproving set of his lips and the gleam in his intense eyes.

And he said: 'Let her go!'

His voice was quiet but commanding, and the monster, accustomed to taking orders, obeyed without a thought. He had all but forgotten the little girl, anyway. She let out a soft moan as she collapsed into the straw – a spark of life remained in her – but the monster's attention was elsewhere.

'You!' he hissed, with as much icy disdain as he could muster. 'The sworn enemy of our kind. You have foiled our plans for the final time. You were foolish to walk into my clutches like this. I will destroy you!'

But the newcomer remained steadfast, silent, unblinking. He wasn't afraid – and, in the face of that courage, the monster knew he was helpless. Worse: his stomach was churning, paralysing him – and he realised now what that feeling was, what it had been all along.

And, in that moment, he was lost.

'I'm afraid not,' said the newcomer levelly. 'You see, I know your weakness.'

It was over in seconds.

The newcomer had given him a chance to surrender, everything about his body language suggesting that he knew he wouldn't take it. The monster, robbed of everything but his jealousy, had hurled himself at his smug foe, doing only what was expected of him. He hadn't seen the device in the newcomer's hand until it was too late, but it didn't surprise him. He had known, with a weary sense of resignation, that there would be something like it.

...and the pain had ripped him through him, and he had lashed out blindly, and there had been a moment, just one beautiful moment, as the newcomer's machine had arced through the air, when he had seen a flicker of... something on his enemy's face...

Just one moment. Too late. The monster's temporary strength had faded, and he had reeled and fallen, and now there were bright colours drowning out his sight and smoke in his lungs, and he realised that the machine had set light to the straw around him, but he couldn't move, couldn't turn his head, couldn't do anything but lie here and whimper and die.

The newcomer ducked past him, and lifted the girl to her feet. She was wheezing, her eyelids fluttering, but she found the strength to resist his urgent tug on her hand. 'What about my monster?' She pointed with an unsteady finger. 'We can't leave him here.'

A cloud passed over the newcomer's face. He looked down at the monster, and their eyes met for an awkward moment. 'I'm sorry,' he said, and the monster was surprised to detect a note of regret in his low voice. 'There's nothing I can do for him.'

'You can see him?' The girl's words caught on the smoke that was rising around her.

'I can see him,' confirmed the newcomer, 'and I know what he is.'

'He's a monster,' said the little girl, sagely.

'Yes,' said the newcomer, 'he is – and there's nothing you can do, nothing any of us can do, to change that. I only wish there were – but he'll remain true to his nature.' His arm was around the little girl's shoulders now, and he was guiding her towards the door. The monster barely made out his next, muttered, words: 'As I must remain true to mine.'

They were lost to the monster's senses, then, as the flames burnt brighter and hotter and louder until there was nothing else in his world. And then, there was nothing at all. To the monster's surprise, he faced his death with a calm acceptance. He only wished he could have shared it with his comrades in that first burst of fire, been spared the torture of self-doubt. But he knew who he was now, and he welcomed the darkness.

The last thing he heard, as he drifted away, was the newcomer's voice. A confident growl, which came to him on a fortuitous air current, almost impossibly loud and clear. It said:

'There's only one way to deal with monsters.'

ISBN 1-84435-111-4

Available now...

DOCTOR WHO™

SHORT TRIPS: REPERCUSSIONS

A short-story collection edited by
GARY RUSSELL

ISBN 1-84435-048-7

Throughout time and space, people have encountered the Doctor. For some, that encounter has enriched their lives. For others, it's been a detrimental experience. Either way, for each of them, nothing has ever been the same again.

Which would be fine – except on those occasions where the Doctor's interference has not just upset or altered the people, but damaged the web of time itself. Like a pebble breaking the surface of a pond, even though the incident has occurred, the ripples still reach further and further out...

These are their stories. Tales of the happy and sad, the broken and the mended. And the effect the Doctor has had, not just upon them but on the whole fabric of the universe...

Featuring stories by Peter Anghelides, Mark Michalowski, Joseph Lidster, Trevor Baxendale, Colin Brake and many more!

Available now...

DOCTOR WHO™

SHORT TRIPS: LIFE SCIENCE

A short-story collection edited by
JOHN BINNS

ISBN 1-84435-047-9

Once, we believed our lives were sacred, that we had souls. Now we know we are mere machines; genetic data. We are science.

But even as we learn, the properties of life remain uncertain. How does life acquire consciousness, or rights? Does a robot dream? If a person transforms into an oak tree, is it science, or the work of gods? Did the Victorians find a way to resurrect the dead?

To science, such questions are invitations to explore. Who better to explore with, than the Doctor?

Featuring stories by Kate Orman, Lance Parkin, Jonathan Morris, Jim Mortimore, Steve Lyons and many more!

Available now...

DOCTOR WHO™

SHORT TRIPS: PAST TENSE

A short-story collection edited by
IAN FARRINGTON

ISBN 1-84435-046-0

Throughout all his travels, the Doctor has had many adventures both on Earth, and in the past. His affection for this particular planet is clear, as is his enjoyment of seeing history happen.

Past Tense features stories set exclusively in Earth's past: from the heady atmosphere of Shakespearian London to the shadowy world of pre-war Istanbul; from the time of King Alfred to the turn of the Millennium.

Featuring stories by Eric Saward, Nev Fountain, Nicholas Briggs, Joseph Lidster, Mark Wright and many more!

Available now...

DOCTOR WHO™

SHORT TRIPS: STEEL SKIES

A short-story collection edited by
JOHN BINNS

ISBN 1–84435-045-2

Imagine you could never breathe fresh, unfiltered air again, or look up into a clear blue sky.

The characters in Steel Skies lead their lives in confined, isolated spaces – from Britain's first underwater prison, to an early human colony on an inhospitable world, and the last ship to fight for Earth in the bitter Draconian War. Confined, isolated, often far from home, they live with loneliness, paranoia, and despair.

And then, they meet the Doctor – and for better or worse, their lives are changed forever.

Featuring stories by Kate Orman, Paul Leonard, Rebecca Levene, Marc Platt, Jonathan Blum and many more!